T0110224

CASTROVILLE, MARINA, THEN— A SHADOW ACROSS THE LAND

The peninsula that was home to Monterey was still there, but instead of one of the most beautiful cities in California, there was blackness and rubble. Nothing else. No pier, no ships.

No people.

Cross gripped his seat. He wasn't sure what sound he made as the helicopter approached the destruction, but he knew it wasn't good. Perhaps he moaned. Perhaps he swore. Perhaps he simply gasped ...

Cross had seen the dust, studied it, even held bits of it in various labs back in D.C. He had watched the battle on television, seen satellite images, still photographs, infrared images, and spectral analyses. Nothing had prepared him for being here in person.

Nothing had prepared him for the blackness that covered the coastline for as far as his eye could see.

By Dean Wesley Smith and Kristine Kathryn Rusch
Published by Ballantine Books:

THE TENTH PLANET
THE TENTH PLANET: OBLIVION
THE TENTH PLANET: FINAL ASSAULT*

*forthcoming

THE TENTH PLANET
OBLIVION

Dean Wesley Smith
and
Kristine Kathryn Rusch

Story by Rand Marlis
and Christopher Weaver

A Del Rey® Book

THE BALLANTINE PUBLISHING GROUP • NEW YORK

A Del Rey® Book
Published by The Ballantine Publishing Group
Copyright © 2000 by Creative Licensing Corporation and Media
Technologies Ltd.

All rights reserved under International and Pan-American Copyright Conventions. Published in the United States by The Ballantine
Publishing Group, a division of Random House, Inc., New York, and
simultaneously in Canada by Random House of Canada Limited,
Toronto.

Del Rey is a registered trademark and the Del Rey colophon is a
trademark of Random House, Inc.

www.randomhouse.com/delrey/

Library of Congress Catalog Card Number: 99-91744

ISBN 978-0-345-48494-9

146673257

For Amy.
Thanks.

Section One

REBUILD

Prologue

April 23, 2018
3:10 P.M. Pacific Time

174 Days Until Second Harvest

Danny Elliot was shaking as he ran, half crouched, to the white house at the very edge of the destruction. The morning was sunny and the air smelled faintly of roses and the sea. If he closed his eyes, he could imagine this neighborhood as it had been ten days ago, as if it had never changed.

But he didn't close his eyes. He didn't dare. He had to remain alert, in case he saw a soldier or heard a truck. This entire area was cordoned off—a quarantine zone—and if he and his best friend Nikara Jones got caught, they'd get into a lot of trouble.

Nikara was right beside him. Nikara didn't look nervous at all. His thin mouth was set in a line, and his brown eyes were intent on that house. Danny was more concerned with the National Guard patrols and the other military vehicles that constantly roared along this deserted street.

That, and with what his mother would say if she knew what he was doing.

He stopped beside a hedge. It had been neatly clipped—probably a week ago, even though it felt like eighteen years ago—and was just high enough to give him protection from

3

any approaching patrol on his left side. He put a hand on Nikara's arm, stopping him.

"What?" Nikara whispered.

"I don't think we should do this," Danny said.

"We're here already," Nikara said. That wasn't entirely accurate. They were heading for the white ranch house that stood out against the blackness beyond like a beacon. They still had some distance to go.

"What if we get caught?"

"We talked about this," Nikara said. He ran a hand through his tight dark curls, then shook his head.

"Yeah," Danny said. "At my house. I'm not so sure now."

Nikara sighed, and rocked back on his heels. He had been Danny's best friend for the last ten years—since they were both five years old—and they had done everything together. Since the aliens attacked, they had spent most of their time with each other. Everyone else was watching television or working disaster relief. Danny's mother would come home at night, sit on their new sofa—a family Christmas present she had bought on credit—and cry. He had seen his mother cry when his dad left five years ago, but she hadn't cried since. Not once. He'd thought his mother was the strongest woman in the world. Maybe she was. Maybe even the strongest woman in the world couldn't handle what the aliens did.

Now there were people starting to say it really hadn't been aliens, but the government that destroyed everything. But that didn't matter to Danny.

What mattered to Danny was that it had all been so unexpected.

Ten days ago, he'd gotten up at six like usual, taken a shower, and had a bowl of Frosted Mini-Wheats. Then he'd gotten his bag lunch from his mother and begged for lunch money like he always did, and when she'd refused like she always did, he'd gotten on his bike and ridden the mile to school. Another year and he'd be old enough to drive, but for

4

now he was still stuck on his bike. He'd had algebra, English, and social studies before everything he knew disappeared.

Alien ships appeared over San Luis Obispo and Monterey. And everywhere in between. Huge black alien ships that blocked the sky. Then they dropped a black cloud on everything, a cloud that ate through wood and skin and bone.

Monterey was gone.

San Luis Obispo was gone.

Only the outlying areas remained. The outlying areas, where the housing was cheap. The poor section or, as his mother used to say, the wrong side of town. Their side of town.

He'd never felt lucky living there before, and he wasn't sure he felt lucky now. But he was glad to be alive.

"Come on," Nikara said. "We only got twenty minutes before the patrol is due."

Danny rubbed his hands on his jeans. His palms were sweating—his whole body was sweating. He'd never done anything like this in his life. He was breaking all the rules.

"From here to the white house," Nikara said. "We can hide near the rhodies. There's a trellis behind them. From there we can climb to the roof."

That had been the plan all along. They wanted to go to the very edge of the Black Zone, as people were calling it, and see the destruction for themselves. Danny wasn't entirely sure if he could tell anyone why he wanted to see the Zone. He just knew it hadn't looked real on television, and from a distance, it seemed as if someone had dropped a lot of gray paint on the horizon. The sea was still there, and the sky, but all the buildings were gone. Some rubble remained—nonorganic stuff, the news reports said—but the trees, the buildings, the *people* were gone.

"Aren't you a little creeped out?" Danny asked.

Nikara looked at him, his dark eyes flat. "No."

Danny felt a flush building. This had been his idea. For days he had pushed Nikara to come. Nikara had finally agreed, on

5

the condition that he'd plan their route and time the patrols before they left. Nikara had put two days of work into this little trek, making sure they had time enough to view the destruction. No matter how creeped out Nikara was, he'd never admit it, not after all that.

Danny should have known better—or he never should have suggested it in the first place.

"Let's go," Nikara said, and started across the street at full run.

Danny followed. So far, Nikara had been right about the patrols. They ran every hour, like clockwork. Otherwise, there was no one here.

Every house was empty.

This neighborhood with its trimmed lawns, and flower gardens, and newly painted small and old houses had always teemed with life. A lot of the people were elderly and spent most of their time outside. Most had owned their houses forever and took a lot of pride in them.

Now everyone was gone and the houses looked abandoned, even though the flowers still bloomed. The yards were getting ragged, and the driveways were empty. Danny wanted to have someone—anyone—open a door and yell, "Hey, kid! Don't you know you're not supposed to be here?"

But no one did.

The doors remained closed and the blinds pulled down. He ran up the curb and onto the lawn of the white house, feeling as if he were trespassing.

Nikara had already made it to the rhododendrons on the side of the house. Their pink flowers shook as he pushed past them toward the trellis.

Danny took one more glance at the street.

Empty.

The cracked pavement seemed almost naked. From this direction, though, everything seemed normal. Behind the ranch houses, he saw the thirty-year-old manufactured homes that

6

marked the beginnings of his neighborhood, and behind that the somewhat larger homes of the next development.

Only if he looked forward, toward the white house, was he reminded of everything lost.

He slipped into the rhododendrons—large plants that had probably been there since the houses were built—and felt the jutting branches scratch his arms. The pink flowers had no real smell, but the leaves gave off a slightly unpleasant odor. He had to push through the sturdy lower branches to get to the trellis.

As he put his hand on the wood, Nikara said, "Careful. It's wobbly."

Danny glanced up. Nikara was already on the roof. He was hanging his head over the side, watching.

Danny took a deep breath and started to climb. The trellis wasn't just wobbly—the wood was rotten and weak. He could feel it bending beneath his weight. A few years ago this wouldn't have been a problem, but this last year he'd really grown.

He shimmied up it as quickly as he could, hearing one of the boards snap just before he reached the top.

Nikara put a hand on Danny's back to help him up, then moved up to the peak.

Danny lay on the roof for a moment, his heart pounding. The shingles felt gritty against his cheek.

"God," Nikara said. "You should see this."

Danny pushed himself up. The pitch of the roof was shallow—which was why they'd chosen this house—and it took very little effort to climb to the peak, where Nikara was now sitting.

Danny climbed, still slightly crouched so that his hands could brush the shingles. That way, he didn't have to look at the devastation until he was ready.

"God," Nikara said again. The word was coming out of him like an involuntary prayer.

Danny sat down next to him, his feet resting on the other side of the roof, the peak against his butt. His hands gripped the rough surface. He waited until he was braced before he looked up.

The blackness spread before him like a shadow across the land. It made everything look flat, even where Danny knew there were rolling hills, slight inclines, and tiny valleys. Then the blackness ended, and the blue water of the Pacific sparkled in the sun. The ocean looked exactly the same. Only it was as if someone had moved a new landscape in front of it, a landscape without houses or stores or tourist attractions; without restaurants or the Wharf or ships; without birds or dogs or people.

His breath caught in his throat. He might have said something—he didn't know for certain. He had gone into those businesses, walked down streets now buried in blackness. He had played at the water's edge.

He had had friends in the neighborhoods covered in soot.

The wind was cooler up here and smelled of the sea. The blackness had no smell at all, at least not one he could detect. A gust hit him, and then another even colder gust, drying his sweat and covering his skin in goose bumps.

"Can you see where Cort's house used to be?" Nikara asked in a voice Danny had never heard before.

Danny made himself look toward the south. Cort had grown up with them, but he lived about five blocks away. He had stayed home sick that day, April 13. And when it became clear what parts of the area were completely destroyed, Danny had asked his mother if she thought Cort got away.

"No, honey," she had said. She had tried to pull him into a hug, but he wasn't a baby anymore. He didn't need comfort. When Nikara had come over to the house the next day and asked the same question, Danny had said, "What do you think?" and neither of them mentioned Cort again.

Until now.

8

Danny's grip on the roof grew tighter. The wind was stinging his eyes, filling them with tears. Cort had rounded out their threesome. He had been cautious when Nikara was reckless, the voice of reason when Danny had one of his crazy ideas, and completely willing to tag along, even on the silliest adventure. In fact, Cort would have been sitting beside them if he hadn't—melted—or whatever those things did to someone.

If he hadn't died.

Danny shivered. He would never see Cort again. Or Cort's father, the only father who was still at home among the three of them.

Or Cort's dog, Buddy.

Or Cort's house.

"Do you see it?" Nikara asked.

"No," Danny said. "I can't tell where it was at all."

He was amazed at how calm he sounded. It was as if he were talking about a landmark or a shop or something he had never seen before. Not a place where he had eaten dinner, where he and Nikara and Cort had logged on to his parents' system and sent phony e-mails to all the good-looking girls in class.

"You can see some of the foundations, if you look hard enough." Nikara's voice was flat. That was why it sounded so weird.

Danny squinted. He could see the shapes of the houses beneath the black dust, something that wouldn't have been as visible from the ground. Large squares here, large rectangles there, a tangle of rubble between.

He rubbed his eye. Damn the wind.

"I still can't pick out which house was his."

"Why does it matter so much?" Danny asked.

"I don't know," Nikara said. "It just does."

They looked at each other. Nikara's eyes were red, too. Cort was the only friend they'd lost. Their school was east of

9

the destruction and everyone they knew had been in class that day. Except Cort.

A lot of kids lost homes, though. And pets. And parents.

"Do you think it hurt?" The question came out as a whisper. He was surprised it even left his lips.

Nikara swallowed so hard his Adam's apple bobbed. He hunched his shoulders, then turned the movement into a shrug. "They showed some film on CNN. That lady, in Europe—"

"Africa," Danny said.

"—she got caught in the black cloud and it dissolved her skin. There was blood everywhere and she was screaming . . ." Nikara's voice trailed off. He glanced at the blackness before them as if he were seeing it for the first time. "Yeah. I think it hurt."

Danny closed his eyes. He didn't want to think about Cort like that lady, Cort on his couch, sick with the flu when suddenly the roof disappeared, and this black cloud came at him—

Danny's eyes flew open. There was no black cloud. Only black dust. "They don't want people walking in that stuff," he said. "You think that's because it might dissolve their feet?"

"I don't know," Nikara said. He brought his knees up and rested his chin on them, as if he were contemplating a problem.

The plan had been to look at the destruction and then maybe walk through it. Unspoken in all of it was that maybe they'd find something of Cort's. Maybe even Cort's house. Maybe proof that Cort had lived through it all.

But that wasn't possible. Danny knew it now. Even though he had seen the destruction from a distance and on television, it wasn't the same as sitting here, on the edge of it—an edge that was as arbitrary as the teams Mr. Goble chose in gym class. If Cort's house had been five blocks east, Cort would be sitting up here with them now. Cort would know if the black

10

dust was safe. He'd know how much trouble they'd be in if the patrols caught them. He'd know everything.

"How much time do we have?" Danny asked.

Nikara checked his wrist'puter. "Ten minutes."

"We have to get down before that," Danny said. "They could see us for miles up here."

"If they're looking up," Nikara said.

"Where else would they look?" Danny asked. "The attack came from above."

"I don't think they're expecting another attack," Nikara said. "At least not right away. They'd be acting a whole lot different if they were."

Still, thinking about patrols put Danny back on alert. If the patrols could see him from far away, he should be able to see them, too. He made himself look away from the black dust covering everything and instead focused on the roads.

The army used the roads closest to the destruction. They had also built a few roads through it—long winding paths where the black dust had somehow been cleared out. Danny remembered his mother telling him about that, and how she didn't approve of the army sending the dust back in the air where it might do damage again.

He scanned those roads and saw nothing. But on the concrete roads at the edge, he saw vehicles moving like ants going back to their hill. Nikara had said that the patrols were very regular—no one, apparently, wanted to go back into the dust, but the government insisted it be guarded.

Nikara was looking in the same direction Danny was. "You know," Nikara said as he squinted at the roads, "they've been riding through this stuff. It's got to be safe."

Danny shuddered. He was getting cold on this roof. "Maybe they wear special suits or something."

"I've seen them," Nikara said. "The first few days they wore masks, but they haven't worn anything since."

Danny looked down. The dust on the other side of the

house glistened, just a little. He had never seen blackness glisten before. It seemed almost evil.

"Maybe they'll get sick later," Danny said.

"They would have done tests," Nikara said.

"My mother says you should never put too much trust in the government. Some people even say the government is the cause of all this."

Nikara sighed. "The aliens did this. I'm going. That's what we came for."

"I thought we came to see it up close."

"You can't see it up close without getting in it." Nikara snorted. "Anybody knows that."

Danny didn't agree, but he knew better than to argue with Nikara when he was in this kind of mood. Nikara half slid, half walked to the edge of the roof.

"Think it's too far to jump?" he asked.

"Yes," Danny said. He hadn't left the peak, hoping that would discourage Nikara.

"If I hang off the gutter, I won't drop so far," Nikara said.

"If you break your leg and those things start eating you," Danny said, "I'm not coming to get you."

Nikara looked at him over his shoulder. "I didn't think you would."

Danny didn't know how Nikara meant that. Did he mean Danny was a coward? Or that it was a sensible thing not to rescue someone who was dissolving?

Nikara gripped the gutter and swung his legs off the roof. Danny's stomach tightened. All he could see were Nikara's brown hands clinging to the rusty metal.

Danny made his way across the roof. He reached the edge just as Nikara let go.

A cloud of dust rose around him, and Danny felt a cry leave his throat. Not Nikara, too. Danny wanted to close his eyes, so that he wouldn't see a friend die, but he couldn't look away.

12

He was breathing shallowly, waiting for the dust to settle, hoping he'd see Nikara in one piece. Danny realized he had lied; if Nikara was injured, Danny would do everything he could, short of jumping in the dust himself, to get Nikara back on the roof.

Finally the dust stopped swirling. Nikara was standing very still. His face, his clothes, his hair were covered in black dust. But his eyes were his own. And they were twinkling.

"It's like feathers!" Nikara said. "It tickles."

Danny frowned. He thought the stuff would be stiff and bristly, like rust flakes. He didn't expect it to be soft.

"Come on down," Nikara said.

Danny put his hands on the gutter as he had seen Nikara do. The metal was cold against Danny's skin. He was about to swing over, to join Nikara, but something stopped him.

"Come *on!*" Nikara said.

Danny looked at the dust. Some of it was still swirling near Nikara's feet. Every time Nikara moved, the dust would move, too. Then Danny let his gaze wander from Nikara to the house foundations. One of those was Cort's. No one had said what the black stuff was. Some of it had come from those ships, yes, but some of it had to have the remains of buildings in it.

When Danny's great-uncle Milton died, he'd been cremated, and Danny's mom, as the only surviving relative, got the ashes. She couldn't decide whether to keep them or scatter them, so for a few weeks, Danny, Nikara, and Cort would open the urn and look inside.

There were gray flakes—soft gray flakes because Danny had touched them—mixed with bits of bone. And that's what this black dust and the rubble reminded him of. Ashes, with a bit of bone.

Bile rose in his throat, and he had to swallow hard to keep it down.

"Danny," Nikara said. "We don't have a lot of time."

13

But Danny couldn't swing himself off the roof. Not and land in ashes. Cort's ashes. One of his closest friends, forever reduced to dust and bone.

"You go," Danny said.

Nikara made a small sound of disgust and slogged through the blackness toward Cort's house. A cloud rose in his wake. Danny watched as the ashes mixed with ashes, and the dust with dust.

And right at that moment he knew that the aliens had to pay for what they had done to Cort and everyone else.

Danny didn't know how. But he knew they had to pay. Cort and everyone else mixed with this gray dust that spread out before him couldn't rest until they did.

1

April 23, 2018
7:30 P.M. Eastern Time

174 Days Until Second Harvest

The Oval Office smelled musty. That was always the first thing Secretary of State Doug Mickelson noticed about the place. Then he noted the large blue area rug with the emblem of the United States in the center, the antique partner's desk beneath the large windows where President Franklin did most of his work, and the white couches nearest the door. The room's oval shape wasn't that obtrusive—the first time he'd been invited here, Mickelson had thought it would be—but the relatively low ceiling and the comfortable furniture kept it from feeling like a mausoleum, as so much of the White House did.

Still, all the years the building had stood in the District's damp heat in the days before air-conditioning had taken their toll. There was a general mustiness about the whole building, something an army of cleaning people couldn't seem to tame. Once, when Mickelson mentioned that the faint pervasive hint of mold played hell on his allergies, his best friend, scientist Leo Cross, had suggested using nanotechnology to clean it out. Mickelson had thought it a good idea at the time. Now, thanks to the alien attack, he understood how nanotechnology

15

worked—had actually seen it in action—and he would rather live with the mold.

He dropped his tall, muscled frame onto the couch, almost tempted to put his feet up. He couldn't remember being so worn out and so angry at the same time. Since the attack he'd had almost no sleep, and had wanted to punch a dozen people, even though he was known for his calmness under diplomatic fire. He was just boiling mad that the aliens had so easily destroyed so much of his home, his country, his planet.

He was amazed the world had survived an alien attack. Thank God it looked as if humans had won when the aliens left, otherwise the world would be coming apart in riots. At the moment almost everyone on the planet thought humanity had chased off the aliens. Doug knew better.

So did President Franklin and about thirty other people around the nation. And maybe a few hundred more around the world. But that was going to change.

The aliens hadn't been chased off—they were just following a plan. A plan that was going to bring them right back to Earth for a second attack as soon as their tenth-planet home got into position again.

And the fact that they were coming back had him even angrier. And scared at the same time. Not for himself, but for the millions and millions who would die in a second attack, not counting all the people who would die in the panic that would sweep the world the moment everyone knew the aliens were headed this way again.

Humanity, civilization as Mickelson knew it, wouldn't survive a second round. It was that simple.

Mickelson heard President Franklin in the narrow corridor off the opposite side of the room, his braying Bronx accent impossible to miss. Thayer Franklin had a patrician name, but that was the only thing patrician about him. His father was distantly related to some of the best families in New England, but he'd married "down," or so the pre-election news reports

16

had said, to a woman from a blue-collar family who'd gotten a scholarship to Harvard. That marriage had lasted long enough to produce Franklin, and to prevent his spunky mother from finishing her Ivy League education. Franklin's father refused to pay child support, and Cara Franklin went home to raise her child.

That was all in the official biography. What wasn't, seemed incredibly clear to anyone who met the small, dark-eyed, clear-spoken mother of the president. She'd poured her ambition into him, and he'd responded. Sometimes, Mickelson thought, the entire success story was an elaborate way for Franklin to thumb his nose at his still-living, unrepentant deadbeat father.

Now Franklin was faced with the largest crisis to ever face a president. Mickelson hoped the man was up for it.

Mickelson leaned his head back and closed his eyes. Most of the time over the past few days, when he did that, either in bed or on a plane, he saw the images of the alien craft pouring the black clouds of nanomachines over people, buildings, entire towns. And those people screaming in pain as the machines ate them alive, from the outside inward.

It was the stuff of horror movies. Skin eaten, blood spurting everywhere.

Faces contorted in pain, covered in blood, skin gone.

Millions of dead.

Nightmares.

Nothing but nightmares.

"Napping on me, Doug?" President Franklin's voice broke through the images of the attack as he closed the door to his inner office behind him.

"Hardly," Doug said, opening his eyes to see the intense gaze of his friend. "Every time I try to sleep I see the attack again."

Franklin dropped down into his normal chair, his back to his desk, and nodded. The exhaustion was clear around the man's black eyes and wrinkled face. Franklin had grown tired

17

looking over his first years in office, but this alien attack had added years to his face.

"So do I, Doug," Franklin said. "And to be honest with you, it's making me damn angry."

"You and a lot of other people," Doug said. He'd spent the last few days on emergency trips to meet with heads of states, calming people, letting them know something was going to be done. "But everyone feels so helpless, at least those who know about the aliens coming back again."

"How many know?" Franklin asked.

Doug shook his head. "Not many at this point. Less than a couple hundred, but it won't take long for others to start figuring it out."

"And the rest of the world, those who don't know?" Franklin asked. "How do you see them taking it?"

"Shock," Doug said, used to having Franklin quiz him on common people's reactions around the world. "Mourning the dead. And celebration that the aliens are gone and that we won."

Franklin snorted. "We didn't win. I'm not sure we even really bothered the bastards."

Mickelson couldn't agree more.

"Well," Franklin said, his voice turning cold and low. "That's not going to happen next time. We're not going to just let them come here, take what they want, and kill our people."

Mickelson knew this wasn't just another of Franklin's speeches. He had known Franklin long enough to see when all the political screens and faces were gone and he was being the real Franklin. And this was one of those times.

But unless something major had changed in the last few hours while Mickelson had been on the plane home from Great Britain, there wasn't any way to stop the aliens that he knew of.

"Oh," Mickelson said, sighing and leaning back. "I wish it were that easy."

Franklin pinned Mickelson with his stare, the anger clearly being held in check just below the surface. "I've seen enough death over the past week to last me a thousand lifetimes. Those bastards aren't going to do it again."

Mickelson sat forward and faced his president. "You have a way to stop them?"

"Damn right I do," Franklin said. "We're going to blow that damn planet of theirs right out of the system before they get another chance to hurt us."

For a second Mickelson didn't understand exactly what the president was telling him. The words seemed to make no sense.

"We're going to attack them?" Mickelson said.

Franklin smiled, but there was no merriment behind the smile or in his eyes. "You bet your ass we're going to," President Franklin said. "And they're not even going to know what hit them."

April 24, 2018
8:10 A.M. Pacific Time

173 Days Until Second Harvest

Leo Cross clung to the edge of his seat, feeling the plastic bite into his fingers. His heart was pounding harder than usual. He'd been in a lot of helicopters and landed in a lot of strange places, but none of the landings had ever made him nervous before. It was the black dust that unnerved him. The black dust and the flat land where houses, businesses, and people should be.

He glanced around the copter. The pilot was concentrating on the path before them. His navigator, an Army man whose name Cross had already forgotten, watched with tight-lipped determination. Cross turned. Behind him, Lowry Jamison looked slightly queasy.

Jamison was a big man—a former college quarterback who would have gone on to play pro ball if it weren't for his heroics in the Rose Bowl several years back. He'd twisted his knee with six minutes remaining. The coach had wanted him out, but the second-string quarterback had already been sidelined with a rotator cuff injury before the game. The third-string was a freshman who'd never played in the regular season. Jamison finished out the game, running fifteen yards to set up a field goal, and giving his team the three points they needed to win. Unfortunately, he'd torn cartilage in the knee, and never played ball again.

Unfortunately for Jamison. Fortunately for the rest of the world. For Jamison had a diabolical mind, and once he could no longer use it toward a career in football, he turned his attention to physics. He worked for NanTech, same as Portia Groopman, another member of Cross's team. Unlike Portia, Jamison didn't work on nanotechnology per se, but on ways to make nanotechnology impossible to detect.

Right now, however, he didn't look like a man who knew how to hide things already too tiny to be seen by the naked eye. He looked like a man who thought the helicopter was going to crash.

Cross had flown with Jamison before. Jamison was not afraid of flying, or even of helicopters. He had the same reaction to this trip the rest of them did.

The thing was, they were prepared. They knew what they were going to face. And they had had warning as the copter brought them in from the north. They were following the coastline, looking at the ocean dash against rocks. They flew low enough that Cross could see homes built on the mountainside, cars parked in the driveways, toys in the yards. As they passed Santa Cruz, he watched the cars crawl on the highways beside the tacky tourist traps. There were more Army vehicles

20

on the roads than he had ever seen before. Humvees, trucks—all green, all moving swiftly. Things looked normal here, but he doubted they were. He doubted things were normal anywhere in the world anymore.

The copter turned slightly, following the coastline inward as they entered Monterey Bay. The pilot, unable to talk because of the thrum of the engine and the *whap-whap-whap* of the blades above them, turned, tapped Cross on the shoulder, and pointed. Cross leaned forward in his chair and saw—

For a moment, he didn't know how to describe it. He had flown this way before, once in a low-flying private plane, and he still remembered it: all the seaside towns nestled against the bay, the sailing ships, the bright, blue ocean. There were the remains of canneries, some of them unable to be torn down because John Steinbeck had written about them in the 1930s, and piers that went out into that sparkling water. The communities, from the air, seemed to blend into one another, and he remembered thinking how lovely they were, how perfect, how typically American West Coast. The kinds of places where people always wanted to live but never could.

Many of the communities remained. Around the curve of the coastline, he saw Castroville, Marina, and then—

A shadow across the land.

The peninsula that provided the home for the city of Monterey was still there, but instead of one of the most beautiful cities in California, there was blackness, rubble, and nothing else. No pier, no ships.

No people.

That was when Cross gripped his seat. He was glad for the noise, the constant roar that copters still made, when all other motorized vehicles were built quieter and quieter. He wasn't sure what sound he made as he saw the destruction approach, but he knew it wasn't good. Perhaps he moaned. Perhaps he swore. Perhaps he simply gasped.

21

All he knew was that a knot had formed in his throat. Swallowing was hard, and so was breathing. His throat was so tight, and his emotions so close to the surface, that he feared a deep breath would make him lose what fragile control he had.

The blackness covered the coastline as far as his eye could see.

The copter was slowing down as it came in for its landing. Cross's grip on the seat grew tighter. He had seen the dust, studied the dust, even held bits of it in various labs back in Washington, D.C. The television stations had shown images of the destruction for the past ten days. Cross had seen satellite images, still photographs, infrared images, and all sorts of spectral analyses. But nothing had prepared him for being here, in person, seeing the destruction up close.

Perhaps he had been too busy to let it sink in before now. Yes, he had watched as the alien ships released the clouds of black dust over six large regions worldwide. The first attack had occurred in the Amazon, Central America, and in central Africa. He and Brittany Archer, the head of the Space Telescope Science Institute—a beautiful woman who had miraculously become his lover through all of this—had watched the attack in the media room of his D.C. home.

They had felt helpless, even though they had been involved with the Tenth Planet Project from the beginning. In fact, it was Cross who had put the world scientists—and ultimately, the world leaders—on alert that something would cause worldwide devastation sometime that year. He had seen the same result in the archaeological record every 2,006 years, and had known it was coming. At first, however, he hadn't known what or from where.

The copter headed toward a white space in the middle of all that blackness. The military had cleared off a section of land on the Monterey peninsula, probably where the Wharf used to be. He didn't know how they had gotten rid of the black dust—whether they had scraped it off into the sea or whether they had scooped it up and saved it for later study. But as the copter approached, he could see the white patch like a ray of light in the middle of a very, very dark night.

He let out a small sigh. Monterey hadn't been destroyed until the second attack. The world governments had united, mostly through the United States, and had fought the aliens as best they could. A number of lucky shots in the Amazon had destroyed alien ships.

The aliens had retaliated by targeting highly populated areas: South Vietnam, central France, and this part of California. The images had been even more horrifying than the first time. Cross had sat alone in his media room, staring at people who were trying to escape: some on foot, others by car. The traffic had been backed up for miles, and most of those people hadn't escaped in time.

The copter hovered over the ground. Its propeller blades whipped the nearby black dust into the air. Cross ducked as the dust hit the plastic windshields, although he had been reassured that it was harmless. It had been through test after test.

In fact, he had already suspected it was harmless. It had been his friend, Edwin Bradshaw, who had discovered the little nanomachines that the aliens sent down. Portia Groopman, NanTech's twenty-year-old whiz kid, had determined that the nanomachines had two functions: collecting and storing organic material.

That was why bits of metal rose from the dust like dinosaur skeletons, why the concrete foundations of buildings remained. Only the organic material had been destroyed.

The gray dust was just a by-product.

The dust coated the windows as the copter bumped to a gentle landing. The pilot shut off the copter. He had warned them earlier to wait until the blades stopped whirring before leaving the copter—not for safety's sake, but so that they wouldn't get blinded by the swirling dust. Cross had been told that the ocean dampness had pasted a lot of it down, but not enough to keep the force of the copter winds from stirring it up.

"It's something, isn't it?" the pilot shouted as the blades slowed.

"You could say that." Lowry Jamison sounded gruffer than usual, as if his throat was as tight as Cross's.

"Saw you duck, Doc," the pilot said to Cross.

"I knew it couldn't get in here, but it still unnerved me."

"It bothers all of us," the pilot said. "I got this gig because I'm the only one who can land here safely. Everyone else blinks at the wrong time. Too many images of dissolving people, if you know what I mean."

Cross did know. The images had been repeated so many times on television that the idea of having the black dust touch him made his skin crawl. Still, he was here to sift through it, to find, if he could, some of the nanomachines that he believed the aliens left behind.

"Dust's settling," the Army man said.

It was, but it seemed to be taking forever. The black stuff was so thin, so light that even when stuck together by moisture it floated up like carbon flakes from a burned building.

The remains of everything organic. Or, as one of the scientists in the Project had called it: the useless stuff, the waste. The organic material the aliens believed they couldn't use.

Cross opened the copter door, disturbing more dust. His task would be more difficult than he had thought.

He climbed outside and stepped onto the clear patch. It was bigger up close than he had thought it would be. They had actually landed on what had once been a parking lot.

The smell of the sea, sharp, salty, and tangy, surprised him. Somehow he had thought the dust would have an odor all its own. If it did, he couldn't smell it. The air was fresh, probably fresher than it would have been if Monterey were still here.

The thought made him sad.

24

He moved away from the copter and stared at the devastation around him. He had expected it to be completely flat, a level black surface as far as the eye could see. But it wasn't. He could actually make out shapes: the steel reinforcements in old buildings; the concrete supports that stood, like columns, in the sea; the metal hulls of boats that had washed ashore. He could see, without much effort, the layout of the city, the Wharf, the harbor.

He could see what once had been.

That, actually, was his strength. Even though Cross had degrees in a number of areas, his specialty was archaeology. He had been trained in using his imagination to determine, from the smallest of hints, what a culture—or a place—had been like.

It didn't take much imagination here.

"Damn," Jamison said. He had stepped out of the copter and stopped beside Cross. Cross didn't know how long Jamison had been standing there.

"It's going to be a needle in a haystack," Cross said, turning the conversation immediately to business. He didn't want to focus on what had been. If they did that, they might not be able to work.

"We knew it was going to be hard," Jamison said. "I just didn't imagine it would be like this."

Cross hadn't either. He had imagined stepping into the dust, using the device Jamison had designed, and searching for one of the nanomachines that he hoped had been left by the aliens. But he hadn't imagined walking around metal bicycle frames and bronze fisherman statues.

"I guess we should start," he said.

Jamison nodded. He handed Cross a thin wand with a large glass base. It looked like a combination of an old-fashioned metal detector and a vacuum cleaner designed to clean stairs. But it was much, much more than that. It had been invented to find machines too small to be seen by the human eye.

"I hope it works," Jamison said.

"Me, too." He had only used it once, and that had been in the R&D room at NanTech. The wands, as Jamison called them, were prototypes. In fact, Jamison and his team had modified an existing device that they hadn't planned on selling.

Jamison's team specialized in hiding nanotechnology, in making it completely undetectable to any modern machine. Jamison had told Cross that in confidence, assuming that Cross had the same high-level security clearance as most people who visited the R&D section of NanTech. Even though NanTech was a private firm, the bulk of its Secrecy Division, as Jamison playfully called it, was funded by the military.

The fear had been, before the aliens had come, that other countries would develop a series of nanoweapons, things that would destroy electrical systems. Yet the nanoweapons would be undetectable, and even if they were traced to the source, they would be impossible to find and remove.

Military intelligence had shown that no other country was close to developing anything like that, so after the initial wave of research on finding nanoweapons, the research shifted to making and hiding nanoweapons. Jamison's division was split: half the division discovered ways to hide the weapons while the other half discovered ways of finding them.

So, after Cross got a chance to think about it, he went to NanTech for help. Finding the nanomachines—an actual nanomachine, not a fossilized one from a previous visit by these aliens—might provide a way to understand what they were fighting.

And better yet, fight back.

That was what Cross thought about the most. Stopping the next attack and fighting back. Humanity had to. There was no choice.

In spite of himself, Cross shuddered.

Cross knew that he and his team weren't the only ones

26

working on ways to fight the aliens. There were branches of military all over the world working on ways to stop the alien ships, but Cross and his team were focusing on stopping what the aliens dropped. The nanoharvesters.

Nonetheless, here in the field, Cross felt out of place. He wasn't a hands-on technology guy, and he'd only recently learned about nanomachines. He was in Monterey because he knew what the nanomachines looked like, at least in fossilized form. He had been studying them since before the alien ships arrived. People like Jamison could study them as well, but they didn't have quite as much experience as Cross did.

And, in fact, the one man who had more experience than Cross—his friend Edwin Bradshaw—was in Brazil with Portia Groopman, the genius of nanotechnology, using the same devices to try to find alien machines.

He hefted the wand Jamison had given him. It was light, so light that it felt as if he were holding a toy. Only the glass base gave it any weight at all.

When Cross had tested the device back at NanTech, Jamison had apologized for the glass. "It's more tempered than bulletproof glass," he had said, "but it does make the wand heavier than we want. We've just found that glass is the best substance for the base."

Heavier. The wand wasn't heavy at all. In fact, if it were any lighter, Cross might forget that he was holding anything.

Jamison clutched his wand as if it were a golf club and he were staring at the first tee on a complicated hole. With his other hand, he shaded his eyes.

"This stuff goes on forever," he said. He sounded mournful.

Cross nodded.

"You know the odds against finding a single nanomachine?" Jamison asked.

In fact, Cross knew them exactly. "They're not as slim as you might think," he said. "Because there is a lot of ground that got covered, the aliens had to use billions and billions of those nanomachines. Even if they left one in a million behind, there should be hundreds of thousands of them scattered in this dust."

"Machines smaller than a speck of dust." Jamison sighed. "Just because we think they're here doesn't mean these wands will find them."

Cross knew that. They'd had that discussion back at NanTech. "Why're you getting pessimistic on me now, Lowry?"

Jamison didn't answer. He just stared at the blackness in front of them.

Cross understood. Over the years, he had stood on hundreds of sites of devastation—devastation that had ruined civilizations thousands of years before. He had sifted through the archaeological record, held black dust compressed by centuries, and wondered at it.

He had never faced it in real time, never thought what it meant—at least not in real terms—to the survivors.

Cross clapped Jamison on the back. "You've faced tough odds before."

"Yeah," Jamison said softly. "But I always knew someone would win the game."

"You know that now," Cross said.

Jamison looked at him, his broad face empty of all emotion, but his eyes were alive with something. Fear? Probably. Cross suspected that emotion was underneath all of their facades.

Fear and anger.

"Right now, we're the underdogs," Cross said. "And this is our Hail Mary pass. We're going to fight back and win this."

Jamison smiled. "Your analogy sucks."

Cross shrugged. "I'm not much of a football fan."

"It shows." Jamison pressed a small area at the tip of the wand, then pressed the base against the black dust. Dust swirled within the glass base, just like it would in a vacuum cleaner,

28

and then it rose around Jamison. He coughed and shut off the wand.

His face was covered with dust.

"We need some kind of suit," he said.

"Already thought of that." Cross nodded toward the copter. The Army guy was there, holding a box. "You just got ahead of me a little. I didn't expect you to turn that thing on so quickly."

"Hey, if we're going to go for the Hail Mary pass," Jamison said, "we've got to move quickly."

"Yes, we do," Cross said. More than he wanted to admit. Because in one hundred and seventy-three days, the alien ships would be back. And if Earth didn't find a way to fight them, the ships would again take what they wanted. Cross felt every second tick away, as if second by second, the blood was dripping from the body of humanity.

April 25, 2018
10:12 Universal Time

172 Days Until Second Harvest

Commander Cicoi stood on the balcony of Command Central, overlooking the valley below. Malmur was a beautiful planet—or it had been, in the times before. He had once been privileged to see the Stored Memories in the sacred vault, images of Malmur when it had its own sun, when it had life every day of every year.

Now the valley below him was just a cut in the dirt, with thousands of solar panels gathering the life-giving energy covering its slopes. There were suggestions of the past. The river that had once flowed through the valley left an impression time could not erase. Smooth stones covered that area

29

under the panel, and a winding depression suggested where the river had once been.

If Cicoi brought down all but two of his eyestalks, he could almost see the water flowing, as it did in the Stored Memories. But try as he might, he could not imagine the greenery that had once surrounded the river, nor the creatures—long sacrificed—that flew overhead or bathed within its depths.

It was said that the Malmuria began their existence in the once-fertile oceans of Malmur, oceans that, like the rivers, were long gone. The tentacles and eyestalks that were such an important part of their race once had different purposes within the water.

So said the Keepers of the Stored Memories, the only ones allowed to study the past for its own sake. Most Malmuria spent their brief time awake struggling for survival, procreating, repairing damage, and eating enough to make it through the next period of darkness.

Once, so said the Keepers, the Malmuria were a magnificent people. They had vast cities and miraculous technologies. They thrived on a healthy planet that orbited its own sun.

But a disaster struck, a disaster so horrible that none were allowed to speak of it, even now. The only way that the Malmuria survived was due to the wisdom of the Ancients. They foresaw the disaster in time to develop a way to survive it: they changed the entire planet into what it was now. And survive was what Malmur did.

Now the planet had a strange orbit in a different sun's system. Malmur's survival depended on a rigorous structure of harvesting that began early in the First Pass near the sun's third planet, ceased as Malmur disappeared behind the sun, and continued when Malmur passed the third planet again on the way back out. Then Malmur was plunged into darkness, a darkness so long and terrible nothing could survive on the planet's surface. The Malmuria themselves went into a cold

30

sleep in specially designed units and were awakened only after the First determined it was time.

Cicoi did not know how the First knew it was time, but in each Pass that Cicoi had experienced, the First had awakened the population at the exact moment.

Cicoi had been among the early arisers for a hundred Passes now. He was considered one of the young leaders, someone who would come into his strengths a hundred Passes in the future.

He was not prepared to be a Commander now.

Cicoi's upper tentacles rose and fell. His eyestalks floated around his face before he turned all of them to the valley below. He had to remember—it was important to remember—that once that valley had been great. And now it was no different from the rest of Malmur. Covered in black solar panels, dark and dusty and empty underneath the panels.

When Cicoi awoke on this Pass, he was a general, yes, but a young general. And since then he had been promoted.

He had become, with no special training, Commander of the South. He had known that he was in line for this position. But he had expected ten Passes of instruction, ten Passes of apprenticeship, and ten Passes of guided rule before he ever took over the position from his predecessor.

But his predecessor, and his predecessor's generals, had all reported to the recycler without having to be instructed to do so. They were no longer useful as living beings. They were killed, their bodies changed to much needed fuel and stored until the long journey into the dark night.

Such was the price of failure.

Cicoi's tentacles drooped further. The very thought of the losses overwhelmed him.

In all of Cicoi's memory, indeed in the memory of all Malmuria, even the Keepers of the Stored Memories, no ship had ever been lost during a harvest. No disaster had ever struck on the third planet. Always, the Sulas had been sent and

31

retrieved. Sometimes the creatures of the third planet had fought, but never in a meaningful way.

This time, the creatures had developed into a stronger people. They had technology, which they had never had before. They were able to destroy seven ships.

It was a disaster of untold proportions. Even now, when he should be examining the losses, trying to compensate for them, Cicoi preferred to stare into the valley below and imagine times long past. For he knew what the losses meant, just as all Malmuria did.

They meant that thousands of his kind would not be able to wake up on the next Pass due to the lack of ships to harvest food. They meant that thousands of his kind on this Pass would have reduced rations, making the long, cold sleep much more dangerous. The birthrate would be reduced for many Passes to come, until a balance was again reached with the number of harvester ships and the population.

He would not make those decisions. He would not decide whose rations would be cut or whose chance at procreation would be denied. Nor would he decide which workers had to forgo rest in order to repair the damage already done, to build more Sulas, and to attempt—since it had not been attempted in a thousand Passes—to build more ships.

No. His task was in some ways ethically easier, but practically much more difficult.

He had to figure out how to minimize those losses. He had to find ways to improve the yield on the next Pass, to harvest enough food with the equipment they had so that some of the losses below would not be as severe.

If he had the experience his predecessor had, he might make the right decisions. But Cicoi was new to the job, without training, and fearful of the consequences. He had seen the battles with the creatures from the third planet. He realized now what he had not seen on the last several Passes.

These were not primitives. These were creatures that had in

common with Malmuria a mind and a heart. They too had died defending their lands. They had technology, and with it, a memory. They would do all they could to fight again.

He could not assume that they would be as easily defeated this time.

At least the energy screens and panels were working at full efficiency. Malmur was taking all that it could from this sun, storing it, and keeping it so that the planet would survive the dark part of its long orbit.

Cicoi raised his eyestalks toward the sky. The light that Malmur received in this, its nearest contact to the sun, was thin and pale and extremely weak. Still, the brightness all but overwhelmed him. He pocketed seven of his eyestalks and continued to look above. Strange to think that something so simple as light, something so small as heat, would affect a world like theirs.

This was the only time in the entire Wakening Cycle that he could stand on the balcony without the warmers being activated. The balcony was usually not used because warmers were a waste of energy.

He usually valued his time here.

But not today. Today he knew how much it cost.

He turned and glided toward the doors. They eased open. His assistants were standing on their circles, working their floating units, attempting to maximize effort. His Second was bent over a representation of the third planet, looking for the lushest region, the place with the fewest creatures and the most food.

Cicoi was beginning to believe such places did not exist any longer.

As he glided to his circle in the center of the room, his assistants rose on the tips of their lower tentacles and raised their eyestalks so that all faced him. He waved a careless eyestalk at them all.

"I thank you for the honor," he said. "But continue your work."

He would continue his. He unpocketed two more eyestalks and raised a small image of the third planet for his own use when he heard ten soft chimes.

Irritation made his lower tentacles curl. Only he could ring the chimes, and then only when he had an emergency. He raised all of his eyestalks and bent them in displeasure at his assistants.

They had flattened themselves on the floor, tentacles covering each other in proper pattern.

The chimes sounded again, ten times, and as he heard each, he realized that these were not his chimes. They were too high-pitched, too warm.

Too old.

A shiver made his eyestalks stand on end. His assistants lowered themselves farther. At first, they had apparently thought, as he had, that the chimes had come from him. But on the second chiming, they realized, as he had, that the chimes had come from a higher authority.

Indeed, the highest authority.

The Elders.

Cicoi let his own lower tentacles slither outward. Nothing was normal about this Awakening. Nothing was going as it should.

He had never heard of a summoning by the Elders. Not in a hundred Passes.

The Elders were the survivors, the brains of the Ancients who had first designed Malmur for its journey across interstellar space. When Malmur was knocked out of its orbit around its original sun, it was the Elders who devised the plan that had saved them all. To make sure Malmur survived its centuries-long travels across deep space, the Elders left their bodies and only lived in an energy-free form, almost

34

pure thought, in the center of Malmur. They had not communicated with any leader since the very first cycle of this new star.

Some even said the Elders had allowed themselves to be recycled long ago, that the Elders no longer watched over the Malmuria, that the Malmuria were on their own.

And many of the dissenters used as proof the loss of seven ships, and the disaster that lay ahead.

Again the chimes sounded. Cicoi pocketed all but one of his eyestalks. His lower tentacles were splayed across the floor. He could not cower here, like his assistants. He was a young leader no longer. He was Commander of the South, and those chimes were for him.

If tradition was to be followed, and it would be, then the series of chimes would ring ten times. If he was not in the Elders Circle by the last of the chimes, he would no longer hold his position as Commander of the South.

He was tempted. He had lost the arrogance that had made him one of the youngest generals in the fleet. He knew that he had been promoted past his skills, that the tasks laid out for him had defeated a better person.

But Cicoi was not a coward. Slowly he slid his tentacles beneath him. Then he wrapped his upper tentacles around his body and glided from the room.

That the Elders had sought him out worried him, but he knew the summons was based on the loss of ships, the destruction that had happened on the third planet. In that, he found comfort. The Malmuria still had their greatest minds to help them solve the problems.

No. That was not what worried him. What worried him was the fact that the situation had become so grave, the Elders had again taken interest in Malmur. Until now, they had been content to allow the Malmuria to handle their own problems.

The Elders must have felt that this problem was beyond the

Malmuria's skills. So the situation was as extraordinary as Cicoi feared it was.

And his worst fear, the one he could barely admit to himself, was that the situation was so extraordinary, not even the Elders would know how to make things right.

2

April 26, 2018
1:13 P.M. Pacific Daylight Time

171 Days Until Second Harvest

For two days, Leo Cross had been working in the swirling black dust. His skin still crawled when he thought about where the dust had come from, but he thought about it less often.

He was standing in the center of what had once been a populated area. He wasn't familiar enough with Monterey to know exactly what the area was, or who had populated it, and for once, he was glad he didn't know.

He wore an environmental suit provided by the Army, but instead of a gas mask, he wore a simple doctor's mask over his mouth and nose. His eyes were covered with welder's goggles, and he had a hat with flaps that covered his ears. The dust still got into everything—his clothing, his shoes, even under his fingernails—but not in the quantity he had first feared. Even though he knew the short-term effects of this stuff were negligible, he was worried about the long term.

If the human race had a long term coming to it.

Jamison was working about a block away. They had discovered that, if they worked side by side, the dust cloud was almost unmanageable. Because the wands hadn't been designed for work in such fine material, the slight pressure with which the wands sorted through the dust created a cloud. Cross discovered that, unless he shut off his wand for nearly five minutes, the dust wouldn't settle. Even though the days had been sunny, he had felt as if he were working in twilight. What light he did get was filtered through the blackness and felt ominous. The times in the day when the ocean breeze picked up and cleared the dust clouds faster were the best.

It didn't help that the wand jammed a lot. Large items like snaps and zippers from clothing, pins that had once been in someone's hip, or even—God help him—dental fillings jammed the machine hourly. He actually began making a pile of the stuff on the first day and quit when the pile had become a mound.

He didn't like to think about what it symbolized. All those lives lost. So many that the U.S. government was now saying it doubted it could account for all of them. There were no bodies left to identify. Whenever people were reported missing from that particular area, they were considered dead. It was the only way the government could deal with the numbers. It also prevented a ton of lawsuits that survivors were going to file against the insurance industry.

Although Cross knew those lawsuits would get filed, no self-respecting insurance company covered its clients for "death resulting from alien attack."

He shook his head. His humor had become mordant, probably due to a lack of sleep. He quit at sundown, just as Jamison did, but every time he closed his eyes, he could hear the clinking and then silence that resulted whenever something got stuck in the wand. That first night, he had slept and dreamed of finding fingers, or bones, or eyes when he went to clear the jam.

He had awakened, a scream buried in his throat, and found it difficult to sleep soundly again. It didn't surprise him to see Jamison up as well. The two of them were now trading a stack of quarters back and forth from their penny-ante midnight poker games, neither of them wanting to admit that anything was better than sleep.

Cross's shoulders hurt, and so did the small of his back, but he kept working. Neither he nor Jamison had found one of the nanomachines yet, but he knew they would.

A hand touched Cross's shoulder and he jerked. He turned to see Jamison, dust covering his mask and goggles, indicating with his head that it was time for lunch.

Eating lunch was almost as difficult as sleeping, but Cross knew he had to do at least one. If he went without food *and* sleep he would be of no use to anyone.

He shut off the wand and let the dust settle. It floated around him like ash on the air. If he breathed just right, he could keep some of the flakes airborne. The entire scenario freaked him out.

He waited until the flakes settled slightly, blown on a slight breeze to his right, revealing the blue sky above him and the miles of blackness in front of him. Somewhere in all of that, a single nanomachine, smaller than anything he could imagine himself making, waited. Maybe more than a single one.

He had to find it.

He turned, felt the dust swirl around his feet, and looked at the ocean. Its blueness met the blueness of the sky at the horizon. Even if the aliens came and harvested again, destroying any possibility for mankind to continue on the Earth, the ocean would still be here, reflecting beautifully toward the sky.

He found comfort in that.

"Come on, Leo!" Jamison shouted.

One of the trucks had arrived with the afternoon grub. Usually Jamison and Cross had to slog to the nearest base. But this time, Jamison was eating a burger from the side of the truck, looking like a chimney sweep at a tailgate party.

The image made Cross smile. He walked carefully through the gunk until he reached the edge of the road. Then he waited for the dust to settle again. No sense in getting it on Jamison's food.

Cross's stomach was growling. He'd only had a banana for breakfast, and only because he knew he had to eat something. He barely remembered dinner the night before. Some spaghetti-like thing in the mess hall. Mostly he hadn't eaten. He had pushed the food around pretending to eat.

A burger actually sounded good.

It sounded normal.

An Army officer sat inside the truck with the door open. He was eating, too. The burgers were wrapped in aluminum with a fast-food logo on the side. He took a bacon cheeseburger, still warm, from the bag, and some soggy French fries. They tasted like a bit of salted heaven.

The officer, a blond man in his early twenties, handed Cross a Coke.

Cross took it and drank. The lemony sweetness tasted good, too. He had to take better care of himself.

He was halfway through the cheeseburger when the officer spoke.

"Dr. Cross?"

"Mmm?" Cross hated answering when his mouth was full.

"That's him," Jamison said, reaching around him for another burger. "Damn, this is fine food."

Cross swallowed. "Is this what football players consider gourmet?"

"Only if it has catsup," Jamison said, unwrapping the burger and taking a huge bite.

Cross wiped his mouth with the back of his hand. "Did you need me for something?" he asked the officer.

The officer nodded. He looked even younger than twenty, with his blond crew cut and his flaming red sunburn. His eyes had shadows beneath them, though, just like everyone else who worked on this project. It was their version of the thousand-yard stare.

40

"I wish I could say I was only here to bring you lunch, but you're wanted in Washington, sir, and I'm not allowed to leave until I take you with me."

Jamison shot him a look. Cross took a final bite of his burger, then set the rest of it down. It no longer tasted as good.

"I've already told them I'm staying here," Cross said.

"I'm not supposed to take no for an answer. General Maddox's orders, sir."

The officer said General Maddox's name as if she were God. And maybe to him she was. She was one of the members of the Joint Chiefs of Staff, and also a representative on the panel that formed the Tenth Planet Project. She had, during the Project's existence, kept it on track and given it validity throughout the military structure. She had also come up with the only game plan that had allowed them to destroy enemy ships.

She was justifiably famous.

She was also an absolute hard-ass whom Cross had tangled with more than once.

"Did she say why?" Cross asked.

"Something about you being the vision of the Tenth Planet Project."

He blinked. The burger he had eaten sat like a lump in his stomach. He had been the vision behind the Tenth Planet Project. He had been the push to get the world governments to do something, anything, before the tenth planet arrived. It had been his foresight that had enabled them to find the planet in the first place.

The tenth planet had an elliptical 2006-year orbit that took it into the very depths of space. Unlike other recurring events in the solar system, from Halley's comet on down, the tenth planet's orbit was so long that only archaeological records held its secret. There was no one alive who remembered it, and there were few written records about it—and certainly no written records from anyone who understood it.

41

Cross had seen the archaeological record, and had managed to tie it, through astroarchaeology, to something that happened in the sky. He had used his friend Doug Mickelson, the secretary of state, to open doors that would otherwise have remained closed.

That was why Clarissa Maddox called Cross the vision of the Tenth Planet Project.

"I think I'm more useful here," he said.

"You can argue with the kid all you want," Jamison said, "but he's not going to stand up to Maddox for you. You'll have to fly back to D.C. to do it on your own."

Cross shook his head. "I'm not beyond my usefulness here."

"We can do this. I can train someone else to use the wand," Jamison said.

"Yes, but I am the one familiar with the fossils. I'm the one—"

"We'll know it when we see it," Jamison said. "If we have any questions, I can always e-mail or call you. Chances are, they need you for some bogus meeting, and you'll be back here when it's done. Trust me, going is easier than fighting a member of the Joint Chiefs."

Cross sighed. He was just getting tired of meetings in which everyone rehashed all the facts that they didn't know. He found it even more discouraging than digging through this dust and finding fillings that had, until a few weeks ago, been a part of someone's mouth.

"You're not going to let me off the hook either, are you?" Cross asked.

Jamison finished his second burger and tossed the wrapper in the bag. "If I'd known this was why you were avoiding your link, I'd've been on your butt in an instant. This is a needle-in-a-haystack project no matter how you spin it, Leo. And you don't know what they're going to discuss in Washington. They might need you more there than we do here."

42

"I think I know," Cross said. "It's just another meeting."

"If it were just another meeting, don't you think your colleagues would let you stay out here?"

Cross looked at him. Jamison was probably right.

This was a meeting of the Tenth Planet Project, and even though Cross had been to a dozen meetings since the aliens left, none of them had been of the original Tenth Planet group. The meetings had been for other things, crisis things, with some or none of the members of the Tenth Planet Project.

That alone made this coming meeting different.

He knew it. He was just avoiding it. And he couldn't any longer. That was what he had been telling his colleagues: no one had time to shut their eyes anymore. And yet he was trying to do it, too.

It was hard to look clearly at something that could destroy life as he knew it.

"All right," he said to Jamison. "But you call me the instant you find something."

Jamison mock saluted, a goofy grin on his face. "I'll call you in a nanosecond, sir."

"You know," Cross said, smiling for the first time in a while, "I believe you will."

April 27, 2018
18:05 Universal Time

170 Days Until Second Harvest

Commander Cicoi had only been in Elders Circle once before, several Passes ago, as he got a tour of Command Central. He had just been made general, and it was customary to let all generals know what they were defending.

He had thought it odd that the Commanders believed the

generals were defending buildings. Cicoi had always thought he was defending Malmuria.

Elders Circle was deep within the bowels of Command Central, ten layers below the tenth public layer. The Waiting Chamber was icy cold, even for Malmur, and the lighting was thin, activated when the first tentacle crossed the threshold. The Waiting Chamber was done in black; the Waiting Circles, dark spots on an already dark floor.

The Commander of the North was already in the room, on the Waiting Circle that designated his position. The Commander of the North was the oldest of the Commanders, the only one of the main Commanders who did not lose his life after the disaster. He was large, as most elder Malmuria were, but his tentacles were graying at the tips. Someday, his upper tentacles would be gray and useless, his lower nearly solid stumps, and he would lose his position through sheer immobility.

It was a fate that awaited them all, a fate that Cicoi was not looking forward to.

The Commander of the North raised a single eyestalk, turned it, and peered at Cicoi. "We await only the Commander of the Center, then."

Cicoi nodded. The Commander of the Center was in a tenuous position. He had risen through the ranks, as the rest of them had, but had done so over the objections of the Brood Nest females. The females, though a younger group, had made it known that they did not accept the results of the last harvest. They were clamoring for one of theirs to become a Commander, even though they had no military experience.

The clamor was coming from the Center, from a group of females who believed that all decisions should consider the impact on the nestlings and the families, and the future of the race. Some of the youngest females, barely out of the nest, their tentacles newly sprouted, believed they should get military training just like the males.

44

Fortunately this rebelliousness had not spread to the other segments. In fact, the Commanders had tried to keep news of this uprising quiet, so that the other females would not learn of it. The females would be busy enough tending the broods and making the food harvested by the Sulas last long enough to compensate for the shortages.

The final set of chimes were ringing as the Commander of the Center entered the Waiting Chamber. He seemed diminished somehow, as if command had shortened him and damaged his tentacles.

He slid onto his circle, his head bowed, all but two of his eyestalks pocketed. More problems in the Center then. Cicoi did not want to know about them.

Cicoi stood on his own circle, head bowed. His tentacles were at his side in proper respectful position. He stood on the tips of his lower tentacles. He had pocketed nine of his eyestalks. When facing the Elders, the ancient instructions said that no more than two eyestalks should be showing. That, of course, was different from the circle of respect for their betters that the Malmuria formed around their faces with all ten eyestalks. It felt awkward and uncomfortable. Cicoi had to work to keep the single eyestalk from floating freely and looking too closely at things it should not see.

The room darkened for a moment, and then ten bells rang. Cicoi felt a sheen of nervous moisture form on his outliner. A waste of energy, but he could not stop it.

Then the floor whitened and dropped away. The standing circles were the only support. If Cicoi stepped off his, he would fall into white nothingness.

Slowly his circle lowered and, he noted with his uncontrollable eyestalk, so did the other two. The Commanders of the Center and North were holding their positions as if a single movement would hurt them.

In exasperation at his own lack of control, Cicoi pocketed

45

his last eyestalk and let the circle take him down in darkness. Only when he felt the circle bounce to a stop did he release an eyestalk—a different eyestalk.

He had sight just in time to watch the room above, where they had been standing only a moment before, disappear. The ceiling closed, leaving them in this expansive luminescence.

It was so bright to his single eye that Cicoi could not make out the details in the room. Except that this vast chamber had a slight breeze and was hotter than any other place he had ever been on Malmur.

Was the energy expended here some of the energy brought to the planet through the solar panels? Or was there something else going on?

He raised a second eyestalk, keeping it in rigid control. He noted that the Commanders of the North and Center had their eyestalks pointed in two different directions. He did the same.

Then, from the depths below, creatures rose. They were shaped like Malmuria, but they were just black shadows, almost outlines of the shape of Malmuria. All of their eyestalks were floating around their heads in an uncontrolled fashion, and their tentacles waved like a child's before the child learned discipline.

One of the creatures assumed the front position. Cicoi saw that the rest, at least twenty, formed a row behind. He turned one of his eyestalks. There were others behind him. Perhaps fifty Elders in all.

It was the force of their presence that kept this chamber warm. Cicoi wanted to hunch forward like the Commander of the Center, but he did not allow himself to do so. To express fear or even awe was to insult the Elders.

Then there was a whisper inside Cicoi's mind. A faint hum, like the touch of a tentacle before a male-female bonding. He tilted his head involuntarily and saw the others doing so as well.

Good, a wispy voice said. Cicoi realized it belonged to the lead Elder. *You can hear us now.*

Cicoi waved his front tentacle in acknowledgment as the other Commanders did the same. The Commander of the Center had raised a single eyestalk in surprise.

We have been content for all this time to watch and let our people make their own way through the problems our new sun has brought. And for thousands of Passes near this new sun, all has gone well. Until this Pass.

The thought felt alien, unlike his thoughts. It was like a voice, but not like a voice. Cicoi tamped down a feeling of fear. These were the Elders, the ones who had made Malmur survive. He had to listen to them.

He tried to control his own thoughts, in case they could hear what he was thinking in return.

The ability of our people to supply our basic needs has been put in extreme danger by the quick and surprising development of the race on the third planet. You must not underestimate these creatures as you have done before.

That was the argument Cicoi had just made to his own Second. But to say that, and to do it, were two different things. The creatures on the third planet had changed so much between this Pass and the last that they seemed to be almost different creatures.

There was no time to study them. There was no time at all.

We feel that for the safety of our entire race, we, as Elders, must again step forward to guide our people past this crisis. It was the way of the past. It is the way of the present.

The words echoed inside Cicoi's mind. He felt no judgment in them; only acceptance of what must occur. The Elders continued flowing, their tentacles moving in the same direction. Cicoi wondered if their wispy forms were simply for the benefit of the Commanders or if the Elders truly looked like that. No one, except perhaps the Keeper of Secrets, would know the answer.

47

The Elders seemed to be waiting for some sort of response to those last words. Cicoi did not know what to say. The Commander of the Center was standing taller on the tips of his tentacles, but he didn't seem to know either. He turned an eyestalk toward Cicoi as if he were expecting Cicoi to do something.

But it was the Commander of the North who finally spoke. He turned his two eyestalks forward in a bad imitation of the circle of respect and pointed his upper tentacles down. He rose as high as he could on his lower tentacles.

"Forgive me, O Great Ones, for speaking to such an august body," the Commander of the North said. "We will do what is needed. We will heed your guidance. We welcome it."

The Elders did not move. In no way did they acknowledge the Commander of the North's polite movements, nor did they respond in kind. The Elders, perhaps, had had different traditions once upon a time.

Finally the lead Elder bowed his head, his eyestalks facing the Commanders. Cicoi's lower tentacles went rigid, and he nearly lost his balance. The direct stare of all those eyes— those ghostly black eyes—was more than he could take.

You must heed us, the Elder said, *if you are to survive.*

His words almost sounded like a rebuke. Was it a rebuke to the Commander of the North for having the temerity to speak to them?

The Commander of the North bent his eyestalks forward and said nothing. Neither did anyone else.

Hear our words, the Elder said.

The phrase was echoed by the others, a faint chorus, that jangled in Cicoi's mind.

The Commander of the North turned an eyestalk toward Cicoi as if Cicoi had done something to provoke the Elder's words. But Cicoi kept his rigid position.

We shall guide you, the lead Elder said. *But before we do, we shall give you an overview, so you know how to prepare.*

48

The Commander of the Center moaned. It was a small, involuntary sound, but it echoed in the large chamber. Several of the Elders turned toward him, and a breeze came up.

"I'm sorry, O Great Ones," the Commander of the Center said, two of his eyestalks waving wildly. "I mean no disrespect."

The Elders turned away from him. Apparently that was all the acknowledgment they would give him.

It was as if the interlude had never happened.

Here is how you will prepare, the lead Elder said.

Cicoi waited, concentrating as hard as he could, so that these words would become part of him.

The next harvest of the third planet must be complete and varied. We must obtain enough raw materials to finish building new harvest ships. An Elder will be on each harvest ship to make certain that the procedures are followed exactly. You will prepare your generals to work with us.

Cicoi shuddered slightly. Commanders, at least, had always been warned of the possibility of meeting the Elders. The generals had not. And one of the Commanders was having trouble, despite the warning. The generals had better be tougher than Cicoi thought they were.

Nine Elders floated from the group and stopped beside the one who seemed to be giving the orders.

We will go with you now to begin preparations. The very existence of our people rests on what we do next. We must not fail.

Cicoi wanted to say they would not fail, but he did not. He did not like the way the Elders had treated the other two who spoke. Instead, Cicoi kept his stance rigid and waited for further instructions.

But there were none. The lead Elder waved his eyestalks, turning them toward all the other Elders. They imitated the movement, and then their tentacles pointed upward.

The ceiling opened, and the breeze grew stronger. The Elders tilted their heads back, pointed their lower tentacles behind them so that they were streamlined, and floated toward the cold darkness above.

Cicoi unpocketed two more eyestalks so that he could watch this tremendous sight. Fifty Elders, their bodies wispy and black, absorbing all light and energy, soared toward the surface of Malmur, a place they had not been in generations.

A place they had not been in living memory.

A place they had not been since Malmur left its home sun a long, long time ago.

Cicoi had thought life for his people was hard before. Now it would become even harder.

April 27, 2018
8:45 A.M. Eastern Daylight Time

170 Days Until Second Harvest

Leo Cross balanced one suitcase against his thigh as he struggled with the old-fashioned lock on his front door. He had already disengaged the security system, but for some reason his housekeeper Constance insisted on using all of the locks when he was gone, including the one on the antique oak door. He should have waited at the airport for fifteen more minutes. By then, she would have arrived and been able to let him into his own house.

Instead, he had to waggle the ancient brass key into the even older brass lock and wait until he heard the tumblers turn. Then he pushed the door open with his shoulder.

The suitcase fell inward with a bang and Cross stiffened, half expecting his mother's voice to yell at him from upstairs. But his parents were long gone. Only their ghosts echoed throughout the house. He had grown up here, and had done little since his parents' death to make the house his. The antiques his mother so loved still filled the foyer and most of the ground level.

Still, it felt good to be home. It felt good to have a home to return to. He shuddered. He'd managed to get some sleep on the red-eye he had taken back from San Francisco, but his dreams had been filled with the slight whirr of NanTech's wand and the clank of wedding bands as they hit the glass front. Wedding bands and engagement rings and anniversary necklaces. So much stuff that had meant so much to people at one time and was now not much more than junk.

His personal phone hadn't rung since he left, nor had his pager gone off. Jamison clearly hadn't found anything—and neither had Bradshaw and Groopman in South America.

Cross sighed and kicked the door closed. Then he lugged his suitcases upstairs and tossed them on the king-sized bed he had bought specially for his room. He had made this room his, with its utilitarian furniture and high-tech gadgetry. It wasn't fair to say he had missed it—he hadn't been gone long enough—but he did feel more relaxed when he was here.

Downstairs the door opened, and he thought he heard female laughter. Constance usually wasn't so merry when she came to work. She had been with the family forever. He could no more get rid of her than he could have fired his grandmother. She made certain he ate well and his home wasn't a complete pigsty.

Cross could have afforded an entire bevy of housekeepers—his parents had left him independently wealthy—but he rarely thought of the money. Instead, it provided him a way to do the work he loved. Or the work he had once loved, before the world had changed with the attack of the aliens.

He pulled off his clothes and took a hot shower, staying for a long time under the spray. He needed to get the feel of the black dust off him. He knew he didn't really have any on him, but that didn't matter. What mattered was the sense of it, the way his skin crawled even when he thought of it.

As he got out, the smell of fried pork sausage reached him, along with the scent of pancakes and fresh coffee. Constance was here, and she knew he was home.

For the first time in days, he felt really and truly hungry.

He pulled on a sweater and a pair of jeans, and walked, barefoot, down the stairs. He would have to change before the big meeting, but he had about four hours. Even in the worst traffic, it wouldn't take him that long to get downtown.

Soft voices reached him as he got to the bottom of the stairs. Female voices. For a moment, he thought Constance had the radio or the television on, and then he recognized the second voice.

His mouth went instantly dry.

Britt.

He hadn't expected to see her until the meeting.

He ran a hand through his wet hair, feeling like a teenager ill prepared for a first date. Dr. Brittany Archer had that effect on him. They had become involved shortly after they met, and they'd been lovers for some time now, but his heart still jumped when he heard her voice. He hadn't felt this strongly about any woman in all his years. All he wished was that he'd met Britt Archer under different circumstances.

Cross made his way through the hall into the kitchen. Constance was pouring batter on the griddle. She already had a pile of perfectly formed pancakes on a platter. Sausages steamed on another platter beside it. Fresh-squeezed orange juice was in a glass pitcher near the refrigerator, and the last of the coffee percolated through the automated coffeemaker.

Britt was sitting at the kitchen table, her stockinged feet on one of the old chairs. Her dark hair was pulled back and held by a gold Irish-love-knot barrette—which would have survived the mess in Monterey. The thought made Cross's gorge rise and he fought it down.

Britt turned to him, her intelligent eyes missing nothing. She stood. She was nearly as tall as he was.

52

"It was tough there, huh?"

Apparently she saw it in his face. He wrapped his arms around her and pulled her close. He didn't want to think about it, didn't really want to discuss it. He buried his face in her neck and let himself feel how alive she was.

After a moment, Constance said, "I got breakfast for you, Leo," as if nothing had changed.

The memory of the past two days had played hell with his appetite again, but he wasn't going to let all this food go to waste. He squeezed Britt, then let her go, and walked over to Constance.

"You're trying to make me fat," he said.

"And I'm failing," she said. "Looks like you lost weight in the past two days."

"Without your cooking, how could I survive?" He grabbed a plate from the cupboard and served himself, slathering the pancakes with butter and pouring maple syrup on top. Then he poured a glass of orange juice and headed for the table.

Britt was just behind him, serving herself, as well.

They didn't even make a dent in the food, although Constance continued cooking, as if she were trying to feed an army instead of two of them. Cross had noticed that Constance had been doing that ever since the alien ships arrived, making too much food and then giving much of it away to shelters later on. It was as if some part of her felt guilty for still being there, for still being alive, for having a place to go and people to take care of.

Cross took a bite of pancake and decided he hadn't had anything that good in a long time. Then he smiled at Britt and put his hand on hers. "I didn't expect to see you until later."

"You think I'd want a reunion with you in front of the Tenth Planet Project?" Her eyes twinkled and she shook her head. "They would have loved that."

She got up and poured herself a huge mug of coffee. Then she held up the pot. "You want any?"

He shook his head. He wasn't quite the coffee freak that she was. He'd wait until he was done eating.

She came back to the table and sat down. She wrapped her hands around the mug and stared at him. "Do you want to talk about it?"

The pancake he'd been eating turned to glue in his mouth. He shook his head.

"I take it you didn't find anything."

"Not yet," he said. "I should still be there."

"I'm sure Lowry will do just fine." Britt had never really believed that they'd find a nanomachine, even after Cross had made the argument to her, the same one he'd made to Jamison. "We need you here."

"Did something happen?"

"Not to my knowledge," Britt said. "But I'm not the one who called the meeting." She shoved her mug away, picked up her fork, and dug into her breakfast. "I suspect it's just a briefing."

Cross sighed and took a sip of orange juice. It was fresh and cool and delicious. "Then why call me back?"

Britt raised her eyes at him without moving her head. "Leo," she said softly, "you just don't get it sometimes, do you?"

"Get what?" he asked.

"How important you are."

"I'm no more important than you or Jesse Killius or Yolanda Hayes," he said, listing two other members of the committee. Jesse Killius was the head of NASA and Yolanda Hayes was the president's science adviser.

"Yes, you are." Britt set down her fork. "It was your insight that warned us of this problem in the first place, and you were the one who figured out that they're coming back."

"No," he said. "You did."

She shook her head. "You solidified it. You're the unifying force on this committee. Without you, it goes nowhere."

"Even if I never have another brilliant idea."

"Even if," she said. "This is no longer about brilliant ideas. It's about survival. You run the team whether you want to or not."

"Clarissa Maddox runs the team."

"Because you think she runs meetings efficiently," Britt said. "They never start until you arrive. It's unthinkable to have a Tenth Planet Project meeting without you."

Cross sighed, and rubbed the bridge of his nose with his thumb and forefinger. Out of the corner of his eye, he saw Constance watching them. She smiled at him.

"Someday you'll figure out that your strengths aren't where you think they are," Constance said.

Cross looked at her. "Oh? You mean I'm not a good archaeologist?"

She shrugged. "Right now, it's not your digging skills that matter. It's your imagination."

"She's right," Britt said.

"My imagination is giving me nightmares," he said.

"From California?"

He nodded.

Britt rested her head on her palm. "Tell me about it."

He couldn't yet. He didn't have the right words, and to explain the horror incorrectly was to cheapen it. "It's not something you want to discuss over breakfast," he said. He pushed his half-finished meal away, and Constance brought him coffee without his having to ask for it. He put his hand around the warm mug.

"So," he said, "did our alien *friends* get home safely?"

Britt blinked, obviously confused, and then she gave him a rueful smile. "I'm sorry to say they did, as far as we can tell."

He sighed. They were talking about the alien ships, heading back toward the tenth planet. Britt's agency, the Space Telescope Science Institute, was using all of its telescopes,

55

from the Hubble III on down, to monitor the alien ships as they left Earth's orbit and headed back to the passing tenth planet.

"I was hoping they'd self-destruct or something," he said.

She shook her head. "That only happens in the movies. Too bad, huh?"

He sipped the coffee. It was better than the stuff the Army had served him. "Do we know what will happen at the meeting today?"

"No," Britt said. "I know we'll get a report on the alien ships—what they're made of, how they're vulnerable, that sort of thing."

"We know that?"

She shrugged. "I don't know. The report might just be about what we don't know."

Cross sighed. For all the speeches everyone was making about his importance, it sounded like the meeting would be the same old thing. "Anything else?"

Britt loudly sipped the rest of her coffee, then set the mug down. "If there's something new and surprising, I haven't heard about it."

Cross closed his eyes. "The end of the world is coming, and all we're doing is having meetings."

"We're doing more than that," Britt said.

He opened his eyes. She looked tired. They were all tired. "Oh?" he asked. "What else are we doing?"

"We're trying to figure out a way to destroy those aliens," she said, her voice so cold it even stopped Constance for an instant at the stove.

Cross looked at Britt. Her eyes were dark, focused on something far away. And the anger was just below the surface of her face, just as it was below all of theirs at the moment.

Cross thought about the fillings rattling around in the wand

56

in California, then sighed. "I would do anything to stop them. Damn near anything."

"So would I," Britt said, coldly. "So would I."

3

April 27, 2018
11:41 A.M. Central Daylight Time

170 Days Until Second Harvest

Vivian Hartlein had spent the early morning standing outside the gates of Graceland until some security guard waved her away. Then she crossed Elvis Presley Boulevard to the now-boarded-up Day's Inn and sat in its parking lot, staring at the long lawn heading up to the old mansion. She'd toured the King's home dozens of times—the first with her parents when she was just a little thing—and she liked the way it always stayed the same. The dark kitchen with its faint never-to-leave smell of grease. The yellow dining room, the beautiful white piano. A permanent place. A historical place. A place where time seemed to stand still.

Vivian had come here every day since the attack. She wanted to go inside again, she wanted to see if time would reverse for her, and she thought maybe it would happen in Graceland. Maybe if she went inside, she would see her mom again. And her dad. They had been gone for years.

Maybe if she went inside, she'd see Cheryl and Lucy and Tommi Jo. She'd told them to stay out of California, but they didn't listen to her. They'd gone anyway, saying there was nothing in Memphis for them. All the jobs were west. And what did Cheryl end up doing, but working in some tourist place near the ocean? She could've worked at Graceland or any of the places around it, or got a job on Mud Island, or even gone to Nashville. It was far, but not that far.

And it hadn't been wiped off the face of the Earth.

Cheryl, her daughter. Lucy, her granddaughter. And Tammi Jo, who was just a baby. Their daddy didn't even have the decency to call, to find out what happened. He was so dumb he didn't even know the attack had happened over Cheryl's house, over her work.

Vivian's husband, Dale, he'd gone out there, trying to find his little girl, and the Army didn't tell him nothing. Vivian stayed home. She couldn't get herself in no airplane. Never had been able to. Dale thought it was maybe connected to that time when she couldn't leave the house, back when she was pregnant with Cheryl, her only child.

Back when she had had hope.

She choked and swallowed hard. Dale was still in California, waiting to get remains, if there was going to be remains. He said he wasn't counting on it. He said there was nothing he could do. He said he'd never felt so helpless in his whole life.

Dale Hartlein, a man who'd never been helpless. One afternoon in California, he told her, he jumped the fence, and went into that black mess himself without protection, tracing the concrete buried beneath the dust, picking up metal road signs with the names pressed into them, and finding, through sheer energy, Cheryl's house.

Or what was left of it.

He said he sat down and bawled like a baby.

Vivian'd never seen Dale cry. He'd teared up when Cheryl was born, and them tears'd come back the day Cheryl said she was marrying that loser ex-husband of hers, but he'd never cried. Not once.

59

Till now.

And when he told Vivian that, she knew her baby, and her baby's babies, was well and truly dead.

He was staying in California until he had remains, but that might mean he'd be gone forever. The bureaucracy ruled, just like she always knew it had. Like her own daddy used to say. *The government ain't nothing but a pack of fools leading another pack of fools by the nose.*

She believed it now. Only now they had gotten worse. Now they had killed her family. And for that, she was going to make them pay.

She had left the Day's Inn at sunrise and come to Riverside Park. The Mississippi smelled faintly of mud and river mold. Barges and tugs still made their way through the shallow water as if nothing had happened. Planes flew overhead. Life went on.

For most people, life went on.

She sat on the old bandstand near a grove of trees and watched as the first car pulled into the lot. She was taking a risk holding the meeting here, in such a public place, in the middle of the day, but she didn't know who would come. She'd keep things toned down. She didn't say nothing in her flyers, or on the web site, or in them radio announcements she made to all the call-in shows about what, exactly, she was going to talk about.

She'd just tell them the truth she learned from Dale. She'd just tell them how the government killed her family and how she was going to get even.

She'd tell them the truth as she knew it from the moment she saw them phony pictures on CNN.

Another car pulled into the lot. Then another. People she didn't recognize was opening the doors and getting out.

She took a deep breath as she watched them, straightening her shoulders, shaking the nervousness out of her. It began this way, with a small group. Jesus taught the world that,

60

two thousand years ago. He started with twelve, and they spread the gospel all over the land.

The tough part was speaking out. Once she spoke out, then the news would spread and everyone would know.

Sometimes she wondered why they didn't already. It seemed so obvious to her.

There was no aliens. There'd never been aliens. Ever since she was a little girl, there'd been talk of aliens. Best-selling books with slant-eyed creatures on the cover. Movies with those same creatures—sometimes friendly, but usually trying to take over Earth. Then those series of "true" stories, mostly on the TV, about people getting abducted.

By the time Vivian was twelve, as many people believed in aliens as believed in angels. She remembered that statistic because Reverend Foster used it in one of his most famous sermons, the one where he lamented the loss of true faith.

Well, she had true faith. And Cheryl had, too. But Cheryl had become an unwitting victim of a plot to take over the world. Vivian was already seeing it. The news carried parts of it. The other countries was listening to the president. Soon he'd take over everything, a man who didn't believe in God or liberty or nothing.

A dozen cars was in the parking lot now, and a group of people was hanging around the edge of the grass, just staring at her. If she was going to do this, she had to take control.

Dale'd tried to talk her out of it, tried at least to get her to wait until he got home. But she wasn't going to wait, not anymore. It was either wait and let the grief eat her up, eat her message and make Cheryl and Lucy and Tommi Jo die for nothing, or Vivian would start taking action. She was angry and someone was going to pay.

She'd always been an action woman. Sitting around just made things worse.

She waved a hand toward the group, and a tall thin man

61

with long blond hair grinned at her. He spoke softly to the others around him, and they came forward like a little troop. She was surprised she didn't recognize none of them.

More cars was pulling in. A man in a business suit got out of one of them, along with a woman wearing too much makeup for a rally. And sure enough, they took out a video camera.

She didn't want them taping the rally. She knew what they'd do. They'd send it on, make her a laughingstock or, worse, sic the government on her. Kill her. That couldn't happen. Not yet. Not this early.

The blond man had gotten to the bandstand. He looked like a take-charge type.

"Hi," she said. "I'm Vivian Hartlein. I'm the one who called this here meeting."

"Jake Styles," he said.

"Well, Jake Styles, there ain't gonna to be nothing happening here if them reporters stay. Think you can get them to go?"

He looked over his shoulder. "Why would I want to?"

"Why're you here?" she asked.

His blue eyes darkened. "My daddy lived on the California coast."

"My daughter and her babies did, too," Vivian said.

They stared at each other a moment. Bonded. She felt it. The loss created a link between them. Without saying nothing more, he turned around and walked toward the reporters.

She'd picked well. He had a charm about him.

More and more cars came. There was maybe fifty people here now. Some she knew, most she didn't. The ones she knew belonged to some of the same groups as Dale. They looked surprised to see her without him.

She wasn't speaking for him today. She was speaking for everyone. And for her dead daughter and grandchildren.

The woman reporter laughed and then patted Jake Styles

on the arm. Oh, charm was useful. But not everything. Still, the reporters got back in their car, backed up, and pulled out of the lot. Jake Styles stood at the edge of the lot until the car disappeared.

By then, her entire crowd was sitting on the dew-damp river grass or standing at the fringes, leaning on trees for support. He came back, shrugged amiably, and said, "I don't think they're coming back."

"What'd you tell them?" she asked.

"That this was the traditional singing rally for the Baptist churches in the area. We're just organizing, and we'd hope they'd come back when we're getting ready to sing in the big sing-a-thon in July."

"You didn't," Vivian said.

"I did." He grinned. "They said that explained the strangeness of the announcements they'd heard on the radio, and they were sorry for troubling us. And they got the date of the big sing-a-thon. They were embarrassed they didn't know about it."

"I can't believe they believed that."

"People believe anything, you say it with enough conviction." His eyes seemed to bore right through her. He was right, of course. That was what she was here to talk about. "You know, if you're gonna talk about how awful things are and not give no ways to resolve things, I ain't staying."

"We got to take things into our own hands," she said.

"Things?" he asked.

"What do you do?" she said. "You ain't government, are you?"

"If I was government, you think I'd be here?"

"Them reporters was."

He took a battered wallet out of his back pocket. Inside was his electricians' union card, tattered now, and a driver's license, a few ripped photos, and nothing else. None of them credit cards or them identification strips that had a person's entire medical history on it. No electronic slider cards at all.

The casual way he handed his life to her was just as it should be. A code among compatriots. A way that believers knew they weren't alone.

"I been thinking about this a long time," she said. "Studying it. Not just when them so-called aliens came, but before. You want to listen?"

"Yeah."

She nodded toward the people before her. "Join them. When I get 'em fired up, I'm going to find out how many of them is truly interested."

"In doing what?"

"Crippling the government. Getting rid of all them who killed our family and aim to kill our country. I know the perfect way to do it."

"Them reporters would say that the government is our only protection."

"Yeah," Vivian said. "They would. They're the ones who aired the phony pictures of those alien ships, and they're the ones who say, 'believe in the president,' and they're the ones who're encouraging allying with other countries. We're going to lose our sovereignty. We're going to become part of a worldwide dictatorship, run by godless people. It's been happening for a while. But now your daddy and my daughter, they been caught in the first assault."

"You think our government did that to our own people?"

She raised her eyes to his. His look was flat, even. He didn't seem shocked. "You do, too."

He nodded.

"Sit down. We got a lot of talking."

He found a place in the crowd. She stared at them for a moment, wishing Dale was here instead of in California. He'd be proud of her. Whenever he had a group needed convincing,

64

whenever he had a difficult customer who needed coddling, he called her.

You missed your calling, baby doll, he used to say. *You shoulda been some sort of preacher, a leader. You wasted it sitting home.*

Don't never say I wasted time raising our girl, Dale Hartlein, she used to say in response. She hadn't wasted time.

But she had lost it.

She stood in front of the crowd and raised her arms. They looked wary. Then she started to speak, and they all looked at her as if she was going to lead them to the promised land.

They was in the promised land. She was going to show them that. And then she was going to show them how to cast out the evil ones and take the land back.

It would not be easy.

But it would be right.

April 27, 2018
12:55 P.M. Eastern Daylight Time

170 Days Until Second Harvest

Dr. Leo Cross wished he had never seen this room.

It was a standard conference room, built in the middle of the last century, and furnished in the 1980s. The conference table, which stood on wobbly legs, carried coffee rings so old that they were practically fossilized. The cushions on the chairs had been worn thin fifteen years ago.

Cross had sat in this room more than he wanted to think about, ever since the Tenth Planet Project was founded earlier that year. The discussions here were often a prelude to gaining more information in the days before the attacks. In those days, he had considered the meetings successful.

Now he wasn't so sure.

He kept going over and over information in his mind, wondering if he had spoken up sooner—maybe even a year sooner—about his suspicions, the first attacks wouldn't have gone as badly as they had.

But if he had spoken up then, he might have been dismissed as a crackpot. He didn't have all the evidence then that he had when he finally approached his friend, Doug Mickelson, who was the secretary of state. Doug had opened a pile of doors for him, and in many very real ways, got the Tenth Planet Project started.

Britt set down the Starbucks travel mug that Cross had bought for her after the last Tenth Planet Project meeting. The mug was steaming. She set down a Starbucks paper cup for him, filled with the latte he'd asked for. He wasn't sure, with the heavy breakfast, the interrupted sleep, and the awful way he'd been eating, that his stomach could take any more caffeine.

Robert Shane of the President's Special Committee on Space Sciences, and one of the Project's cooler heads, sat down across from Britt. Shane was a tanned, athletic man whose blond hair was cropped short. He had sharp blue eyes and a quick wit that, Cross suspected, served him well in his government post. Shane was first and foremost a scientist, and in all the meetings, through all the debates, Shane never forgot that, which was something Cross appreciated.

Britt took a sip from her mug, and tapped on her wrist-'puter. Taking time away from the office to spend the morning with Cross had cost her a lot. She had been working around the clock, canceling research times on the various space telescopes and trying to determine which agency now had priority with the vast machines. Before the aliens had arrived, the telescopes' time was carefully parceled out to scientists and researchers all over the globe. Now the crisis took precedence, and Britt found her orderly life in complete disarray.

"I hope this damn thing starts on time." Yolanda Hayes, the president's science adviser, walked into the room. She had her dark hair pulled away from her face, and she was wearing minimal makeup. When Cross had first met her—what seemed like years ago, but was actually only seven months before—she was one of the most stylish women he had ever seen. She still wore the clothes, but the details were gone: no painted nails, no lipstick. It was as if she no longer had time for anything but the essentials. "I feel like I'm coordinating an army."

"Maybe that's because you are." Jesse Killius, the head of NASA, followed her into the room. Jesse looked more tired than Cross had ever seen her.

"I guess." Hayes smiled, but the smile was small. "My job used to be committees and advice. I never expected to coordinate a nationwide research effort in so many different areas."

"None of us did," Shane said. "At least we have the information about most of the nation's scientists at our fingertips."

Hayes nodded. "I'm just worried that we don't have enough."

No one answered her. It was the fear they all had, on various levels, and it really had nothing to do with their areas of expertise. It had to do with the aliens, the tenth planet, and the fact that they were in the lull between storms they didn't entirely understand.

"I can't believe Clarissa's the one who's late," Killius said. "She had her aide call me last night to remind me about this."

"She's balancing too much," Shane said. "She probably shouldn't even be in this meeting anymore."

"I'm glad she is," Cross said. "She's still representing the president."

At that moment the door slammed back and General Clarissa Maddox strode into the room. She was a powerfully built woman who wore her general's uniform like a shield. Her back was so straight that Cross sometimes wondered if it had been surgically altered.

She took her seat and nodded to the group. "I see I'm just in time for the uplink," she said, which was probably the only acknowledgment she would make of being late.

"Coffee, General?" Shane asked.

Half a smile crossed Maddox's face. "Right now, I'm subsisting on the stuff. I'd love some."

Shane got up, went to the refreshments table, and poured her a cup. Even though there were pastries on the table as usual, no one had taken any.

The two flat vid screens were already down. As the clock hit 1 P.M., images appeared in various corners: the Japanese representatives, the European representatives, the Africans, and the newest members, the Chinese. Most of the groups were sitting at long conference tables like the U.S. group was, and Cross was surprised that he knew the rooms in those faraway lands as well as he knew this room here. In fact, it almost seemed as if the rooms were somewhere in this building, in parts he hadn't been to yet.

The customary greetings in the various languages echoed. The official language of the Tenth Planet Project was English, partly because it had become the language of science, and partly out of deference to the Americans, who were the ones who first put this meeting together. But the greetings were always in the native tongues, and it was a custom no one wanted to forgo.

When the formalities were done, General Maddox sighed so softly that only those at the U.S. table could hear her. Then she smiled, a businesslike smile that had an edge of weariness to it.

"I have a personal announcement first," she said.

Cross stiffened. Britt put her hand on his arm. *Here it comes,* Shane mouthed. Apparently he thought what they all were thinking: they were going to lose the general.

"I've been asked to leave the Project," Maddox said, her voice strong.

68

Shane rolled his eyes and shook his head slightly, his commentary on the stupidity of government clear, at least, to the people across the table.

"But I have refused. I believe that the work we do here may be the work that saves this planet. I want to be a part of this as much as I want to be a part of the military team that eventually destroys those alien bastards."

Shane turned his head toward her in surprise. Cross let himself relax. Britt squeezed his wrist, bowed her head, and smiled slightly. None of them wanted to lose Maddox.

Maddox said, "I suspect that I will have to defend my place on this Project for some time to come. That's my problem. However, I do have one favor to ask of the group."

Cross noted that everyone in all the various conference rooms around the world was watching her intently.

"In the past we've had a bit of banter and a rather loose format for the meetings."

"Loose?" Britt whispered so softly that only Cross could hear her. It was his turn to smile. Scientific meetings were never as structured as the meetings of the Tenth Planet Project had been.

"I would like now to run these meetings as efficiently as possible."

One of the Russian scientists started to protest. Maddox held up a hand for silence.

"I understand the need for informal discussion," she said. "I can no longer be present for that. So instead of holding those discussions within the structure of the meeting, I have arranged to keep the uplink going for as long as necessary after the formal meeting, so that the informal talks can continue. All I ask is that I am briefed on any new and important information that comes from the informal discussions. Is that acceptable to the group?"

All of the members of the Project nodded, and many spoke the word "yes" aloud.

69

Maddox's smile was real this time. "Good," she said. "Very good. Then let's get this meeting under way."

She touched her wrist'puter, where it seemed as if she had a list of notes. Britt also had notes, and several of the others at the international tables seemed to have notes as well.

"Since I started," Maddox said, "let me continue with a matter the president has asked me to bring to your attention."

Cross cradled his cooling latte. He wondered if Jamison had had any luck yet in Monterey, and if so, why he hadn't paged Cross.

"All of the world leaders have discussed this, but the president asked me to make a special point of mentioning it here."

Britt's grip on Cross's wrist eased.

"The Tenth Planet Project is something the press does not know about. Our governments have managed to keep a lid on our work, as well as on one other thing: no one has yet, in any credible way, leaked the news that the tenth planet will make a return visit in five and a half months. All our analysts believe there will be massive riots and destruction, with millions dead, if the world finds out that what happened two weeks ago was only a prelude to another alien attack. We cannot allow this to happen."

There was a general murmuring of agreement. Cross waited for the rest.

"We have been ordered not to speak to the press about the future of the tenth planet. No hints, no leaks. We need to keep this information contained, and part of containment is this: if there is a leak, we have to squelch it, and quickly."

"You want us to lie," one of the Chinese representatives said.

"If necessary," Maddox said.

"The news will get out eventually," Britt said.

Maddox frowned at her.

Britt shrugged. "Scientists all over the world are familiar

with the tenth planet now. They may not be part of our organization, but they're not dumb. They're going to come to the same conclusions we do."

"We've already spoken to the best and the brightest in astronomy and physics, at least in this country," Yolanda Hayes said. "They're under instruction to send any new information to the president's Science Office first. We're forming a brain trust to be coordinated by me, Robert Shane, and two other members of the White House's scientific community."

"You're going to control the free flow of information?" Cross asked, unable to keep quiet any longer.

"In a nutshell, yes, Dr. Cross." Maddox crossed her arms. "What's your problem with this? I assume you don't want the millions of dead, which rioting would cause, any more than I do."

Her remark was like a slap, but he went on anyway. "Science doesn't function with restrictions on information."

"Are you familiar with the Manhattan Project?" Maddox's voice was cold.

"You're comparing us to a group of scientists hidden in the New Mexico desert, a group whose mission was to design the deadliest weapon of all time?" Cross turned toward her.

"Leo," Britt whispered. "Not now."

He ignored her. The other members of the Project were silent.

"Yes," Maddox said. "I am."

"In many ways our mission is similar," Hayes said.

Cross turned to her. "I can't believe you want to stifle the free flow of information," he said. "You of all people know how valuable it is to scientists."

"I believe in a trade-off," Hayes said. "If we don't control this information, we'll have rioting in the streets, and I personally can't live with the idea I could be even partially responsible."

71

Maddox looked pointedly at her watch. Cross ignored her. "I understand the press blackout," he said. "It's the rest of it. The brain trust, the control of information even among scientists—"

"Someone will leak it," Killius said. "You know as well as I do that scientists don't always have the best social skills. They sometimes don't think about the people applications. Do you want some lower-level astronomer posting his notes on the tenth planet's return on the Internet? Others'll check it and—"

"How do we prevent it?" Cross said. "Just because you have the best and the brightest already on tap doesn't mean that some amateur astronomer won't figure it out on his own."

"That's a problem," Hayes said.

"Yeah, it's a problem," Cross said. "It's a twofold problem. The amateurs are often the ones who come up with the most creative solutions. And right now, that's what we need. We need creativity, not some brain trust sitting around in a damn meeting!"

He slammed his hand against the table and the sound silenced everyone. They were all staring at him.

His heart was pounding, and he was breathing hard. They clearly knew that he was frustrated being in the room, but he wasn't going to back down. He had a point. They had to see that, too.

"Pardon me," one of the British physicists said, "but I do see both your points. Dr. Cross is right; it is always better to share information among like minds. However, if perhaps we set up a web site or a contact number for people who believe they have valuable information, we will still be able to get the input of the creative amateurs."

"And who'll monitor the sites?" Hayes asked. She sounded as frayed as Cross felt. "That'll be a full-time job in and of itself."

"Graduate students," Shane said. "Research assistants.

Maybe some high school science teachers. Folks who we can trust with the knowledge but who won't be on the brain trust."

"This is a compromise, Dr. Cross," Maddox said, "and I believe it's the only one you'll get. It's better than anything I would have mentioned. But then, I have a military mentality, as some of you are fond of pointing out."

Cross made himself swallow hard. Maddox was right. This was a compromise, and it was probably the best one he was going to get. "We're going to need someone to coordinate this effort in each country."

"I'm sure that's something that can be determined after I leave," Maddox said.

"I think it can, General," Shane said quickly, with a look toward Cross. "I have some ideas that might make it work."

"As long as any new information is contained, I don't care what you do," Maddox said. "But believe me, if something leaks, I'll have that leak traced and the leaker's butt in a sling so fast that he won't even know what hit him. Is that clear, Dr. Cross?"

"I won't leak anything, General," he said. "I kept this a secret for a lot longer than anyone else."

Her gaze met his and in it, he thought he saw a trace of sympathy. So the general understood his argument and the problems with silence. Good. He hoped the others did.

"Good," she said. "Moving on. The second item on my agenda is, ironically enough, the sharing of information between governments. We need to keep our people in the dark to prevent rioting, but we, as governments, need to share as much as possible. With that in mind, I'd like to update you on the U.S.'s military position."

As she talked about troop counts and training and increased weapons buildup, Cross finished his now-cold latte and calmed himself down. Without the free flow of information,

Cross would never have put together the facts that led to the discovery of the tenth planet. He had contacted archaeologists via e-mail, amateurs and professionals alike, asking simple, pointed questions. He'd brought Edwin Bradshaw into his circle—Bradshaw, who had been a man ahead of his time, and then had been disgraced for research that was now proving central to the tenth planet itself. Cross could have done none of that with the strictures the governments wanted to impose.

". . . in the history of the world," the German military representative was saying, "there has never been a military buildup like this one. Not this quick, not this uniform, not worldwide."

"Every country that has a military is deploying it," said the British Cabinet member who was fulfilling the equivalent of Maddox's duties in his tenth planet group.

"We've stepped up production of aircraft, weaponry, and anything else we can think of that might defeat these aliens," Maddox said.

Cross wondered why. The weapons had done no good against the alien ships last time. Or at least not much good. He guessed building weapons was the only thing the military knew how to do.

"Please," the head of the Japanese group said, "my people have a special request."

Everyone was silent. The Japanese listened more than spoke at these meetings.

"We are not only conscripting our young people for military duty," the Japanese leader said, "but we are also taking our youngest scientists, the award-winning students, and putting them to work on various projects that might help us defeat the aliens. We believe we are alone in this program. We ask that other countries do the same."

"A modified way of dealing with your objections, Dr. Cross," Shane said.

Cross shrugged. "It'll do."

"It's a wonderful idea," Britt said.

"I think," Killius said, "we might also want to consider funneling some of our young people into accelerated astronaut programs."

Her words were met with another silence as the members contemplated them. Then, one by one, the leaders of the various groups nodded.

"Excellent," Maddox said. "We're accomplishing more here than I thought we would."

Yeah, Cross thought. And if the world survives, everything will be different. We won't recognize the military culture we've built. Or be able to control it.

But he said nothing, because as far as he could see, there was no choice.

"Dr. Cross," Maddox said. "Has there been any progress on the nanomachines?"

He sighed. "Not the kind I want," he said. "We haven't found one. But we do have a device that might make finding one possible. We have teams at the various damage sites"—he was already using euphemistic language himself—"searching for the machines. I was there myself until I was called back here, a move that the general probably regrets."

There was laughter all around. Maddox even smiled.

"We can disagree, Dr. Cross, but your opinion is extremely valuable to this Project," she said.

"Thanks," he said. "Statistically, we should find more than one nanomachine—enough were left to form a fossilized record in the past—so it's only a matter of time. The key is, the sooner we find one of these things, the more time we have to study the aliens' technology. And if we're going to defeat them, we're going to defeat them through knowledge, not guesswork."

"That said," Maddox said, "does the South American team have information from the downed alien craft?"

75

On the vid screen in front of them, one of the men sitting at the South American conference table stood up. He folded his hands together and nodded toward someone off the monitor.

That someone, a man, joined him. Both men were thin and wore dark suits. They could almost have been twins if it weren't for one man's thick head of hair, and the other's baldness.

"We have just begun work on the ships," the first man said. "We have very little by way of preliminary findings, only that it was not what we expected."

"What did you expect?" Shane asked.

The other man smiled. "Perhaps something out of your American movies." Then he shrugged. "But we have been working with a large group of scientists. We have found little enough to report, but our biologists have studied the alien remains."

Cross felt the hair on the back of his neck stand on end. He had been so focused on the technology and preventing the aliens from returning, he hadn't even thought of the possibility of alien remains in those downed ships. But, of course, they would be there.

"They are quite different from us, and yet, I think we may have had similar origins." A third man had joined the group. He was speaking with an Australian accent. "I lead the biological team," he said by way of introduction.

"Continue," Maddox said.

He nodded. "I would guess they originated in their planet's oceans as we did in ours. Only when they climbed into the primordial ooze, they kept their tentacles and a few other features. They breathe through slits, like gills. There are many other features to their anatomy that we don't completely understand yet, but we have done one thing. We have, using the information we got from the remains and from the structure of the ship, created a composite sketch of what we believe these aliens look like alive. I will uplink it now."

The vid screen blanked for a brief moment.

"Sorry," Maddox said to the group in front of her. "That's the security protocols kicking in. Our techs are instructed to double-check the secure lines before images other than our own go over them."

Cross folded his hands and rested them on the table. Britt put the plastic cap on her mug. She slid her chair back slightly.

Then the screen lightened again.

The image facing them was not what Cross had expected, even hearing about the tentacles. The creature before him had smooth, rubbery black skin—if skin was what you called it—that covered an oblong center. Cross was reminded of the middle portion of the butterfly, the part that held the antennae and wings in place.

Tentacles floated off the middle of the torso, and the bottom of the oblong center. At the top were what appeared to be more tentacles until the image shifted.

They were long stems, with eyes on the top.

Cross shuddered.

The biologist was explaining that the breathing slits were on the sides near the top of the oblong center and that there were pockets at the very top of the creature's torso thingy, ten of them, probably for the eyes.

The alien looked like a squid crossed with some sort of nasty stinging bug.

Cross shuddered. He was completely repulsed. And he didn't know why.

But he did know he was going to do everything in his power to strike back at these creatures for what they had done to his planet. And his people.

April 27, 2018
21:05 Universal Time

170 Days Until Second Harvest

Malmuria filled the streets. Overhead the great solar panels had tightened down, so that a brown light filtered through. The light was greater than Malmuria were used to, but it was still thin and provided little illumination.

Barely enough to see the Elders, floating toward the Great Monument, their wispy bodies like black smoke pouring across the city.

Cicoi had never seen so many of his people outside. Young females, their tentacles tight around their bodies, stood beside older females who had briefly left the nests untended. Worker males had left their jobs and were standing in clumps, as far from the females as possible. And family males, what few of them had been allowed to awaken, were standing with their females, huddled close as if they derived comfort from the bodies around them.

All of the Malmuria had unpocketed two eyestalks—any more would be an insult—and all of those eyestalks were raised toward the sky, turning, watching, as the Elders moved forward.

Cicoi had never seen such a sight. The buildings behind the Malmuria were filled with more timid members of the communities, leaning out windows that hadn't been opened in generations, standing on balconies whose use was long forgotten.

So much change. Cicoi raised a single tentacle and let it fall. More change than he had ever wanted to see.

He stood on the tips of all of his lower tentacles on the slide leading up to Command Central. The Commanders of the North and Center were beside him, their posture the same as

78

his. None of them spoke to the others; they didn't dare. The Elders weren't done with them yet.

How Cicoi knew that, he had no idea. But he suspected it had to do with the Elders touching the inside of his brain.

The Elders floated as a group toward the Great Monument, the last thing ever built by the ancient Malmuria, in the days before they left their original sun.

It was a statue of the ten greatest leaders, each with their ten best advisers, eyestalks pointed toward the stars as if they could see into the blackness of space, tentacles flowing freely as was once allowed. Cicoi loved that monument; it spoke of things lost and things gained, at least to him. He had never heard any of his own people discuss its actual meaning.

The Elders encircled it. Some leaned against the central ten figures. Others touched the tentacles of the advisers. There were not enough Elders to touch all of the advisers.

My people, said the Elder who had spoken before.

In unison, all of the eyestalks were pocketed. Heads went down, tentacles flattened in a submissive position. The sound of so much movement echoed in the square.

Cicoi kept one stalk out. He wanted to see, and he knew it was allowed.

We shall do all we can to preserve our people. You must trust in us, as you have in the past. Now. Go back to your work.

Single stalks rose and pointed away from the Elders. Keeping heads bowed and tentacles as flat as possible, the Malmuria filed toward their work.

Cicoi took a deep breath. He turned toward Command Central's main door only to find a single Elder before him. He did not recognize which one this was: they were so wispy as to be almost formless.

Other Elders stood before the Commanders of the North and Center.

You seem hesitant, the Elder said, and Cicoi wondered if it was speaking to him, or to all three of them.

79

None of the others answered. Cicoi could only assume that the Elder was speaking directly to him.

"I am not hesitant," Cicoi said softly.

Ah, the Elder said, and his head moved slightly forward. *But you are. You have concerns about the creatures of the third planet. You believe because they have developed technology, because they have learned, they should not die.*

Cicoi flattened his tentacles and moved his eyestalk into a position of respect. "It has always been our policy to leave the natives as untouched as possible."

We no longer have time for niceties, Commander. The Elder's mental voice seemed colder than it had before. Cicoi did not know how that was possible, but it was. *We are speaking of the survival of our own people.*

"I know," Cicoi said.

You are young. Inexperienced. You do not know.

Cicoi raised one of his eyestalks enough to peek out of the pocket. The other two Commanders appeared to be getting instructions from their Elders, not having conversations.

Are you paying attention? This time the Elder's voice held the sharpness of command.

"Yes, O Great One. I'm sorry."

We were speaking of our survival.

"I know."

Survival occurs at all costs.

Cicoi almost lost control of the single fully extended eyestalk. He forced himself to hold it in place. "All costs?"

You are *young,* the Elder said. Six of its upper tentacles floated free. Cicoi couldn't tell if they indicated annoyance, amusement, or both. *We were speaking of the creatures on the third planet, and your sympathy for them.*

"It's not sympathy."

Empathy then. A reluctance to kill sentient beings.

"It is a tenet of our training."

80

It is a luxury. All ethical considerations are luxuries in grave situations.

Cicoi felt his lower tentacles wobble. "We have to make choices that do not diminish us."

Do you think anyone will care what our choices were if our species does not survive? The Elder moved closer to him. Cicoi had to concentrate to prevent himself from backing away. *I am not telling you to kill indiscriminately. I am ordering you to view all options. The creatures of the third planet have proven themselves to be resourceful. If they hold us off, if they destroy more of our harvesters, the choice will come down to one thing: their survival or ours.*

Cicoi's eyestalk toppled, and he pocketed it quickly, making himself temporarily blind. He raised a different eyestalk.

Theirs or ours, the Elder repeated. *If it comes to it, can you order the destruction of the creatures of the third planet?*

"All of them?"

We might need them gone because of their fighting capability. Or we might need their organic material for food. The third planet is not as rich as it was in my time. The Elder's transparent eyestalks turned toward him. *Which is a long way of saying, yes. You might have to destroy all of them. Can you do so?*

Cicoi wobbled again on his lower tentacles. He couldn't maintain the position of respect much longer.

The Elder's ten eyes were staring at him. They seemed eerie, with their whitened pupils, their transparent lids.

"Yes," Cicoi finally said. "I'll do what I have to. I will protect my people first and foremost."

The Elder's eyestalks bent slightly, and then he turned them toward his companions. *We have agreement from the Commander of the South.*

And the North, came a different Elder's voice.

And Center, came a third.

81

Cicoi bowed his head and folded his tentacles into a position of submission. Survival at all costs.

It was the only way.

4

April 29, 2018
11:16 A.M. Pacific Daylight Time

168 Days Until Second Harvest

Somehow, seeing the destruction a second time wasn't as devastating. Perhaps that was because Cross was prepared for it.

He sat in the back of a helicopter, again, the same pilot in front of him. Sunlight played across the majestic Pacific, sparkling on the waves. He saw the white spot among all the black as the copter turned and began its rapid descent.

Cross wasn't nervous this time. He was feeling optimistic and it felt strange.

Jamison had paged him less than twenty-four hours ago, claiming he had found what they were looking for. A cache of the little alien nanomachines.

Cross's stomach had settled down for the first time in weeks. He even ate some leftover pot roast from the dinner Constance had prepared for him while he was packing for his second flight across country in less than a week.

He was glad to be returning to California. The Tenth Planet Project meeting had left him unsettled. Britt claimed it was because of the discussion about secrecy.

Cross knew that it was his reaction to the aliens.

Something about them had penetrated his scientific aloofness. If he had to guess, he would say something buried within him recognized that visage as the face of the enemy. He had mentioned it to Shane in passing, and Shane had laughed.

"You mean we've got an instinctual reaction to those things?" he asked. "Like a rabbit instinctively knows the shadow of a hawk means danger?"

"I don't like your analogy," Cross said. "But yeah, I think that might be what's going on. Didn't you have a reaction?"

"Of course," Shane said, "but my rationale for it was different. I know what those creatures can do. I think I have a right to be repulsed. And angry."

"It's not a scientific reaction," Cross said.

"Since when did an emotional response become unscientific?" Shane asked. "You might have been looking on the thing that will kill you. Don't you think that'll create a reaction—in anyone?"

Shane had a point, but, days later, Cross wasn't sure he agreed with it. His reaction concerned him because he worried that he wouldn't be able to look at the aliens rationally. In a war situation, the enemy was always made out to be subhuman. In this war situation, the enemy was *non*human, and that might be a problem. If Cross—and his colleagues— couldn't get by their feelings of disgust, couldn't look at things rationally, then they might miss something important, something that could only be gained through understanding. Not through fear or anger.

But Cross wouldn't, and couldn't, put away the desire to pay those creatures back somehow.

Someway.

The copter set down on the white patch, and Cross got out. The black dust whipped around him as the copter blades slowed. His skin crawled, just like it had before, only this

84

time, he ignored it. He stepped out from under the blades, and into the truck that was parked alongside the spot.

Jamison was at the wheel, looking jaunty. "We have loot," he said.

"Let's hope it's the right kind," Cross said.

Jamison backed the truck up and drove down the narrow path that led out of the destruction. "We found it in the remains of a restaurant, of all things."

"A restaurant?" Cross asked. "How'd you know?"

"The industrial-sized stove, refrigerator, and dishwasher were largely intact, along with some steel tables. The nanoharvesters got blown underneath the door of the freezer somehow."

"If they were inside something, how'd you find them?" Cross asked.

"I opened the door. I wanted to see if the food inside had gotten destroyed."

"It had, I take it," Cross said.

Jamison shook his head. "Apparently those nanoharvesters eat on the way down. They don't have independent propulsion. They somehow got through the door. Maybe it was left open when they were dropped and got shoved closed by something falling before they were picked up. Who knows. But they were trapped in there. Some of the food they had missed, and it smelled like a son of a bitch."

Cross didn't have to be in that freezer to know what it smelled like. He was glad he hadn't been there after all. "Good work," he said.

"You've been saying that, but let's wait until you examine those things." Jamison bumped the truck over a curb and onto a real road. Suddenly buildings surrounded them. It felt as if they had sprouted suddenly, when of course they hadn't. But Cross hadn't been looking at the road—purposely. He hadn't wanted to see the black dust, the twisted metal, lining the

85

sides. So it was out of the corner of his eye that the buildings suddenly appeared.

Jamison took the truck on a road Cross hadn't been on. They parked in front of what had once been an insurance office. Jamison had gotten permission to set up camp here before Cross had left the first time, but this was the first time Cross had been in the building.

It was a single story with tacky plastic desks from the early '90s. The door's window even had the business's name painted in gold.

Jamison unlocked the door and went inside. His computer setup was in the back office, the one that had probably belonged to the long-vanished insurance agent. Cross didn't want to think about what had happened to that person.

"I suppose you want to see them," Jamison said.

"Yes," Cross said.

"Okay." Jamison sat down at the desk, spun his chair to the right, and grabbed two sets of thin rubber gloves. He handed one set to Cross, who put them on, and then slipped the other set on himself. Then Jamison picked up a microscope slide. It really didn't look as if anything was on it, the nanomachines were so small.

"These were in the freezer by themselves?" Cross asked. "How did you even see them?"

"I kept the wand running. I found a whole pile. It was like a little anthill."

Cross took the slide and held it gingerly. He brought it closer to his eye. He could barely see what looked like dirt flecks that sometimes got on his sunglasses. Smaller by far than the period at the end of a sentence, these nanoharvesters seemed completely harmless.

He still found it amazing that something that small could do so very much damage.

"Okay," he said, handing the slide back to Jamison. "Let's see these vicious machines up close and personal."

"I thought you'd never ask." Jamison put the slide into the microscope built into the side of his computer. An enlargement of a section of the slide, a thousand times bigger than could be seen by the naked eye, appeared on the screen. The nanomachines were gray and oblong, with ten slashes along their upper surface. Viewed this way, they looked like carved rocks or the badly designed New Age jewelry of his youth.

Except for their color and their three-dimensional appearance, they looked just like the fossils that Edwin Bradshaw had found embedded into a bit of rock decades ago.

"That's them, all right," Cross said.

"I figured," Jamison said, "when I brought them back here and gave them a quick look-see. Our nanotechnology is becoming pretty sophisticated, but it's nothing like these little creatures here."

"What can you tell me about them?" Cross asked.

"Not much," Jamison said. "Analyzing other people's technology is not my strong suit. That's why you have Portia."

"She's in South America with Bradshaw," Cross said.

"I think it's time she comes home," Jamison said.

"I think you're right." Cross tapped his wrist'puter and had it dial out for Bradshaw. Jamison continued to stare at the nanomachines.

So did Cross.

They were creepy in their own way, a completely different way than the aliens themselves were. The nanomachines didn't move. They seemed inanimate. Something that small, Cross thought, should be moving, like viruses in a drop of blood. But these things just rested on the glass surface, waiting for something to activate them.

"Will they eat us if we touch them?" Cross asked.

"I don't want to find out," Jamison said. "We've been using strict contamination procedures whenever we work with

87

these things. I don't even know if this group has chewed its quota or hasn't even begun its work. That's for Portia."

"What is?" a tinny voice said. Cross glanced at his wrist. He had an audio connection with Bradshaw.

"We hit the jackpot, Edwin," Cross said.

"Jackpot?" Bradshaw sounded confused.

"We've found an entire stack of our little friends," Cross said. "Have you had similar luck?"

"No," Bradshaw said. "Although I keep thinking we should."

"Well, worry about it no longer," Cross said. "Pack up the equipment and come home. Bring Portia. Tell her I'll bring her some new toys to NanTech tomorrow."

"Tomorrow?" Bradshaw said.

"We've only got a few months," Cross said. "We can't afford to waste any time at all."

Cross heard mumbling in the background, then Bradshaw said, "Portia wants to know if you can download any of this to us now?"

"Is this a secure line?" Cross asked Jamison.

He shook his head. "We'd have to go to the Army for that."

"Sorry," Cross said to Bradshaw. "No can do. Just go back to D.C. I'll meet you both there tomorrow."

"Got it," Bradshaw said. "And Leo, congrats."

"Thanks," Cross said. "But the congrats go to Jamison. It's a good first step."

Jamison smiled slightly as Cross severed the connection. "When I found these things I got completely overwhelmed." He swept his hand toward them. "They're so alien."

"Funny," Cross said. "I thought they seemed eerily familiar."

Jamison shook his head. "Not to me. They're so unlike our nanomachines. It's as if they're based on a different thought process."

Cross stared at the gray shapes on the screen. They weren't much different than he had expected.

"It's kind of like what we'd get if a dolphin invented a vehicle," Jamison said.

"Why would a dolphin do that?"

"Rapid propulsion," Jamison said.

"That's a hell of an assumption," Cross said.

"But make it for a moment," Jamison said. "They'd start from the idea that the car would have to move quickly in water."

"It wouldn't be a car, then," Cross said. "It would be a submarine."

"Not for them," Jamison said. "They can already be underwater for long periods of time. It's as if these creatures had a similar principle in mind—something small that works quickly—but began from a different technology. The result is familiar enough that we can understand it, but not so familiar that we can make it work on the first try."

"Got it," Cross said. Jamison's analogy was faulty, but Cross understood. It was like finding bits of pottery or ancient tools in a dig. Sometimes, if the culture was an unfamiliar one, the archaeologist could only hypothesize what the particular tool was used for.

Only here, they didn't have to hypothesize. They knew. They just didn't know how the thing worked.

Which reminded him. He had one more phone call to make. "Can I link into your system?" Cross asked. "I have one more call."

"Just use it," Jamison said. He removed the nanoharvesters from the computer, and deleted the image. The video link system showed on the screen. Cross dialed, and the numbers were blacked out. Efficient.

He got through to the Pentagon in one try. Apparently it was easy when you had the right numbers. The face that filled his screen belonged to Clarissa Maddox's aide, Paul Ward.

"Leo Cross for General Maddox."

"She's in conference," Ward said.

"It'll only take a minute," Cross said. "This shouldn't wait."

Ward didn't even ask him to hold. Instead, the screen went black, and then the United States Government seal filled the blankness.

"What?" Jamison asked. "No music?"

"Your tax dollars at work," Cross said.

"Do you want me to leave?"

"It's not necessary."

Then the screen blanked again for a moment before Clarissa Maddox's face appeared. She looked tired.

"Dr. Cross. I trust you have good news."

"Excellent news, actually, General." He leaned toward the computer. "I'm in California. We found what we were looking for."

To his surprise, she smiled. It was a warm and joyful smile that made her look years younger. "You don't know how I've needed to hear something good, Doctor. This is wonderful news, and it'll be very helpful in our efforts."

"I know," Cross said.

"All right. I will order the Commander on-site to have you and the items flown back to Dulles. Then you bring all of the items directly to the Army lab. Is that clear?"

"General, I thought that NanTech would help with some of this. After all, they're on top of the current research."

"It's a military problem now, Doctor. If our scientists need outside experts, I'm sure they'll bring them in." The smile had faded from her face. "You're not going to give me another argument, are you, Leo?"

He made himself smile, even though he didn't feel like it. He felt as if he'd been run over with a tank the last few times he'd talked to Maddox. "Of course not, General. I see your point."

Her face softened. "Good. I look forward to seeing those

little beasties." She reached for the off button and then she paused. "Tell your team that it has done spectacular work."

And her image vanished.

"Spectacular work," Cross said dryly.

"I heard," Jamison said. "What a tight-ass."

Cross shook his head. "She's getting pressure from all sides. The only victory we had in that conflict came from her quick thinking. She's just doing her job."

"And now she expects you to give this to government scientists? No offense, Leo, but we turned down a number of their nanotech guys when they applied at NanTech. The government is very behind in this area. I can only think that the Army's guys are even farther behind."

"I know," Cross said. "I'm not a member of the U.S. military."

"Which means what?" Jamison asked.

"I'm going to look the other way as you divide these 'beasties,' as the general calls them, in thirds."

"Thirds?"

"You're taking a large pile to NanTech, and I'm taking a small pile to the Army."

"And the third pile?"

"I think Edwin and I deserve just a few, too, don't you?"

"You guys aren't that familiar with nanotechnology," Jamison said.

"Nope, but we know fossils. And we might see something in the old ones that is missing from the new or vice versa. It might be something you guys miss."

Jamison grinned. "I like how you think, Dr. Cross."

Cross stood. "I'm glad someone does."

April 29, 2018
6:09 P.M. Eastern Daylight Time

168 Days Until Second Harvest

Britt Archer hadn't put on a slinky dress in half a year. She'd spent all of her time at the office or at Cross's house. Her cats barely knew her any longer. Poor babies. They didn't know why she was so frazzled, and she was glad she couldn't explain it to them. They, at least, weren't panicked, like the rest of the world.

She adjusted the strap on her high heels, clutched her purse, and ran her tongue over her teeth, making sure she didn't have any lipstick where none should be. A long time since she got dressed up, and Cross wasn't even in town to see it. He had called as she was leaving her apartment. He would be back by morning.

She didn't tell him how much she missed him. She had decided, in the middle of the bombing, that while personal feelings were nice and good, they didn't help wage a war.

And that's what they were in now. A war. With an enemy no one understood.

She shuddered, and got out of her car. The valet had been waiting for her to do just that. He looked about twenty-one, athletic, and impatient with everything. If he were living in Europe right now, he'd be in the military. The U.S. was delaying the draft for just a few more weeks while it put training programs in place. Maddox had said she wanted some of the new recruits to go into astronaut training, others into science work.

In a month, this kid wouldn't be parking cars. No one would.

But Archer couldn't tell him that. Instead, she handed him her keys and stepped onto the red carpet someone had laid over the concrete sidewalk. It led under a matching red awning with the restaurant's name emblazoned in gold. Another young man held open the oak door for her, revealing a coat check area and stairs leading up to the main dining room.

She felt awkward being in a place like this, and somewhat amazed that fancy restaurants were open and doing business. But why wouldn't they? Fancy restaurants were the mainstay of Washington society. They wouldn't shut down unless the entire country were under continual bombardment.

Which it just might be in a few months.

She shuddered, removed her shawl, and handed it to the young woman behind the counter. Then Archer walked up the stairs, careful to hold the railing so that she wouldn't trip in her stylishly uncomfortable shoes.

The maître d's station was at the top of the stairs. A dapper man in his midforties fussed behind an oak podium. When he saw her, he raised a single eyebrow as if inquiring what had possessed a woman like her to come into a restaurant like this.

"I'm here to meet General Maddox," Archer said.

The maître d's face eased into a wide smile. "Ah, the general. We don't see enough of her these days." He made it sound as if it were Maddox's fault for failing to patronize the restaurant in times of crisis. "Follow me, please."

He grabbed a menu swathed in leather, and a smaller book that had to be the wine list. Archer wondered if she was the first to arrive. When they reached the table in the very center of the room, she realized she wasn't.

Jesse Killius sat there, looking awkward, her chewed fingernails tapping on the wine list. She looked as uncomfortable in her black silk dress and pearls as Archer felt. When Killius saw Archer, she smiled in what seemed like relief.

"I was beginning to feel like my date stood me up in front of the entire school," she said.

Archer laughed and sat down. With a flourish, the maître d'

handed her the menu, and then disappeared before Archer could ask for a drink.

The restaurant was full, and Archer recognized a number of Washington power brokers as well as a few journalists scattered among the tables. Everything was done in heavy oak and linen, very traditional, very old-fashioned.

"Would madam like a drink?" a voice asked at her elbow.

Madam would like the whole damn bottle, Archer was tempted to say, but didn't. Instead, she said, "Yes, please. A glass of Chardonnay."

She didn't even get to see the voice's owner before he was gone.

"After all that's been going on," Killius said, "I would have thought you would order something stronger."

Archer shook her head. "For all its trappings, I suspect this is a business meeting."

"You don't think we have enough in common with the general to warrant a girls' night out?" Killius asked.

Archer liked Killius's fey sense of humor. They had spoken on the phone a number of times, but never enough for that humor to come out. Whenever they were on the phone it was either STScI business or NASA business, and they were talking in either scientist or administrator shorthand.

"I think we probably do," Archer said, "but I don't think we have the time to find out."

Killius's smile faded and she sighed. "When I was in college," she said, "we had to interview people who had gone through a twentieth-century historical moment for a history term paper. I interviewed an old guy who had been a German POW in World War II."

Yet another waiter set down Archer's white wine. She picked up the glass and twirled the stem between her thumb and forefinger.

"He had a lot of stories, most of them about the harsh conditions, but the one thing that stuck with me is that they piled a bunch of sawdust into something shaped like a bread loaf and as they ate it, they talked about the best meals they had ever had."

Archer sipped her wine. It was the best house Chardonnay she had ever had.

"So after that, at times when I was cooking Thanksgiving dinner or when I came to a fancy restaurant—" Killius swept her hand toward the door "—I would remember what he said and wonder if I would ever be in a situation where I would be starving and remembering that meal as one of the best meals I ever had."

Archer shuddered. "I think if something happens to us this time, it'll happen so fast we won't have time to think about meals or our lives flashing before our eyes. We'll just be gone."

Killius's gaze slipped away from hers. "Sorry. I didn't mean to be so glum."

Archer shrugged. "I'm the one who brought it up. I mean, aren't you a little uncomfortable being here, knowing that—"

"Ladies." General Maddox approached the table, leading the maître d', who now looked like a whipped puppy. "I'm glad you could make it."

If she hadn't spoken first, Archer wouldn't have recognized her. Maddox was dressed up, too, in a slinky blue dress, with a sassy set of sapphire earrings, and a matching sapphire bracelet that accented her strong arms. She wore her hair up and her makeup light, but she looked nothing like the tough general who had been running the Tenth Planet Project meetings all these months.

She let the maître d' pull out her chair, then sat, and nodded when he asked her if she wanted her usual. He was gone before anyone else had a chance to say a word.

95

"This is some place," Killius said.

Maddox smiled. She was a beautiful woman in a nonconventional way. Archer had never seen that before. "I've always liked it," she said.

"They seem to know you here," Archer said.

Maddox shrugged. "I've learned that sometimes having a conversation over a relaxing meal is a lot better than a meeting in a stuffy office, especially in the evening." She picked up her menu. "The crab cakes are always good here."

They looked at the menus as yet a third waiter brought Maddox a gin and tonic. A fourth waiter described the specials, and Maddox assured all of them that this would be on the government's tab.

Archer ordered a filet mignon, medium rare, and felt slightly guilty at the expense. Killius ordered lobster and smiled in obvious anticipation. Maddox ordered the roast duck special.

Then the waiter took their menus and wine list, and disappeared. The conversation around them was a low hum.

Archer decided she'd begin. "You called this a meeting?"

"I called this a conversation," Maddox said. "But you can call it a meeting."

"Just us, not the Project?"

Maddox sighed, but she didn't look irritated. She took a sip of her drink. "I'm coordinating a lot of things right now," she said. "My biggest concern is that the aliens are an unknown. We can make assumptions about them based on very little evidence. And we only have a short time to gather more evidence. I know that Cross is right. They're not done with us yet."

"All we have are the bodies," Killius said.

Maddox shook her head. "The bodies, the ships, and the historical record. I've been thinking about that first presentation of Cross's. Do you remember?"

Archer did. She'd seen it more than once as Leo was

96

drumming up support for the Project. In it, he had used the historical record—actually the writings of civilizations dead for thousands of years—to show that a "black death from the sky" happened at all. Now they'd seen the black death and knew why it came from the sky.

"Yes, I remember," Killius said.

"There's bound to be more information in there, if we just know where to look." Maddox sipped her drink as a waiter set down some warm bread. She took a piece and slathered it with butter, then set it on her bread plate. "We also have observation. Obviously these aliens have a civilization. We should be able to see it."

"With the telescopes?" Archer said.

Maddox nodded. "They are the best vision we have into deep space. The planet is moving inside Venus's orbit and won't be this close again for four months. We need to get better information about the aliens before then."

Archer frowned. They had had this discussion once before. Briefly and on the phone, but they had had it. Then Maddox glanced at Killius, and Archer realized what was going on. This meeting wasn't for her. It was for Killius. Was there a problem at NASA?

"I empathize," Archer said. "But the scopes can't help you, not for another three months. They just aren't powerful enough. The tenth planet doesn't reflect light, and soon it'll disappear behind the sun. We have to wait until it's much closer before we attempt to see anything on its surface. But to be honest, I don't think we're going to get much more as it comes toward us this time than last time."

Maddox sighed and took a bite of the bread. Killius dug in the bread basket until she found a piece of rye. She pulled it out and buttered it lightly.

Yet another waiter appeared with their salad course. As he mixed the Caesar salads and queried them about the amount

97

of pepper, the women watched him. When he left, leaving large plates of greenery before them, they continued.

"What about probes?" Maddox asked.

Killius picked up her salad fork. She stabbed at her plate. "We lack the funds, General."

"If funds weren't an issue."

Killius raised her head. A single lock of hair had fallen alongside her face. She was thinner than she had been when Archer had met her, a long time ago. "Not at all?"

Maddox ate her bread and didn't touch her salad. In fact, she pushed the salad plate away. "Jesse," she said softly. "We've just suffered through the worst attack ever on the continental United States. Congress is going to roll over and bark whenever we ask it to. Money is not an issue. Most of the defense funds that had gone to conventional ground weapons are useless in this campaign. We can now turn that toward space. Toward NASA, if that's the place to go. If it's not, I suppose we can go directly to private industry—there are a number of companies that have been launching their own satellites and a few probes—but I worry about their commitment to our cause."

"They should be just as involved as the rest of us," Archer said. She'd talked to some of her nonscientific friends. They were scared.

"Should be. But I have a healthy mistrust of private industry. I prefer to keep things under government control."

Where she or someone like her could oversee the work, Archer thought. The key word in Maddox's last sentence wasn't "government." It was "control."

"We can do probes," Killius said.

"What about a defense system?"

Killius frowned. "A planetary defense system? That's not something we can do alone. I'm sure the other nations would

98

have something to say about it. In the '80s, when President Reagan suggested the Star Wars system—"

"I know your institutional memory is long," Maddox said. "So's mine. And Reagan's system, in addition to being forty years out-of-date, never got off the ground. And it wasn't designed to protect us from things arriving from *outer* space. Instead, it was to protect us from things launched *into* space from other countries. It's not applicable. If we're doing a planetary defense system, the other nations will benefit from it."

"If we present it to them properly," Archer said, finally understanding one of the reasons she was here. Her work at STScI was largely a matter of international cooperation and coordination. "If we give them a say-so in much of what we do."

"I'd prefer this to be an American-run project," Maddox said.

"Forgive me, General," Archer said, "but you can have a project that's run formally by the Americans, and you'll get a lot of protest. Or you can have one run informally by us, with much of the control situated in this country, and you'll get almost no protest at all."

"This has happened with your telescopes?"

"Yes," Archer said. "And I'm speaking from experience in times of peace. We're not at peace now. There should be even more cooperation."

Killius was studying her salad, working her way methodically through all the lettuce and pushing the croutons aside. She looked like a woman who knew she was being double-teamed. Archer wanted to take her aside and assure her that it hadn't been set up beforehand, that she hadn't agreed to the meal to badger Killius into a position she didn't want to be in.

The very first waiter, the one who had brought Archer her

drink, appeared and whisked away their salad plates. He cleaned the crumbs off the tablecloth with a little brush and then put large platters down before leaving as silently as he had arrived.

"So," Maddox said. "A defense system. We have ideas, and we've already talked to a few of your people. What we really need from NASA isn't a design for the defense system, but your cooperation in using manned shuttles to set it up."

"Oh," Killius said. "We don't become a long arm of the Defense Department, then."

Archer stiffened, wondering if Maddox would take offense. But she wasn't even looking at Killius. She was looking at the headwaiter, who was carrying a tray of food on three fingertips. He bowed and placed the tray on its little cart. On top were dishes covered with silver warmers.

"The filet," he said with just a hint of a British accent. Archer wondered why it was that all headwaiters spoke with that same accent, that same precision. Was it taught to them in headwaiter school?

"Mine," she said.

He waved it in front of her, before setting it down and removing the cover with a flourish. Then he repeated the procedure with the lobster and the duck.

"Do your meals look satisfactory?"

"As good as usual, Claude," Maddox said. Her tone clearly held dismissal. The headwaiter nodded, grabbed his tray, and left.

"The long arm of the Defense Department?" Maddox said softly. Archer winced. She had hoped Maddox hadn't heard that. "You sound as if that's a problem, Jesse. NASA and Defense have always worked together closely."

"And been separate agencies."

"This is not the time to worry about who's in charge of what," Maddox said. "The lines are probably going to blur mightily before this thing is over."

100

Killius stared at her lobster as if she suddenly didn't know how to eat it.

"They've already blurred," Archer said. "Even between countries."

The cooperation they had all seen on the Tenth Planet Project wouldn't have been possible a year before.

"Jesse," Maddox said. "What's bothering you?"

Killius pushed her plate away. She hadn't touched the lobster. "Change bothers me," she said, her head down. Then she raised it. "It's not you, General. It's the new ways of thinking. I'm a better bureaucrat than scientist, I guess, but I'm both, ultimately, and both operate by strict rules. Suddenly I find myself in a world in which the old rules no longer apply, not to science, and not to bureaucracy."

"The old rules do apply," Maddox said. "But it's the old wartime rules, not peacetime rules. None of us worked during the Cold War—in fact, we were all children when it ended—but that's the model NASA has to look to now. An enemy so great that we might not be able to destroy it, but we have to put our best effort into it. That attitude got us into outer space in the first place."

"We're not trying to go to space, General," Killius said.

"No." Maddox spoke softly. "We're trying to save Earth."

Archer let out a small breath. Her hands were trembling.

Killius looked at both of them for a moment. She was pale beneath her makeup. "Probes, and manned shuttle missions."

"Yes," Maddox said. "That's all we're asking."

"That's a lot," Killius said. "We're stretched now."

"I'm trying to change that," Maddox started, but Killius raised a hand to stop her.

"If you can guarantee the money," Killius said, "I can guarantee results."

Maddox met Killius's gaze for a moment. Archer found

101

herself holding her breath. The two women were staring at each other as if they could read each other's minds.

"I can guarantee the money," Maddox said.

"Then you'll have your probes. I'll make sure we'll know everything humanly possible about those aliens by the time they make their return trip around the sun. And you can have all the shuttles you can pay to get into orbit."

"Good," Maddox said. "I can't ask for more."

She picked up her fork and poked at her duck. Archer cut another piece of steak. It was one of the best steaks she had eaten for a long time. After a moment, Killius pulled her plate closer and began to pick apart the lobster.

Maddox took a bite of duck and then smiled. "The meeting's over," she said. "Let's have a real conversation, about men, and vid stars, and whether or not we should have dessert."

Archer looked at her.

Killius seemed startled.

Maddox raised her eyebrows. "We don't get chances like this very often," she said, "and I suspect our chances will be fewer and fewer over the next couple of months."

She took a bite of duck, chewed for a moment, and then cut another piece. It was as if she couldn't get enough.

She said, "Eat well, ladies. We have to enjoy the good things in life while we still have them."

The words didn't encourage Archer to eat more. Instead, they nearly stole her appetite. *While we still have them.* Even Maddox thought that ultimately they'd lose.

Archer shuddered.

She had a hunch Maddox was right.

April 29, 2018
22:07 Universal Time

168 Days Until Second Harvest

General Gail Banks felt the shuttle shudder as it attached itself to the docking bay outside one of the units of the International Space Station. Sloppy work, that. A shuttle should never shudder when it docked, especially in space, where so many things could go wrong.

She waited for the all clear, then unhooked all her seat belts locking her into the passenger chair. She had purposely stayed out of the cockpit—she'd learned through bitter experience that she couldn't be hands-off when faced with a less competent pilot than she was, and most pilots never came up to her exacting standards. When she had been in charge of the shuttle program, pilot testing had been rigorous. So rigorous, in fact, that some idiot had complained to the media, which then sicced the congressional doofuses on the case. Congressmen who had Air Force bases in their home states, and tons of pilots who someday dreamed of flying to the moon as their constituents, suddenly demanded an investigation.

And so, Banks had to spend a week out of her life sitting in front of microphones in the House of Representatives, defending her standards to a bunch of people who wouldn't know what standards were if a lobbyist didn't tell them. It had been all she could do to keep her contempt to a minimum.

Not that it did any good. She was the public face for the program, and so, of course, she was the one whose head went on the block. She got several apologies from her superiors, all of whom said they wouldn't have removed her from duty if it had been their choice. But it hadn't been. The suits had decided that standards were too rigorous. Our pilots weren't getting a fair shake.

And now she had to tolerate a shuddery docking on the International Space Station. A shuddery docking on the wrong part of the ISS could create all sorts of internal problems for the station. If she had time, she would try to affect the piloting problems from here.

She wouldn't have time, and she knew it. She was on the tightest deadline of her life.

"Ready, General?" The pilot poked his head through the separator.

"Are you certain we're properly docked?" she asked. "That was a rough connection."

"All systems go according to the board."

"I don't give a damn about the board," she said. "You eyeball it, mister, and then we disembark. I've got nuclear missiles onboard this beast, and I'm not going to lose one of them to your carelessness."

The pilot's face flushed. "Yes, sir." He disappeared into the cockpit again.

She clutched a rung and waited. He hadn't turned the low gravity on yet either, and they would need it to unload those missiles. This part of the ISS, the newest part, had continual gravity—not as strong as Earth's—but enough so that the permanent members of the ISS's staff didn't get osteoporosis or other degenerative bone and muscle diseases. No matter how much exercise folks did in zero g, it didn't substitute for the good old force of gravity herself.

Through the closed cockpit door, she heard the slide of the pilot's exit. Well, at least he took her advice. Only she didn't think it was her tone that worried him. She thought it was probably the mention of the missiles. Most folks didn't like the mention of nuclear and warhead in the same sentence, let alone in the same phrase.

She smiled to herself, and floated toward one of the windows. The ISS was a strange place. The first pieces, Russian-built, went up before the turn of the century. The ISS was, as its name suggested, an international project that had been initially designed for research. But as more private industry got into space travel, and as governments saw the point of it, the suggestion of turning the ISS into an interplanetary way station gained legs. The problem was that the ISS wasn't designed for it. Sure, it had modules upon modules upon modules, but they were held together with spit and glue, and a whole lot of prayer. The newest pieces could barely talk to the younger pieces, and the oldest piece, called *Zarya* by its designers, was mostly shut down because it had become so dangerous. Unfortunately, it was smack-dab in the middle of the main section of the station, so it couldn't be disassembled or jettisoned, at least not without great effort, great expense, and great risk.

Zarya wasn't her problem. The ISS really wasn't. She was running ops from here, and her biggest problem wasn't the missiles. It was the deadline. When General Clarissa Maddox assigned Banks the task, she'd said, "I know this deadline is tight. In fact, it's damn near impossible. But you're the only person I know who can make the impossible happen efficiently and well."

It was, Banks knew, both a vote of confidence and an apology for all the things that had happened with the shuttle program. But Banks also knew she wouldn't be assigned a mission this critical strictly as an apology. She had to be the best for the job, just like Maddox said she was.

There was no margin for error. She wouldn't allow any. She'd make sure these missiles were unloaded, and then when the next shipment came up, she'd make sure those missiles were properly taken care of, as well.

And she would keep doing that until all the area around the space station was filled with missiles. And then the aliens would see that they attacked the wrong people.

Maddox's plan was a good one, and Banks was proud to be the one who would make sure everything got done right. She wouldn't make any friends on this job, but she might just save a few billion human lives.

She grinned.

As long as they were killing a few billion aliens in the process, she could live with that.

5

May 6, 2018
9:02 A.M. Eastern Daylight Time

161 Days Until Second Harvest

Leo Cross was late and of all the places to be late to, Nan-
Tech wasn't one of them. He had forgotten how these old
streets outside the Beltway jammed during rush hour. He was
five miles from NanTech and it felt like he was five hundred
miles away.

His car was on automatic, following the directions given
by the guidance system installed somewhere in Detroit.

"What do those idiots know about D.C.?" he muttered and
shut off the guidance system. The Mercedes squawked, "Are
you certain—?" before he shut off the vocal controls as well.
Then he took over the steering himself, turned right onto a
side street, and drove fifteen miles over the speed limit through
a residential area that had been built around the time he
was born.

He hoped no children were playing hooky from school,
no dogs decided to take that moment to cross the road, no
cats chased a mouse across his path. He hadn't driven hands-
on in months, not since the last time he'd rented a car in,
what? Oregon? when he went out to see Bradshaw for the
very first time.

It was rather liberating. He hadn't realized how controlled he felt by this expensive car, by its automatic everything—so smooth you can forget how to drive and still get where you're going in comfort, according to the stupid radio ads. Well, he was getting where he was going, in comfort, and *on time*, because he was taking matters into his own hands.

The back streets had none of the crunch of the main thoroughfares. He was beginning to see the problems inherent in automatic guidance systems.

He turned into the NanTech employee lot, bounced over a few speed bumps, and parked behind the building. There was no gilt here, no fancy scrollwork to mar the glass-and-steel design. It looked so '90s. He'd always found that amusing. He was coming to the cutting edge of nanotechnology, and the building looked dated.

He walked in the back door, ignoring the building as it greeted him—everything at NanTech talked—and happy to avoid the bug sculpture in the lobby. That's what Bradshaw called it anyway. The sculpture was supposed to be of a human form covered with nanomachines. Instead, Bradshaw said, it looked like some poor guy covered with ants.

Cross pressed a button for the elevator. He debated, as he waited for the doors to open, whether or not to shut off the vocal unit, but then decided not to. He was late. He deserved it.

Besides, he didn't know where everyone was meeting.

The elevator doors slid open silently. The elevator was empty. Cross cursed under his breath, and stepped inside.

Dr. Cross. You are half an hour late. I will take you to the fifteenth floor.

"Thanks," he muttered, knowing he didn't sound grateful at all. He hated having inanimate objects talk to him. Portia Groopman, she of the genius mind trapped in a twenty-year-old's body, said she found all this idle chatter "comforting."

108

Cross was really afraid to think about what the world would be like in his old age.

If the world survived to his old age.

He shuddered, wishing that for one day he could forget how very close they all were to losing everything.

The elevator doors opened. The nanomachines had formed a series of teddy bear sculptures, all of them pointing to the left.

"Cute, Portia," Cross said.

She had designed the nanosculptures, as she called them. They changed daily, sometimes hourly. Nanomachines were programmed to form several different images. Usually the changes followed a prearranged program, but sometimes someone—usually Portia—made them do something special for a guest. In this case, a late guest.

Cross followed the pointing bears down one hallway until he reached an open doorway. Inside, he saw Bradshaw, Portia, and two other members of NanTech's whiz squad, as Bradshaw called them. None of the NanTech employees on this team, at least, were older than twenty-five.

"Hey, Leo, it's about time," Portia said. She looked up from the screen she'd been studying. She was a slight girl, whose delicate frame made her seem even slighter. She wore rose-tinted glasses and had her black hair cut in a perfect wedge. Her skin was tanned from her trip to South America with Bradshaw.

Bradshaw looked up at the mention of Cross's name. Bradshaw was the oldest member of the Tenth Planet Project. He was nearly sixty, although he didn't look it. He had lost weight since coming to Washington, D.C., but he still had love handles, as Britt called them, and his graying hair needed a trim. He, too, had tanned on this last trip, and it accented the laugh lines around his eyes and mouth.

"Leo," he said. "You're late."

109

"It's the damn car," Cross said, and came into the room. "It insisted on driving us the slow route."

"You know, you can program the guidance systems to do anything you want." Jeremy Lantine, the head of the biology division at NanTech, was a scrawny black-haired man who, in a different generation, probably would have been a poet. His goatee was an affectation that matched his beret. His beat-up leather jacket hung on the chair beside him. He wore a see-through muscle-T that revealed his muscleless chest. "You can even make them ignore all the rules of the road. It takes some jury-rigging, but—"

"Some day," Cross said, "I'll let you adjust my machine."

"Excellent," Lantine said.

"I wouldn't let him loose on it," said Yukio Brown. Yukio wore his dark hair in a modified Mohawk, and he had tattoos on both cheeks. The designs matched—two **S**-shaped squiggly lines on one side, and two inverted **S**-shaped squiggly lines on the other side—but Yukio said they signified nothing except his lame attempt to get his father's attention. "He might instruct your guidance system to drive only on lawns."

"I wouldn't do that," Lantine said. "I never repeat myself."

"See why I don't have a car?" Portia said. "These guys would just screw it up. Although that was kinda funny, watching you chase after your car as it dug ruts in all that nicely mowed grass."

"It was not funny," Brown said. "That old lady on Third made me pay to have the whole thing resodded."

"Made me pay, you mean," Lantine said.

"No," Brown said. "I made you pay."

"Enough, children," Bradshaw said. "Leo wasted enough of our time being late. When this crisis is over, you can tell us all you want about your car wars. Until then, the stories get canned."

Cross whistled. "You're being tough, old man."

"I've had to listen to them for a week, Leo." Bradshaw

looked aggravated, but his eyes were twinkling. "While you've been—what have you been doing since you got back?"

Cross came around the table. They had several screens set up, all with different views of the nanomachines. Many were models that were rotating. Some were changing as if they were going through a cycle.

"I've been visiting our friends at the Pentagon mostly," Cross said, "trying to find out what the government's doing with the other nanoharvesters. No one'll tell me. Clarissa Maddox says that I'll know when she knows."

"But you're the guide behind this thing," Lantine said.

"I am not a specialist in nanotechnology," Cross said, modifying his voice so that he sounded like Maddox. "Really, Dr. Cross. You can't oversee everything."

"Yes, Dr. Cross," Bradshaw said, and then shook his head. "How do they expect anything to get done if they're going to clamp down on the information flow?"

"They have to," Cross said. "They don't want it in the wrong hands."

"Since when did you become the wrong hands?" Brown asked.

The room was silent for a moment. Cross felt his breath catch in his throat. He hadn't thought of it that way.

"It's the military way," Bradshaw said. "One branch doesn't tell the other branch what's going on, not without a big conference about something or other."

"It's the government way," Cross said, thinking about the stuff his friend Mickelson went through as secretary of state.

"I suppose," Portia said. "But it seems weird to me. They don't know we have these, do they?"

Cross shook his head.

"You expected this?" Lantine asked.

Cross's smile was small. "No, I didn't. But Maddox warned me. She didn't have to. She could have ordered me to bring

111

everything to her after I'd arrived in D.C. But she told me before."

"You think that was a warning?" Brown asked. "Sounds like that good old-fashioned oxymoron, military intelligence, to me."

This time, Cross glared at him. "Clarissa Maddox is one of the smartest people I know. And she's damn political. She doesn't make a mistake like that. She let me know she was going to cut me out of the loop, it was part of her job, and she gave me a choice of going around her."

"Which isn't to say you won't get nailed if she catches us working on this," Bradshaw said.

"Right," Cross said. "Unless we find something really good."

Portia sighed. She eased herself into a chair. Lantine adjusted his beret. Brown flopped beside Portia.

"We did find something good, right?" Cross asked.

"It depends on your definition of good," Bradshaw said.

"Anything that'll help us win this next battle," Cross said. "Or prevent these things from working."

"We're not miracle workers," Lantine muttered.

Portia punched him in the arm. He glared at her, rubbed his rubbery bicep, and said, "I mean, we've only had a week, sir."

"Actually, I think we've got a lot," Portia said. "It just isn't what you need yet. But we'll get it."

"What do you have?" Cross asked. He turned his fullest attention to her because she was the real whiz kid in this group. Her office—which was in a different part of this building—was decorated in early chocolate and stuffed animals. But she was no child. She had one of the most far-reaching minds he'd encountered in all his years in the sciences.

She glanced at her colleagues. "Everyone okay with me telling this?"

"You're the one who found the stuff," Brown said. There

was no animosity in his tone. "We're just here to ask the questions that get you going."

Portia laughed. She got up and went to the nearest screen. On it, one of the nanomachines rotated slowly. It was clearly a model. She picked up a laser pointer and turned its red beam on the screen.

"What's bugging me the most are those marks," she said. "I think they're a language, and I'm not a linguist. Still, I look at them and wonder if I'm missing something."

"Tell me what you do have," Cross said.

"Okay," she said. "This is a simple machine, just like I told Edwin from the fossil he showed me. It's designed to harvest. Matter goes in, gets processed and the good stuff stored, and the waste comes out. That's all."

"These things can't fly or move on their own?"

"Nope. They're like a single-celled organism. They may have a molecular attraction to their target, like a magnet to metal, but they have one function and one function only. Harvest."

Cross nodded. "That's good news, right?"

She shut off the laser pointer. "I don't know. These things are really, really efficient. Once they're dropped, they go to work, and they don't quit until their little bellies are full."

"Bellies?" Cross said.

"Portia anthropomorphizes everything," Brown said, fondly.

"She's saying that they eat until there's nothing left. That's why it's good these things don't move around much." Lantine stretched out his legs. "And don't reproduce themselves from what they eat. When we discovered that part, I had this nightmare that these little buggers grew legs, reproduced, and started walking. And when I woke up, I got even more scared, because I thought about it, and if they did, they'd have gone through more than the California coast. They'd have eaten their way into Nevada, and up into Oregon, and down into

113

Mexico, and God knows what they'd've done under the ocean, and we'd have no hope at all."

Cross felt his shoulders tighten. "No hope?"

"None," Lantine said. "Kabingo, we're dead. These things eat organic material. If they walked, reproduced themselves as they went along, nothing would survive. I'm just glad they don't."

"We'd have designed them to move more, I'm sure," Brown said.

"Remember," Portia said to Bradshaw, "when I looked at that fossil, I said these things were designed different than people would design them?"

"I remember," Bradshaw said quietly.

"Jamison said the same thing to me just last week," Cross said.

"Well, that's one of the things I meant," Portia said. "We put a lot of emphasis on equipment that moves on its own. I'm guessing that movement is less important to these aliens. Having the harvesters have a molecular attraction is more than enough to make them efficient."

"Interesting hypothesis," Cross said, "but I'm loathe to make generalizations based on one bit of equipment. After all, we know these aliens are good at other kinds of movement, like using their spaceships. Just because they didn't design their nanomachines in the way we would doesn't mean they're that different from us."

"They've got to be different," Brown said. "We'd never devastate a planet like this."

Cross had to prevent himself from snorting. Bradshaw looked at Brown as if the boy were the most naïve person on the planet.

"You need to take a class in archaeology," Bradshaw said.

"Archaeology, hell," Cross said. "How about the history of food? Take a look at what the introduction of farming did to this planet."

114

"Not to mention certain methods of hunting," Bradshaw said.

"We're notorious for stripping land bare—on our own planet," Cross said.

Brown held up his hands. "I stand corrected."

"Better sit, then," Lantine said.

"Are you boys done?" Portia asked.

Cross grinned at her. She smiled back, then ducked her head shyly, her bangs falling across her eyes.

"Sorry, Portia," he said. "What else have you got?"

She tossed the laser pointer from one hand to the other. Lantine grabbed a small stuffed dog, about the size of a golf ball, from a nearby table and tossed it at her. She caught it and nodded her thanks.

Cross suppressed another smile. The team knew one another well. Whatever Portia had to say, it bothered her, and Lantine knew she needed comfort. He also knew the dog would provide it.

"Okay," she said, taking a deep breath. "Dr. Cross, I'm not sure we can turn these harvesters off."

"They stop, don't they?"

She nodded. "But only when they're full. Once they start chewing or dissolving or whatever they do, they keep doing it. I have not been able to find an intercept."

"No emergency shut-off valve?" Cross asked.

"Not that I can find." She cupped the dog in her right hand and rubbed a thumb along the dog's nose. Cross half expected it to wag its stuffed blue tail. "And I'm not even sure these things shut off in the way that we're thinking."

"What do you mean?" Cross asked.

"I think they shut off when they're full, like I said. But there's no way to test it. Because they seem to be full when the organic material goes away."

"In other words," Brown said, "they stop running when the food is gone."

"But if there were unlimited food," Portia said, "I'm not sure they would stop until they were completely full."

"Like the locusts of Biblical fame," Bradshaw muttered.

"What?" Lantine asked.

"You know, the ones that God sent against the Pharaoh," Brown said.

"Actually," Bradshaw said, "I was thinking of the one mentioned in the Book of Joel."

"It left the land barren," Cross said. His gaze met Bradshaw's. "You think they saw these things?"

Bradshaw shrugged. "I don't know. It might have been actual locusts. But I was thinking about the devastation, how nothing was left and there was starvation all over the land."

"If they drop more of these things," Lantine said, and then stopped.

Portia was staring at all of them. Her hand had closed around the dog. The poor thing looked as if it were strangling. If, of course, it had actually been alive.

"If they blanketed the entire United States," she said, "we'd have nothing left. It'd look like it did in South America. We'd be gone, and there'd be dust everywhere."

"And that'd be all that's left of us," Brown said.

Cross shuddered. Not all. There'd be zippers and earrings and buttons, and concrete, and cable, and steel. Enough for archaeologists to sift through a thousand years from now and misjudge what the entire society was about.

"Okay," Cross said. "Let me get this straight. Either these things stop when they're full or they stop when they run out of material to chew."

Portia nodded.

"Can you make them think they're full?"

"Or think they're out of raw material?" she asked. "I don't know. This technology is truly alien, Dr. Cross. I mean, they

116

have spaceships and we have spaceships, but that doesn't mean one of our astronauts can get into their ship and fly it."

"Not without some study," Cross said.

"Right," she said. "And I'm just beginning work on this."

"We don't have a lot of time," Cross said.

"She knows." Bradshaw now sounded fatherly, as if Cross were pushing too hard. "These kids have already managed to cram a year's worth of work into a week, Leo. You're expecting miracles."

"We need miracles." He leaned against the desk and stared morosely at the slowly rotating image of the nanoharvester. Whoever thought that destruction of the human race might come from machines so tiny that they were almost impossible to see with the human eye?

"There's one more thing, Dr. Cross," Portia said softly.

He looked up. She had opened her hand and was still petting that little dog. She looked like a girl who was asking for the keys to her dad's car, not about to explain a scientific discovery.

"It's really clear that these nanoharvesters can be programmed."

He felt his heart leap. "By us?"

She shook her head. "By the aliens."

He frowned. "What do you mean? I thought you said these harvesters had only a single purpose."

"They do," she said. "They're harvesters. But they don't have to harvest organic material. They can harvest anything. What they harvest is programmable."

"How'd you figure this out?"

"Don't ask," Bradshaw said, meaning he already had.

But Portia had turned toward the third screen. A set of the nanoharvesters was shoved to one side, next to several of the fossils. "Edwin's been teaching me how to examine fossils," she said. "I looked at the fossils we have and compared them to the harvesters we have."

117

Cross's stomach was jumping. He wasn't sure he liked what was coming next.

"About four thousand years ago, we have a fossilized harvester preserved with the body of a small rodent," Bradshaw said. "I didn't think anything of it at the time. But when we got back from Brazil, I looked at it. And this was one of the few cases where we had a written record. The aliens needed something special. The harvesters fell, but they took minerals out of rock instead of organic material. At least, that's what I'm guessing."

Cross peered at the harvesters and then at the fossil. "I don't see a difference."

"There is none," Portia said. "That's what I'm saying. These aliens can program these things. If the aliens need organic material, they take that. If they need water, I'll bet they can take that. If they need only ocean salt, I'll bet they can take that. All with these things."

Cross stared at those alien machines. They were growing more and more hideous, the more he heard about them. "So," he said. "If they want to take all of Earth's resources, they can."

Portia nodded. "I think so. If they have enough harvesters. And enough time."

"My God," Cross said. How come the more they discovered, the more difficult things became?

He stood. "See if you can find a way to shut those things off," he said.

"We're doing our best," Brown said. "It would help if we knew what our military colleagues were doing."

"I know," Cross said, "but I don't think we'll know any time soon. Just assume you're working alone on this."

"There are some great nanotechnology guys in other labs," Brown said.

"Bring them in," Cross said.

118

"We're a for-profit company," Lantine said.

Cross stared at him for a moment.

Lantine raised his hands in a gesture of surrender. "I know, I know. If we don't survive, profit won't matter. But if we do—"

"You have my permission to patent your findings. This is a rogue operation anyway. You may as well make use of it." Cross again had the feeling that, if the Earth survived this threat, he and the others were creating a culture he wasn't sure he was going to like.

But he'd rather take that—a culture he hated—than a silent Earth blanketed in dust.

May 6, 2018
20:34 Universal Time

161 Days Until Second Harvest

The old glide paths were dust covered and rusted. Cicoi was able to use his glide platform for only half of the distance. For the rest, he had to pick it up with two lower tentacles, and cross debris, gingerly, with the remaining eight. The Elder who had been assigned to him waited in the air before him, flapping his own ghostly tentacles, as if Cicoi's slow progress irritated him.

Cicoi had no idea where they were going. All he knew was that his Elder, who refused to tell Cicoi his name, had simply said, inside Cicoi's brain, *You shall come with me.*

Of course Cicoi obeyed. All of the Commanders obeyed the Elders, and did not discuss their hesitations, although Cicoi had many. He assumed the others had many as well. The Elders seemed to have taken complete control, and they didn't seem concerned about the destroyed ships, the lack of

119

food gathered on the First Pass, or the decreased possibilities for the future.

The Elder was taking Cicoi to a part of the planet Cicoi had never been in before. Actually, it was a part of the South Cicoi had never been in before. When he had inspected this area before he became Commander, he had seen the solar panels laying dark on the planet's surface, as they did over most of the planet, and believed what he was told.

That this part of the South was empty land—once farmland, generations ago, under a different sun. Now abandoned and left, empty and resting, until, perhaps, that day came in Far Beyond, when life grew on Malmur again. When the solar panels could be removed and light actually allowed to reach the surface.

Sometimes Cicoi did not believe in the Far Beyond.

The glide paths leading to this region confused him. He knew that workers had once been here—as evidenced by the solar panels' existence over them—and he knew that workers occasionally had to come effect repairs, but he did not expect someone—even long ago—to have gone to the expense of a glide path.

It had been built properly, too, with the right downsloping trajectory so that travel on a glide platform required only a single puff of energy at the start, and the rider would use slope and momentum to maintain speed. Cicoi felt rather guilty that he had had to restart his platform six times already, but the Elder didn't seem irritated by it. He seemed more irritated by Cicoi's slow progress down the glide path.

It was almost as if the Elder wanted to pick him up and drag him toward whatever it was the Elder wanted to show him.

As Cicoi went farther down the glide path, he began to wonder about the return trip. Sometimes, glide paths had a wide slingshot angle, so that he would have to go far out of his way in order to rise high enough to find the return downslope. He saw no return slope on either side, and that made him worry that it was either too far above him or too far away for him to see.

The Elder had said nothing during this long trip. He had to know that Cicoi was worried about everything, from the return glide path to the amount of time he was taking away from his post. Right now his Second was running too much of the planning. His Second was ambitious and sometimes short-sighted. He might be planning for glory rather than for the future.

Cicoi had been spending too much time with the Elder to double-check on his Second.

The time with the Elder was, to Cicoi's mind, wasted time. The Elder wanted to relive the First Pass, to see what exactly the creatures on the third planet had done. Then the Elder wanted to see Cicoi's plans for the Second Pass. When Cicoi had showed him, the Elder had grunted and flown off. Later, Cicoi had learned that the Elder had joined the other Elders, and they had had some sort of conference.

Cicoi had a blessed two days without the Elder, and then he returned, along with his cryptic message. *You shall come with me.*

And Cicoi had. The deeper he went along this glide path, the colder he got. His upper tentacles wrapped around his torso in an effort to keep warm. Cicoi was used to cold temperatures; he had grown up in them. But these were uncomfortable and—he worried—maybe even dangerously cold.

He only had two eyestalks up, but he might have to send up more just to see. Even though the solar panels above him were collecting the light, they weren't funneling it this deep. The brownish half-light down here did come from the surface, but Cicoi knew the farther he went, the dimmer it would get.

Then he would have to choose between insulting the Elder

121

and seeing better. Cicoi had lost some of his awe of the Great Ones. He would insult the Elder and see what happened.

Suddenly, the glide path veered to the right. Cicoi went with it, into an even darker area. He was about to unpocket three eyestalks when the Elder waved his tentacles at the far rock wall.

Lights flashed on beneath the solar panels. Lights, clearly being fed by the panels. Lights, whose energy hadn't been used in hundreds of Passes.

Cicoi felt a shudder run through him at the thought of all the wasted energy. He personally knew of several lives that might have been saved if he had simply known this energy existed.

You would have used it unwisely, the Elder said to him.

Cicoi didn't argue, at least out loud. But if the Elder could read his thoughts, as it seemed he could, then the Elder would know that Cicoi was losing his patience for all this mystery.

The Elder flattened himself to fit on the glide path and placed himself in front of Cicoi.

Come with me.

Cicoi had no choice but to follow.

The glide path led inside a massive cavern, carved out of rock. Lights went on in here, as well, flooding the cavern with light.

Cicoi's tentacles waved slightly, mourning the waste of energy. And then he let his tentacles drop.

Before him were a hundred ships. Bullet-shaped in the front, like a torso with no tentacles, swept back and expanded in the rear. Clear black reflecting material over the nose, and propulsion at the base.

Cicoi had never seen anything like these.

As you stand here, the Elder said, *your companions to the North and Center stand in similar caverns.*

"These aren't harvester ships," Cicoi said. That was obvious. They were too small and sleek. They were shaped like

Malmuria with their tentacles pointed downward and their eyestalks pocketed. Poised to move as swiftly as possible.

No, they are not, the Elder said.

"You built them, obviously," Cicoi said. "But how come we didn't know about them?"

There has been no need for them. We have had no enemies. Until now.

Cicoi shuddered. He did not think of the creatures on the third planet as enemies. They were obstacles.

Or they had been.

The Elder was right. "Enemy" was the better word.

"If these aren't harvester ships, what are they for?" Cicoi asked, fearing the answer.

The Elder spun toward him, tentacles flowing freely, as if his answer gave him great joy.

They are for war, the Elder said.

"War?" Cicoi repeated. He shuddered. He had heard stories of great wars, but had never lived through them. "Surely we don't have enough energy to run a war."

We have stored it, the Elder said. His tentacles were still waving. *We are prepared.* He waved two tentacles toward the ships. *These are more powerful than our harvesters. They are the best ships we have ever built.*

"More powerful than the harvesters?" Cicoi asked.

And faster, too. The Elder's tentacles flowed toward Cicoi. He had read the emotion right. It was joy. *We shall destroy the creatures on the third planet, and they will never, ever know how we did it.*

Or why, Cicoi thought. But he said nothing. For the first time since the last Pass, he felt hope.

May 6, 2018
22:07 Universal Time

161 Days Until Second Harvest

They were going to fight back.

That was all General Gail Banks kept repeating to herself as she stood inside the small cubicle that had been assigned to her as an office. Initially she had sworn she hadn't needed one. Now she was glad she had it. The cabin they had given her to bunk in was little more than a closet, even though it was top-grade and private. Here, though—here she had room to think.

And she was thinking about humanity fighting back, destroying the aliens that dared attack Earth. She'd seen pictures of their bodies. Information about their ships. She knew that even though they had the dampening screens, the coming attack would work. Some of the missiles would get through. And all they needed was for some of them to explode. It would be enough, she was sure.

But her job was to make sure the odds were in humanity's favor.

She moved to the porthole in her office that looked out into space. The plastic porthole wasn't really a hole at all. Instead it was a long clear section that ran the entire length of the wall. Through it, she could see the missiles that had been launched into orbit, at least part of them.

They glinted against the blackness of space. All had their internal telemetry on, and some had lenses and cameras pointing toward the tenth planet, ready and waiting.

Banks spent a lot of time before this window, just staring. She had gotten the station organized. She had workers on regular schedules, she was monitoring the incoming shuttles, she double-checked the orbits of incoming missiles before they arrived. She dealt with the recalcitrant permanent staff,

124

the hardworking temporary staff, and longed for her own people. She put in requisition orders and sent messages to Earth, demanding more missiles.

About three hundred missiles had arrived and, she was told, that was about all she'd get. A few more here or there might arrive before the fight, but probably not. Maddox had confided that two countries were being "somewhat difficult" but that was it.

After that it was up to her and her people.

From her window, she could see half the missiles at one time, hanging in the blackness of space. They were all cylindrical, but after that, the similarities ended. The most current ones, all of U.S. design, were sleek things that looked like they could respond to a whispered command with complete accuracy. Beside them were some ancient rockets that were so ungainly, they seemed impossible to move, even in space.

Then, of course, there were the handful of missiles that used to belong to the countries that had once formed the Soviet Block. Banks couldn't believe the organizers let some of those antiques lift off. They'd come from the smaller, less powerful countries of Eastern Europe—Lithuania, Latvia, and a few others whose names she couldn't remember. Even though the missiles should have been disassembled twenty years ago, they suddenly "reappeared" when they were needed to defend the Earth.

Banks hoped that they wouldn't explode at the wrong time.

She had workers outside, placing the warheads on top of the missiles. It was precise and difficult work, and she had only her best people on it. But the demands of time made it clear that she had to push them. She didn't worry about shortcuts— none of the people tethered to those rockets, working on the parts, would ever take shortcuts. But she knew what it was like to work under an impossible deadline, to know that the fate of everything you knew and loved depended on your success.

She knew that fear drove them—fear and panic and anger—and she knew that no matter how hard she tried to reassure them, she wouldn't be able to cut through that. Especially the anger. All of them wanted this work. All of them wanted to strike back at the aliens.

The best she could do was push them, but be aware of their needs. No one had less than six hours sleep, fewer than two meals. No one worked two shifts in a row, no matter how much their skills were needed.

No one cut corners, even if they were sure the corners could be cut.

She had promised Maddox she'd make the impossible deadline, and she would.

The missiles were here, hanging in space near the station, and everyone said that wouldn't happen.

The warheads were here, being put on the missiles, and no one believed that would happen, either.

The workers were here, some of them finishing their training in a New York minute, and the entire senior staff said that couldn't happen.

So far, three small miracles.

She hoped those three miracles would equal one giant miracle: stopping the aliens cold in their tracks.

She folded her hands behind her back and watched. Occasionally she saw movement as one of her workers, in a white environmental suit, slowly moved around the cone of a missile. Dozens of small shuttles floated among and around the missiles, helping with the work. At least thirty people were doing space walks at the moment, and she had thirty more taking their eight-hour break—six hours of sleep, plus two meals—inside.

More people were in space than had ever been here. Ever, in human history.

Once she would have been proud of that. Once she would have been happy to command such a force. Once she

126

would have used that fact as a major point in her military résumé, a case to be made for yet another star.

But she wouldn't speak of it. She had a hunch that fact would be forgotten in a very short time.

Once the missiles were launched.

Once the codes were activated.

Once the warheads exploded.

Right now, this mission was Earth's best hope.

Earth was fighting back and it was up to her to make sure the attack worked.

Section Two

WAR

6

May 20, 2018
8:01 A.M. Eastern Daylight Time

147 Days Until Second Harvest

Again, when entering the Oval Office, the first thing Mickelson noted was the faint smell of mold, covered by the cleaning fluids and furniture polish. But it was still there, just under the surface, waiting for the heat of the summer to bring it out into full bloom.

He was the first to arrive. Timeliness, which served him so well overseas, was a curse here. It meant he would have to wait alone, in a room he had never thought he'd find himself in ten years before.

Mickelson took his usual place on the white couch nearest the main door. Long ago, Franklin had told him to make himself comfortable no matter when he came into the room. Franklin hated walking into his office to find his Cabinet members standing on the blue rug like children waiting to be told to sit down.

"You're running this meeting?"

Mickelson started, and turned slightly. General Clarissa Maddox had entered the room. She was in full uniform—all five stars glistening on her broad shoulders—and she seemed to be in a take-no-prisoners mood. But there were shadows under her eyes, and new lines around her mouth that Mickelson had never seen before.

"If I were, we wouldn't be meeting in here," Mickelson said.

Maddox sank onto the couch beside him. The cushion didn't sag as much as he thought it would. It always surprised him how she could look so powerful and be so slight at the same time.

"I've got so much to do," she said, so low that only he could barely hear her. "I hope he doesn't make us sit here for an hour like the last time."

"The last time he got a call from Britain's prime minister. He couldn't exactly blow it off," Mickelson said. He hadn't been able to tell anyone during that last meeting what was going on. But now he could. A lot had come out of the call. And it seemed like months ago, instead of just ten days. Strange how time slowed when every minute of every hour was being used.

"I suppose not." Maddox looked at him sideways. "Do you even know what time zone you're in?"

Mickelson grinned. "Lessee. A round room, lots of blue, gold, and white decor, and oh yeah, an American flag behind the desk. Must be Washington, which puts me in Eastern Daylight officially."

"And unofficially?"

"I think I'm still working on strict Greenwich Mean."

"Your last stop was England?"

"I hope so," Mickelson said, "or that rather shy man I was referring to as Your Royal Highness was too polite to tell me I should have been calling him something else."

Maddox laughed. "If he was too polite to say anything, you were either in England or Minnesota."

"What about Minnesota?" Shamus O'Grady, the president's national security adviser, sat down across from them. He was a slender redhead with hazel eyes. His light skin, which

132

he never allowed in the sun, gave him a more youthful appearance than he deserved. It also showed every line, every mark of fatigue. And there were dozens of them. If everyone else on the president's team looked this tired, Mickelson thought, he wondered how bad he looked as well.

"Just saying that the folks there are polite," Maddox said.

"Wow," O'Grady said. "Are we talking about regional customs? Because I know a few that might shock you."

"I doubt you do," Maddox said.

Mickelson held up a hand. He'd been in this conversation with these two before. They had a sort of one-upmanship going that he found amusing most of the time, and disgusting the rest. He once told them that it seemed as if they brought out the high school in each other, or maybe even the middle school. It was as if gross-out humor were the highest form they could aspire to.

"Let's not go there," he said. "It probably won't shock General Maddox, but it'll shock me. Think of me as though I'm as naïve as your twelve-year-old son, O'Grady."

"Then nothing'll shock you, Mickelson," O'Grady said.

"We're playing that game again?" President Franklin walked into the room. Everyone stood. He waved them back down. "The last time you played it, I walked in to hear my staff discussing which was more disgusting, eating monkey brains or goat brains. And if I remember correctly, it was you, Doug, who actually had an opinion."

"I was just trying to shut them up, sir."

"Well, it seemed like encouragement to me." President Franklin sat down in the armchair. He was a slight man who had his mother's button eyes and mobile mouth. His dark hair fell across his forehead naturally, and that, combined with his incredible personal charm and aquiline nose—apparently the only thing he'd inherited from his father—got him voted *People Magazine On-Line*'s Sexiest Man in America in 2016, the year of his successful reelection campaign.

"I'm sorry, sir," Mickelson said with mock humility. "I won't do it again, sir."

"See that you don't," Franklin said, his black eyes twinkling. "I chance upon too many of these conversations as it is."

Maddox's cheeks were slightly rosy, and O'Grady's neck was flushed. Mickelson suppressed a smile. Franklin could embarrass them any time.

Of course, he could embarrass Mickelson, too. Franklin had a wicked sense of humor, and it was so dry that most people rarely caught it. His staff usually caught the blunt end of it, and Franklin liked nothing more than to razz people who gave him the opportunity.

He leaned back in the armchair and seemed to gather himself. Franklin had looked exhausted since the day of his inauguration, and Mickelson thought that a good sign. In all his years in Washington, Mickelson noted that there were two kinds of presidents—those who aged five years for each year they were in office and those who looked the same when they emerged as they had on the day they entered. Or, as Mickelson once put it to Cross, there were those presidents who haunted the hallways at night and those who slept like babies.

Mickelson preferred to work for the ones who aged and didn't sleep. They were the ones who were in office to do some good, not because they'd reached the political Holy Grail.

"All right," Franklin said. "I guess we'd better do this. You've got the ball, Doug. How do we stand?"

Mickelson straightened, as if his posture suddenly made a difference. The last ten days had felt like ten years. He'd hit most of the major nations, inspecting their weapons, their military, their production facilities, talking with their leaders about the best methods to approach the next attack by the aliens.

When he was visiting the U.S.'s traditional allies, he had

little trouble. Britain welcomed him with open arms. But in countries with which the U.S. had shaky relations, or a history of bad relations, Mickelson also had to have meetings in which he reassured the countries' leaders that cooperation didn't mean a loss of sovereignty.

Mickelson's argument had been simple: this was a global threat, and it needed global leadership. The United States was the logical choice.

China's leaders had argued for a U.N.–led effort, which would have made sense fifteen years before. But the last two U.N.–led efforts had dissolved into infighting and slow movement. Mickelson argued, parroting Franklin's words, that slow movement in this case would be deadly.

China really didn't need much more convincing. And since the entire argument hadn't taken longer than lunch, Mickelson suspected the entire interchange was intended only to save face.

"I spent most of my time touring military facilities," Mickelson said, "and talking to each country's leadership about the best methods to proceed. Everyone seems to understand the need for speedy action. Even China."

Maddox made a soft sound and leaned back on the couch. "They're going to cooperate?"

Mickelson nodded. "It took very little persuasion on my part."

"So they think the world's going to end," O'Grady said.

Mickelson smiled. He'd had the same thought. In fact, before he left he'd said to Franklin that it would be a cold day in hell before China cooperated. Apparently that long-predicted cold day had finally arrived.

"I saw weapons facilities and military outposts that we've been trying to get into for years," Mickelson said.

"I need a full debrief," Maddox said.

Mickelson nodded as Franklin grinned. Franklin had warned Mickelson of that the night before. "You'll get it," Mickelson

135

said. "Although you might get more out of Lieutenant Rogers. She, at least, knows more of what she was looking at."

"I didn't realize you'd taken her as your aide," O'Grady said.

"With the president's permission."

"But not mine," Maddox said. "They're taking all my best people for these political tasks, when I need them onboard for military work."

"This is military work, Clarissa," Franklin said without a trace of irritation. That was more than Mickelson could have done. Maddox simply had no comprehension of diplomacy.

"Forgive me, sir," Maddox said. "But that's not military work. You could have sent a flack with Doug. But to send a perfectly good officer, that's bullshit and you know it."

Mickelson thought he saw a smile play around Franklin's lips, but he couldn't be certain. "Was it bullshit, Doug? Could you have used a flack?"

Mickelson suppressed a sigh. Meetings should be banned, and yet the government thrived on them. "No," Mickelson said. "Lieutenant Rogers had some valuable insights that I don't think I would have gotten without her along."

"Such as?" Maddox said.

"Such as," Mickelson said, struggling to keep the irritation from his voice, "the fact that much of the First World's military might is very out-of-date. We haven't had much more than border skirmishes since the turn of the century. The last significant worldwide military buildup was during Kosovo, and the last great one was during the Cold War. I saw missile silos in Russia that had completely rusted out. Most of this world, to put it flatly, isn't in shape to fight the aliens if we let them get back here."

O'Grady leaned forward. "Then this is terrible news. The plan won't work without functioning warheads."

"We almost have enough warheads in orbit now to do the job," Franklin said.

Doug sat in stunned silence. He had no idea the launches had gone so fast.

"But we can always use more," Maddox said. "And we need to have everyone ready to fight in case our first plan fails. We've known for a decade about the world's aging military-industrial complex. We even have a scenario on what to do if some of the oldest equipment malfunctions and starts a war."

Franklin spoke softly. "Granted, we knew about this. Mickelson's junket only confirmed it. In fact, the news about the Chinese is good. We hadn't counted on them."

"They really must think the end of the world is near," Maddox mumbled.

"I think they do," Franklin said. He was looking at her. "I think we'd all be fools not to consider that."

"Aging warheads? Come on, Mr. President. We can't send ancient warheads to the ISS." O'Grady had shifted in his seat.

"We already have. And we'll send more, if we need to," Franklin said.

"We have more than we planned on," Mickelson said. "We have full Chinese cooperation. Russia has been maintaining its weapons production—at lower rates than fifty years ago, but nonetheless, they have some up-to-date equipment. So do the Saudis and the Israelis, and most of Southeast Asia. Japan is the only country that's a bit farther behind than we expected. Even Germany is going to contribute more than we had planned on. The aging warheads do exist, but they're going to be our last-ditch effort if, and this is a big if, we don't have time to step up production worldwide."

"You think we can?" Maddox asked.

Mickelson nodded. "That was the most encouraging news I got from this entire trip. A lot of factories can be converted quickly to military supplies and weapons productions. I'm gathering our biggest problem worldwide isn't going to

137

be weapons or equipment or production. It's going to be manpower."

"And getting through the alien screens to use the weapons," Maddox said.

No one said anything to that.

"I don't completely agree with the manpower problem," O'Grady said. "We have satellite photos showing almost every nation on Earth has fully deployed its military. If anyone is behind the eight ball, it's us. We haven't deployed enough."

"We've explained that, Shamus," Maddox said.

"It's making me nervous, Clarissa."

The whole thing made everyone nervous, but Mickelson didn't say that.

"The problem isn't numbers," Mickelson said. "It's talent. We need astronauts and shuttle pilots and ground control crews. We need very specialized talent to fight this war, and it's precisely the kind of talent we haven't trained. And not just us. The Japanese and the Russians are the only other countries with a significant number of trained astronauts and pilots. The rest of the world didn't have the money or the time to pursue a space program like we did."

"Exactly," Franklin said. "If our attack doesn't work, the coming war with the aliens isn't going to be fought on the ground. It's going to be fought in the air and in space."

"The Australians have something."

"The Brits have something, the French have something, the Germans have something, even Israel has something," Mickelson said. "But something isn't enough."

"I've already got my people changing the focus of training," Maddox said. "They think they can find candidates and train them to operate in zero g within six months."

"That's a short time frame," Franklin said.

"It's more than what we've got, sir," Maddox said.

Her words hung in the air for a moment. Then Franklin

leaned back and templed his fingers. "The question is, Doug, whether or not the other countries are with us."

"If they have the capability to build a warhead, they have the capability to send it into space," Mickelson said. "I've got to tell you, I didn't expect that, and that turned out to be good news. A lot of countries can convert the system they use to launch satellites to get the warheads to the ISS. We'll have some accidents, but a small number is to be expected. We can be ready for a second wave of attack if we need it."

"You're kidding," O'Grady said.

Mickelson shook his head. "The best part of this junket was that I learned that any functional transport that can get a payload into low Earth orbit is being used. A lot of countries have commandeered their private industries' transports as well. As we're sitting here, atomic warheads are being launched into space from all the countries that have them. This is the biggest mass deployment of nuclear weaponry in human history."

O'Grady shuddered. "At least it's not being deployed against human beings," he said softly.

Franklin tapped his fingertips against his lips. It was almost as if that comment displeased him—not for its sentiment, Mickelson knew Franklin agreed with that, but for the interruption it caused in the flow of the session.

Franklin let his hands drop. "All right, General. We know what our allies are doing—"

Mickelson winced at the word "allies." Many of the countries he visited weren't really allies at all. He had a sense this was like World War II: incompatible governments uniting against a common cause. If that cause went away, all hell would break loose.

"—so now I want to know what we're doing. How're those attack rockets coming?"

"Better than can be expected," Maddox said. "We'll have enough boost power to get every warhead we have in orbit to its target."

139

"Excellent." Franklin truly sounded pleased. "And the work on the International Space Station?"

"General Banks is there and—"

"Banks?" O'Grady said. "The one who testified before Congress?"

Maddox leaned forward, her face inches from O'Grady's. "She got busted, mister, because she was too competent. And frankly, I would rather have someone who is too competent, who demands too much of our people, on that space station than one who believes in coddling everyone. Wouldn't you?"

Mickelson moved out of the way. He'd never seen Maddox in her professional soldier mode. She was tough and hard. He was impressed.

"Well," O'Grady said. "When you put it that way . . ."

"There's no other way to put it," Maddox snapped. "There's government and then there's the military. We're at least efficient."

"Ouch," Franklin said.

Maddox sat up. "Sorry, sir."

Franklin shook his head. "It's a point well taken. We need competent efficient people, folks who can get the job done. You're exactly right, General. If we have any chance of success against those aliens, we have to be operating at peak efficiency, not just in this country, but all over the world."

That was Mickelson's cue. "I think it can be done," he said. "And most every country will be looking to us to coordinate things."

"To lead," O'Grady said.

Mickelson smiled. "In effect, yes. But don't tell them that."

"They're not dumb, Doug."

"I know," Mickelson said. "But in diplomacy, a polite lie gets a lot more accomplished than the bold truth."

Franklin nodded. "We're close, then. All the details are in place. I don't want to hear about leaks from anyone's office. And I want no statements made to the press. They're going to

140

notice all the activity, and there will be questions, but a good old-fashioned 'no comment' will work. I want to be the one to make the announcement."

"All right," Maddox said.

"The less I talk to the press, the happier I am," O'Grady said.

"I already told the heads of state I met with that you'd make the announcement when the time was right."

"I take it they had no problem with that," Franklin said.

"If they did," Mickelson said, "I would have told you."

"Good." Franklin sighed. He looked at every one of them, holding each gaze for several seconds. It was an old political trick, designed to make the person feel as if he were friends with the person in charge. Mickelson knew that and was usually immune when other people did it to him. But when Franklin's gaze caught his, he felt absurdly flattered and mentally shook his head at himself.

This was why he was sitting here, now, handling a crisis he wouldn't even have been able to imagine two years before. This was why he accepted Franklin's offer to become secretary of state, why he put himself on the line. He trusted Franklin, as much as someone could trust a man who desired to become president. He knew Franklin was one of the smartest, most committed policy men to ever hold office.

But Mickelson wasn't sure policy was what was needed now. He wasn't sure Franklin would prove himself to be a good wartime commander in chief.

Yet Mickelson had gone all over the world, making certain that Franklin would metaphorically lead the troops into battle. He hoped that this was the right choice. Other world leaders had more charisma. Several others were smarter. But none of them led the most powerful nation in the world.

Mickelson wondered if Franklin knew how much of the fate of the world rested on his shoulders. He seemed more focused than he had ever been, and that was saying something.

But being focused and being the right man in the right spot at the right time were two different things.

A lot rested on Franklin's speech. Mickelson hoped that when the time came, Franklin could pull it off.

May 24, 2018
12:57 P.M. Eastern Daylight Time

143 Days Until Second Harvest

Britt Archer's cat Muffin hated Leo Cross. From the first time he had come to Archer's apartment, Cross had had to contend with the small, gray tabby with the face of an angel and the temper of a lion. Any time he got close to Britt, the cat tried to bat him away. He didn't have this problem with Britt's other cat, Clyde. Clyde seemed to know that they were both guys, and as such, had to bond. But sometimes, Cross was afraid that Muffin would slice him up in his sleep.

Britt's large two-bedroom apartment was close to her job at STScI. Even though she'd been at the job for nearly ten years, she'd never bought a house, because she'd always believed she'd have to move for her work. So far, that hadn't happened, but, Britt said, the moment she bought something, it would.

Cross loved the apartment. It had bay windows with a view of the tree-lined street, lots of light, and a functional design. Its only flaw was the kitchen, and since Britt didn't cook, that meant that she only had to squeeze herself into its dark and cramped quarters twice a day—once to pour cereal in the morning, and the other time to feed the cats at night.

However, Muffin thought the kitchen was her domain, and whenever Cross padded in there, as he had now, she attacked his ankles. He was careful to wear shoes and socks any time he headed in this direction. He'd once said to Britt it was like the cat believed he'd die if she cut him off at the feet.

142

Britt found all of this cute and funny, but Cross looked on it as a war in miniature. He was trying to get along with this alien being that Britt had brought into her house. So far, things weren't going well. At least he had Clyde.

Britt was in her bedroom, getting dressed. She rarely wore makeup and never fussed with her hair, but for her, getting dressed took much longer than it should have. Cross finally figured out why. She dithered over what to wear, so much so that she often tried on three or four separate outfits before picking the outfit of the day. When Cross finally asked what the reason for the dithering was—expecting some sort of clichéd female thing, like she had to make certain she looked perfect—he was surprised by the answer.

It seemed that the brilliant and competent Britt Archer was confounded by the weather.

She listened to the weather reports as if they were gospel, then tried to dress accordingly. She worried that she would be too hot or too cold, wearing too many layers or not enough.

Cross had learned, in the few months of their relationship, to offer no opinions about this morning ritual. It didn't piss Britt off, but it did make her try on at least two more outfits before she decided what to wear.

Since they had yet another Tenth Planet Project meeting this morning, he had to get Britt going on time.

He'd actually bought donuts the night before, knowing that getting out of the apartment would be a problem. He'd tried to talk her into staying at his house, which was closer, but Britt had had a mountain of work to finish, and she hadn't wanted to make the drive that late at night. Cross understood. He could be flexible, and often was, and decided that staying here was the better part of valor.

Even if he had to fight with Muffin.

She was crouched in the corner of the kitchen, her tail switching back and forth, her eyes slits. Of course, she was right beneath the part of the counter where the coffeemaker lived.

If Britt didn't have her caffeine in the morning, she was no good to anyone. Cross was about to make the dangerous trek to the coffeemaker, when the doorbell rang.

Britt cursed from the bedroom.

"I got it," Cross said, and gladly left the wilds of the kitchen. He had to step over Clyde, who was sprawled on the fake Oriental carpet that was the living room's centerpiece, before opening the door.

Portia Groopman stood in front of it, her dark hair mussed, its oblong cut growing out unevenly. She had a monkey on her back—a stuffed white monkey with long arms and equally long legs. They had Velcro on the palms so that the hands looked like they were clasped together.

"Oh, good, Dr. Cross. I caught you."

He blushed. For a brief moment, he felt like he was still in high school and had been caught doing something he shouldn't. "How'd you know I'd be here?" he asked. Most folks knew about him and Britt, but they had never made a big deal about it.

"Edwin," she said.

Bradshaw. The eternal matchmaker and gossip. Cross nodded. "Is something wrong?"

"I got a wild hair," Portia said.

Cross frowned.

"An *idea*," Portia said as if he were dumber than a post. "Can I come in?"

"Oh, sure." He stepped away from the door.

She entered the apartment, looked at the books and the computers and the ivy crawling its way across the ceiling, and said, "Nifterino—Dr. Archer knows how to live."

"I'll tell her that she has your seal of approval," Cross said dryly, but Portia didn't seem to hear. She had already crouched on the rug, and was petting Clyde's stomach. Clyde's front

144

paws were kneading the air and he was purring so loudly, Cross thought the cat might make himself sick.

Muffin was watching the entire display from the entrance to the kitchen. She looked as disgusted as a cat possibly could.

It was probably his only chance to get to the coffeemaker. "I was about to make some coffee. Want some?"

"Sure," Portia said.

Cross slipped past Muffin, who was focused on this new intruder, and made coffee as dark and rich as Britt liked it. Then he grabbed the giant box of donuts and placed them on the oak table that stood in front of the bay windows.

"There's some breakfast, too, such as it is," he said.

"Great," Portia said, but didn't move from her spot beside Clyde. She looked like a little girl, her stuffed monkey hugging her, and the happy cat beneath her. At moments like this, Cross could see the impact her lonely childhood had on her. She had been homeless until she was ten. As good as she was at her work, she still didn't have a real place to call her own, not with family and cats and plants. And she needed it.

That was only one reason to make sure those damn alien harvesters didn't destroy the planet.

"What was your idea, Portia?" he asked as he sat down beside the open box of donuts.

She looked up, seemed to remember herself, and then tucked some loose hair behind her ear. "Oh, you'll probably think it's crazy."

"Crazy enough for you to track me down."

"Yukio and Jeremy said I shouldn't, but Edwin said I should. He said you like wild-hair ideas and that those are the only kind that make any real sense. He also said that if you didn't believe in wild hairs, no one would have known about the aliens until it was too late."

It almost was too late when they found out, but Cross didn't say that. Instead, he said, "Edwin's right."

She nodded. "We've been trying to find out more about

145

those nanoharvesters, and we've made some progress, but we're still a long way from being able to shut them down like you want."

The coffeemaker gurgled and shut off. Muffin raced for the kitchen. It was Cross's sign that the coffee was done.

"It's still early yet," he said, even though that wasn't true.

"I worry about the reality of learning everything there is to know about an alien technology in time to do some good," Portia said. She sat down across from him, pulled the monkey's hands apart, and took a long moment settling him in the third chair. She made certain he sat upright, that his paws rested on the table, and that his face was turned toward her.

"How do you drink your coffee?" Cross asked. While she was settling the stuffed animal, he might as well deal with the live one.

"Lots of sugar," she said.

He should have known. He got up and headed into the kitchen. There was a yowl, and Muffin wrapped herself around his right leg. He ignored her, even though she was biting so hard he could feel the scrape of teeth through his socks.

He poured three cups of coffee, got out the sugar, and poured some whole milk into Britt's so it would be the right temperature by the time she got dressed. Then he brought his and Portia's to the table.

"What's with that cat?" Portia asked.

"She doesn't like me."

"No shit."

Muffin finally let go of his leg and moved away from him. She was cleaning her fur, as if it were his fault that she was ruffled.

Portia put three teaspoons of sugar into the mug, took a sip, and added three more. Then she took a Bavarian cream donut out of the mess of donuts, and started to pick it into small pieces.

146

"Okay," Cross said, grabbing an éclair. "What's this crazy idea?"

"Well," Portia said around a piece of donut. "You know, if we can't shut the harvesters off, maybe we can attack them."

"Attack them?"

"Sure. You know, develop our own nanomachines designed to attack alien technology. We'd have this megawar being fought on the molecular level."

Cross frowned. He had no idea how this would work.

"You can develop this?"

Portia shrugged. "Don't know until we try. But I wanted to check with you first. Any word from the government guys?"

"None," Cross said. "That door is completely closed. Whatever their nanotech researchers are discovering, they don't want to tell us about it."

"Damn," Portia said and popped the rest of the donut in her mouth. She chewed, chipmunklike, and then swallowed, washing everything down with coffee.

Cross suddenly understood. "You don't have enough workers to study the nanoharvesters and create some machines of your own."

"No," Portia said. Then she shook her head. "Well, that's part of it. But not all of it. I mean, we've got some good people, especially after you told Jeremy that he could do what he wanted with what we discovered. But they're not me, you know."

He did know. There was no arrogance in what Portia said, only truth. She had the right kind of vision for this project. She would probably be the one to discover the shut-off mechanism for the nanoharvesters, or be the one to discover the kind of nanomachine that would defeat the alien machines. But she wouldn't be able to do both.

Britt picked that moment to come into the living room. She was wearing a summer sweater with a pair of khaki pants, some Birkenstocks, and gold jewelry.

147

She looked gorgeous, but Cross knew better than to tell her that, this close to decision-making time. He had to bow his head so that she wouldn't see him grin. He was in love with the woman. She was one of the most capable scientists he knew, and yet she had some of the best quirks he'd ever encountered.

"How're the Muffin wars this morning?" she asked.

"Your coffee's on the counter," he said, "and I've already poured the milk."

She kissed him on the top of his head. "You're a god," she said.

"Wow," Portia said.

"And you can take that however you want to," Britt said. "Good morning, Portia."

"Hi, Dr. Archer. I hope you don't mind me being here."

"I hope you don't mind if we eat and run," Britt said. "We have to get across town."

"We're nearly done anyway," Portia said as Britt disappeared into the kitchen. Muffin followed her, purring.

Cross shook his head. Cats. He'd managed to live his entire life without them. Why was he investing so much time in them now, when he had no time?

Britt, of course.

"So what do you think, Dr. Cross?" Portia asked. She was cradling her coffee mug.

He sighed. Resources. It all boiled down to resources. Then he smiled slightly. Resources for Earth—and for the tenth planet. "Can you work on the new nanomachines alone?"

"No," she said.

He cursed softly. "I don't know, Portia. Nanotechnology is your area."

"But the aliens are yours."

He didn't know how that had happened, but everyone seemed to assume he knew more about the tenth planet than he did. Still, inventing their own nanomachine to fight

148

the aliens' might have more of a chance. Portia would be developing something with technology she understood, not trying to figure out technology she didn't.

"Leo," Britt said as she came out of the kitchen. "If we're going to fight the traffic, we've got to go now."

Portia was still looking at him.

"I like the idea," he said to her. "But I need some time to think about it. The choice is a tough one. Off the top of my head, I'm leaning toward developing our own technology, but I don't like taking you off the current project."

"It's not as if we're the only ones working on it," Portia said. "And besides, we're not even supposed to be. So I keep worrying if we do figure something out, no one will listen."

It was a good point, and if the people weren't so damn scared, it would be a valid one. "If you do figure something out," Cross said, "I'll make sure someone listens."

Portia smiled and stood. She slung the monkey on her back, and only then did Cross realize that it had another Velcro slit on its back. It had a tiny carrying case built in, and Portia was using it as a backpack.

"I'll get back to you," Cross said. "In the meantime, continue on the same project."

"Okay," she said.

"Need a lift?" Britt asked.

Portia shook her head. "I've got my own, thanks." She stopped to pet Clyde, then let herself out.

"Strange girl," Britt said.

"Lonely one," Cross said.

Britt looked at him. He shrugged, and handed her a glazed donut. "We don't have time to eat," she said.

"You don't have time not to."

"I'll eat in the car."

"Fine," Cross said. He finished his coffee and waited while Britt poured hers into a travel mug. Then they gathered their things and left the apartment.

They took Cross's car, but Britt drove. She liked the new conveniences, and had, in the last week, taken five minutes to reprogram his navigation system so that he wouldn't be stuck in traffic. He had had no idea you could program the system to monitor links that showed which roads had the most traffic, or traffic tie-ups, or road construction. When Britt realized how much he let technology abuse him, she had taken over, and he hadn't minded.

He settled into the passenger seat, and thought about Portia's idea. If it worked, it would be the answer to everything. But he'd learned long ago not to trust answers like that.

With Britt's reprogramming, the car's natural speed, and its programmed ability to hit the timed stoplights correctly, they made it to the meeting in record time. They arrived as General Maddox did. She nodded curtly at Cross, then smiled at Britt as if she were an old friend.

Most of the rest of the group was there. Three large pots of coffee sat in the center of the table, their plastic sides bearing the Starbucks logo. A plate of donut holes sat beside them.

"See?" Britt whispered to Cross. "Told you I didn't need breakfast."

He didn't argue, but he remembered how many times in the last few weeks there'd only been institutional coffee and stale food.

"I tapped the military budget," Maddox said as she took her seat. "If we have to be locked up in this remnant of the 1980s, we should at least be comfortable."

The group chuckled. Britt smiled and looked down. Cross found that curious. Normally, she would agree on that point.

"What is it?" he whispered.

Britt shook her head, but he nudged her. Finally, she sighed, grabbed a donut hole, and then leaned toward him. Nice move, he thought as she did so. No one would know that her movement was connected to Maddox's comment.

"The general believes," Britt whispered so softly that he

had to strain to hear her, "that we have to enjoy the good things in life while we can."

Cross shuddered. He didn't like the idea that Maddox was planning to lose this battle. He resisted the urge to look at her. Maybe she had always felt this way. Maybe she was naturally pessimistic. But now he wished that Britt hadn't shared.

"No secrets." Robert Shane rounded the table and poured himself a cup of coffee. Then he grabbed four donut holes with his left hand.

"Leave the lovebirds alone," Jesse Killius said as she took her seat.

"Lovebirds?" Cross asked.

"Denial is not your forte, Dr. Cross," Hayes said. "Leave it to the politicos."

"Denial?" Britt asked.

"Hey," Cross said spreading his hands, his half-eaten donut hole dropping crumbs on the table. "I'm not denying. I'm just stunned at the word choice."

"What would you prefer?" Killius asked. "The 'couple'? That's so mundane."

"And unclear," Shane said. "The couple of whats?"

Maddox was smiling. "You know, we do need to get down to business here. I understand our international uplinks are ready."

Cross finished the donut hole, then poured himself a large cup of coffee. The last few meetings had gone on longer than he wanted, and he'd nearly dozed in one. Not because the information was dry—it wasn't—but because of his lack of sleep, the stuffy room, and the fact that he had always despised meetings. He was stuck in them now. Maddox led the Tenth Planet Project meetings, but everyone still turned to Cross as the de facto leader.

He was beginning to mind that. This whole thing didn't belong on his shoulders. He wasn't superhuman. He was having as much trouble with this as everyone else.

151

He let out a soft breath, trying to calm himself. Portia's visit bothered him more than he wanted to admit. Why did he have to choose which job she should do? If he chose wrong, Earth might lose everything.

Then of course, there were no guarantees that either path would work.

". . . right, Dr. Cross?" Maddox was saying. The links were up. Conference tables in various rooms had people surrounding them, just like this one, and half the faces were turned toward him. Or so it seemed.

"I'm sorry," he said.

She grinned. "I said, we're ready to start, right, Dr. Cross?"

"Whatever you say, General," he said, wondering why she was tormenting him this morning. Or maybe it was evidence of a good mood. Was there a reason the general was in a good mood? A reason he should know about?

He frowned, and decided to watch her more closely.

"The last few meetings have run over time," Maddox was saying. "I'm going to do my best to push this one through. First, an update on the spaceships. What have you found?"

The same man who had been doing all the reports from the South American team stood. His name was João Agripino, and he was renowned in both physics and biology. Cross had read some of Agripino's e-mail updates. It was inaccurate to call the team "the South American team." That was simply where they were operating. The team itself was large—over a hundred of the best engineers and scientists from all over the world. Even a few of the SETI people were down there, and a few science fiction writers with strong science credentials. As Maddox had said, imagination was as important as direct knowledge, at least in this instance.

"The going's slow," Agripino said in heavily accented English. "This technology is quite foreign to us, which makes sense when you consider how different these aliens are from us physically. It took us most of the last week to determine where the command center of the craft is. There are still many sections of the spaceship that seem to be wasted space or have uses that we do not understand."

"I don't care if you can reproduce the entire ship," Maddox said. "What we need, and we need now, is to know how those shields work. We want to know how they stopped our fighters."

"Yes, General. We have received this request not just from you but from several other military leaders. Even from your president. But this is not one of your American stories where the hero figures out how alien technologies work an hour after seeing them. In order to understand a detail of the technology, which this is, we must see the larger picture."

Two spots of color appeared on Maddox's cheek. How many people had told her that this was not a movie or a novel? The comparisons to science fiction thrillers were being made in all corners, probably because of the aliens, and scientists were especially defensive about it. Cross personally had heard half a dozen scientists use this analogy, and he'd used it a time or two himself. He bet Maddox had heard it more because so many scientists saw her as military and therefore assumed she was stupid.

"I do understand your dilemma, Dr. Agripino," Maddox said. "But you need to understand this: you don't have the luxury of time. If you can't gather all the information you need with the team you have, then get more people on this. If we don't understand those shields by the time the tenth planet returns, we may as well hand this planet over to those aliens. It's the same thing."

Agripino's body stiffened. On the small screen, he looked as if he had been jerked into position by an invisible string.

"Now," Maddox said. "What do you know about those shields?"

"We have yet to figure out the controls in the command

153

room, General," Agripino said. "We are a bit leery of randomly touching buttons."

"Defensive," Britt whispered. Cross nodded.

"In other words, you don't have anything beyond discovering where the control room is," Maddox said.

"That is a major breakthrough, General," Agripino said.

"Not major enough," Maddox said. "We need to understand those shields. Conrad, what have you got?"

Stephen Conrad was a Londoner in charge of monitoring the worldwide situation. *The human problem,* as the head of the English team had referred to it.

Cross glanced at Maddox. She wasn't going to let anyone slow down work. She *was* scared, but she wasn't admitting it.

On the screen, Conrad sat up when Maddox said his name. He looked surprised. Agripino sat down in his chair, keeping his face from the camera.

"Um, well, it's not good news on this front either, I'm afraid," Conrad said. "We're discovering growing pockets of discontent worldwide. A rise in hate groups, most of them fortunately concentrated on the aliens, but a disturbing number who do not believe that aliens exist."

"What do they believe?" Britt asked, sounding stunned.

"Well, that's a bit of a hodgepodge, really," Conrad said. "Near as we can tell, they believe that this is a hoax perpetrated by world governments to encourage the rise of dictatorships. But nothing is uniform. We're talking about fringe groups here. They only become a worry if they gain legitimacy."

"Do they have any legitimacy?" Maddox asked.

"More than they had before the aliens arrived," Conrad said. "People are always looking for explanations. You've got to remember one other thing. We're tracking the groups that have gone public in one way or another, whether on the Internet or on the airwaves or written letters to their MPs or some such. But the problem with most of these fringe groups,

154

particularly in Germany and in the United States, is that they operate underground. They're particularly mistrustful of any organization and prefer to create their own. We have no good way of tracking those."

Cross felt cold. He hadn't thought much about this. "Is this going on in every country?"

"So far as we can tell. China has quashed all unusual Internet activity, and many of the African countries still have limited access," Conrad said.

"What does this mean for us?" Cross asked.

"What it means," Conrad said, "is that there is a greater tendency than ever for overreacting. Our governments have to be very careful how they present things. Mass hysteria is just around the corner. Riots, burning in the streets, attempted coups, all are possible and likely at any moment."

"Because we're facing a common enemy?" someone from the European Block asked, as if she were stunned.

"Because we've suffered such a mass defeat," Conrad said. "And because our worlds are changing because of it. We're losing national identities."

Cross frowned. He hadn't had this sense.

But Conrad continued. "For example, we're all in our separate countries here, working on this Tenth Planet Project, and when we do communicate face-to-face, we do it in my native language, which happens to be English. However, we do it in a branch of my native language that many of my own countrymen deem inferior: American English. Multiply that tiny dissatisfaction among all the other countries in the world, and you suddenly have a problem. Add to that problem the fact that everything is changing, from the way we deal with one another to the way that our jobs and resources are being used, and we have the makings of serious social discontent."

"Well," Maddox said as if this didn't concern her. "We'll have to—"

"Pardon me, General, but I would like to finish because

155

this last point is the most important." He looked a bit embarrassed, but that didn't stop him.

Maddox's fingers tapped against the table, just once, a rapid drumbeat. Conrad probably didn't see or hear it. "All right," she said.

"We have lost our sense of ourselves," Conrad said.

Maddox closed her eyes, but Cross had the sense she would have rolled them if she had kept them open.

"I know you Yanks don't think of this as being all that important, but we Brits know the dire consequences of this. We suffered through it all during the last century, when we went from being an empire that ruled most of the world to a commonwealth."

There were mutterings from other groups. Some of them, Cross noted, former members of the British Empire. Apparently Conrad noticed, too.

"I don't mean to say that the Empire was well and good for all those involved. We don't need that sort of political discussion here. But we do need to acknowledge that, until a few short months ago, we thought ourselves alone in the universe. And not just alone, but the most superior race in this universe."

"You'd better have a point," Maddox said tightly.

"I do, General, and I do want you all to hear me. What I'm saying may not be politically popular, but it does factor quite strongly into much of what is happening worldwide." Conrad leaned against the table. His colleagues had moved away from him slightly.

Cross found that fascinating. Were they afraid of being associated with the superior race theory?

"If we look at human history, one perspective is that it's a continual struggle for world domination. But we have always assumed that the world domination we've been speaking of is human domination. None of us ever thought that apes would

156

rise up and take over the world, or that we'd suddenly be attacked by squadrons of killer dolphins."

Surprisingly, no one laughed. Cross almost did: the mental image was one he appreciated. Killer dolphins on scooters, coming to take over the world.

"I believe," Conrad was saying, "that this assumption is behind much of the denial that's going on in the fringe groups. Aliens can't be out there because they might take over our world. And we all know that no alien will take over Earth. We—the Americans, the Japanese, the Germans, whomever—we will take over the Earth, but certainly not some outsider."

"You're calling us xenophobic," Hayes said.

"Yes," Conrad said. "And some of us are ignoring it because we need to defend ourselves. Some of us are expecting humans to triumph because we've always seen ourselves as the superior species. And some of us are so xenophobic we can't imagine any other species—from anywhere, Earth, Mars, or the tenth planet—being greater than we are. So we deny that the aliens exist."

"Clearly their technology is superior to ours," Cross said.

"Clearly," Conrad said. "And it always has been. One of the most bitter pills about this entire affair, Dr. Cross, are the discoveries that you made, the discoveries that led us all to look toward the skies before the tenth planet even arrived."

Someone whistled—it looked like someone in the Australian feed—and Cross felt his stomach turn.

"The fact that they've been here before," he said.

"Countless times," Conrad said. "Defeating humanity each and every time. What this means, my friends, is that we are not the superior species. They are, and have been, for millennia. It requires an entirely new way of thinking, about humanity, about Earth, about ourselves. England went through this on a very small scale when it lost its empire. So, I would assume, did Rome, centuries ago. But never have humans, on

157

this scale, been forced to examine themselves. And never before have we come out looking quite this bad."

Across the table, Robert Shane sighed and looked down. Britt put her hand on Cross's. Yolanda Hayes pursed her lips and looked toward the ceiling.

Maddox had threaded her fingers together. "Let me see if I get this, then," she said. "You believe this reassessment, this new way of looking at things, is causing more nutballs?"

"Absolutely," Conrad said. "I keep going to the British model because it's the one I'm familiar with, but the discontent in England during the 1920s is related to an economic crisis, yes, but also to the fact that our national psyche was injured. People were quite angry, and they took to the streets over the smallest thing."

He paused. No one was fidgeting any longer.

"Right now, people are very angry. We've been attacked from above, from the heavens, something we have never expected. We've had significant loss of life and property. We've been destroyed by weapons we don't understand, by a species we've never heard of, and for no apparent reason. The average citizen in almost every country feels quite powerless. There is no rising against the oppressor because the oppressor is invisible. So the uprising could occur against the people who are visible."

"The governments." Maddox didn't look bored any longer.

"Not just one," Conrad said, "but all of them, and for different reasons."

"This is a political problem," one of the Japanese scientists said.

"No," Conrad said. "This is a problem we must all be aware of. Fringe groups often tie with terrorist organizations, and if they direct their wrath against a major government, we might be fighting on two fronts: against the aliens, and against ourselves."

"What do you expect us to do?" one of the African representatives said. "Most of us are scientists."

"Or advisers," the South Korean representative said.

"We need to warn our governments to pay attention to these threats, and to neutralize them where possible. I will send you all e-mail with some of this material in it." Conrad threaded his fingers together. "We also need to make certain that the people know we're doing something."

"The massive deployment of troops should tell them that," Maddox said.

"The massive deployment of troops figures into the conspiracy theories," Conrad said. "I've read some of the paranoia on this. We need to let people know, as time goes on, that we have successful plans for fighting the aliens."

"Most of the world doesn't even know the aliens are coming back yet, even with some of the tabloid coverage," Cross said.

"That status is not going to last much longer," Conrad said. "There's too much coming out from too many sources. And anyone with a slight knowledge of orbits will figure out that the tenth planet will be close to Earth a second time in a few months."

"We can't divulge what we're going to do," Maddox said. "We're at war."

"No, we can't," Conrad said. "But we can make reassurances. And we should from time to time."

"I'll speak to the president," Yolanda Hayes said.

Others echoed her sentiments.

Maddox's mouth was a thin line. "Well," she said. "That was cheerful. Let's talk about something we do have control over. General Obote, what's happening with those fighter planes?"

A heavyset man wearing a uniform that Cross didn't recognize stood. He was in the African group. He nodded, as if

159

he felt there needed to be a bit more formality in these proceedings.

"Thank you, General Maddox," Obote said. "I have been placed in charge of coordinating the joint military effort to build more fighter planes. Several governments are involved in this project, and we have made contact with several more. We have also spoken to international conglomerates, like your Boeing, and they have, as you say, stepped up production. Things are proceeding rapidly. We should have many more planes by the time the tenth planet returns. More planes than I would have been able to predict a week ago."

"Excellent," Maddox said, and Cross knew she wasn't surprised by this. She had been saving it for just this sort of moment in the meeting. "Anything else?"

"All of the countries we have spoken to have taken old fighters out of retirement and are fixing them, putting them in working order. We shall have, by our target date, more fighter planes than the world has ever seen."

"What about pilots?" Shane asked.

"Many are returning from retirement, and many are on an accelerated training program. Many of the smaller countries are sending their most promising candidates to flight schools in the larger, more developed countries. We shall have pilots to fly our fighters, sir. We shall have a fighting force that the aliens will not expect."

"Thank God," someone said.

Cross only thought about how worthless that would be without the ability to get through those alien ships' screens.

"Good news at last," Maddox said. "Thank you, General."

Obote nodded again, then sat back down.

"Dr. Archer, what do we have on the planet itself?" Maddox asked.

"Not much, General," Britt said. She slowly stood up as the others had been doing. Cross got the sense she was still unnerved by Conrad's argument. It had been as if he had

160

spoken about a taboo subject. No one wanted to think about the changes the arrival of the tenth planet brought, especially the less visible, psychological changes.

"We're attempting to get as much information as we can," Britt was saying. "All of the telescopes are focused on it, but right now it's too close to the sun. We can only get minimal information, most of which I've already reported. Soon the tenth planet will go behind the sun, and then we'll have three months to sift through the information we have before the planet reappears."

"I expect that sifting to take less than three months," Maddox said.

Britt smiled as if she had expected that slight rebuke. "You've already gotten the important information, General. It's the subtler stuff we'll be working on while the planet is out of our range. We're going to be double-checking facts and figures to see if we've missed anything. We're going to go over our previous work to make certain we're on the right track, and we're going to see if we can clean up these last images we get in the hopes that we gain more information from them than we initially thought possible."

"Excellent," Maddox said. "Is there anything else?"

As usual, there were small items, things that had more to do with coordination than information. Finally Maddox insisted that the specific groups work the details out among themselves. Cross noted, as things wound down, that Maddox had said nothing about what the military was doing. She had, in fact, steered the meeting away from all but the good news about the fighter planes.

When the international contingent signed off, Cross reached for one more donut hole to tide him to lunch.

"I didn't adjourn us, Dr. Cross," Maddox said, and he felt like a high school student who got caught cutting class.

He took his donut hole and leaned back. "Just getting more

161

food," he said, holding it up to her as evidence. He would have done the same thing in high school.

"Well, when you're done, you can tell us what NanTech has discovered on those harvesters," she said.

Britt gasped.

Thank you, Dr. Archer, Cross thought, but didn't say. If Maddox hadn't known before, she definitely did now.

A small smile played at Maddox's lips. "Don't be coy, Dr. Cross. I happen to know that you took some of those alien nanomachines to NanTech. If I had been thinking, I might have instructed you to do that. So, what has the team found?"

"Not much," Cross said. "Just the fact that the harvesters don't move on their own, that they do seem to shut off when they're full, and they can be programmed to eat anything."

"Anything?"

"Right now they're designed to eat organic material. The NanTech team believes they can absorb minerals as well, or saline from the ocean. Anything the tenth planet needs, in other words."

Maddox didn't look surprised. Apparently her spies had told her that as well. But the others did.

"My God," Yolanda Hayes said. "You mean they could destroy the very Earth itself?"

"If they wanted to," Cross said. "It would take a lot of nanoharvesters."

He turned to Maddox. He wasn't military and he wasn't her underling. He didn't appreciate being ambushed like that, and he was going to make it as plain as he could without direct confrontation.

"What about your people? I've heard nothing since I brought the harvesters back from California. What have your researchers found?"

"About the same thing yours have," Maddox said. Then she slapped her hands on the table. "I suspect we all have better

162

things to do than finish the last of the donut holes. *Now* the meeting is dismissed. Oh, and Dr. Cross?"

Why did he have the feeling he wasn't going to like this request either?

"Make certain you have a report on NanTech's work next time we meet."

"It would be easier if they had access to the military's work," Cross said.

"I doubt that," Maddox said.

Cross let out an exasperated breath. It was Shane who came to his rescue.

"General Maddox," Shane said. "Remember the discussion we had about sharing information? It's critical in the sciences."

She nodded curtly. "I'll take that under advisement." And then she stood. "Thank you all for coming," she said, and left.

"Dammit," Britt said. "Just when I was starting to like her."

"That wasn't so bad," Hayes said. "If you'd been military, Dr. Cross, you'd have received a strict dressing-down for taking those harvesters to private industry."

"It feels like I did get a dressing-down," Cross said.

"I suspect that General Maddox wasn't even trying to upset you, Leo," Shane said. "She's got bigger balls than most of the guys on the Joint Chiefs. She could have humiliated you with a single sentence. Trust me, I've seen it."

Cross shook his head. "It's not something I want to see."

"Well, your dressing-down is good news actually," Killius said.

"Why's that?" Britt asked.

Killius sipped the last of her coffee and tossed the paper cup into the wastebasket near the door. "I'd been getting the sense from the general that she wasn't sure we could win this battle against the aliens."

"Yeah," Britt said. "Ever since that dinner."

"Dinner?" Shane asked.

163

Cross shook his head. "It doesn't really matter," he said softly.

"Exactly," Killius said. "That dinner creeped me out, too. It kinda felt like the opening round of the party at the end of the world."

"Oh," Shane said.

"But if the military doesn't want private industry to get its filthy paws on those nanoharvesters, then that's a good sign," Killius said.

The logic was too circuitous for Cross. "How's that?"

Killius looked at Cross as if he were dense. "It means they think we're going to survive this, and after it's all over, the private industry will exploit things that the government feels are dangerous in the wrong hands. The government wants to control this technology. And I'm convinced, after that little performance, that the only people working on those nano-harvesters are Americans."

"Je-zus," Hayes said.

"That's just plain wrong," Cross said. "If we fail in the air, we have to be able to defeat those aliens on the ground. And the nanoharvesters are the key to that. We should be making it a top priority in all this research. I'm half tempted to ship information off to labs all over the world."

"Do that," Shane said, "and you will get a real dressing-down. Don't worry about it for now."

"It seems you were hiding information as well," Hayes said.

"No, I was just pissed that we were going to be out of the loop." Then he paused, a bit confused. "You know, it was Maddox who told me we were going to be. Why would she do this now?"

"Maybe because the orders didn't originate with her," Killius said. "And maybe she doesn't agree with them."

Shane made a dismissing sound. "She's too by the book for that."

"No," Britt said. "Jesse's right. Maddox is by the book, but

164

she's a human being, too. And she's scared. That's what we got from that dinner, just how scared she is. Maybe she was hedging her bet without the government's approval."

"Then your sign isn't as good," Shane said to Killius. "Maybe we've come up against good old-fashioned stupidity."

Killius shook her head. "Nope. I hold to my opinion. The fact that they're hiding information like this means someone thinks we can win this thing. And if that's the case, that means someone above us is optimistic. I see that as good news."

"If that's what you need," Shane said. "But I've been in this too long. I have the hunch it's just a case of business as usual."

"We haven't been doing business as usual on anything else," Cross said, "even to the extent of sharing information about military equipment. I can't believe we'd do it here. I vote with Jesse. I see something good in all of this."

Shane's eyes twinkled. "Well, if far-seeing Dr. Cross believes that we'll survive, that's good enough for me."

Cross grinned. "Sometimes, Shane, I wonder how you made it this far in this business."

"Usually," Shane said, "I keep my mouth shut and my head low. I have no idea what was wrong with me today."

"Too many donut holes," Britt said, grabbing the last one. "And me, I've got to get to work."

The others agreed, and followed Britt out of the room. Cross lingered for a moment and stared at the now-blank screen. Optimism. Hope. No one was using those words. Maybe Conrad was right. Maybe the fear came from the sudden, new knowledge that not only were humans not alone in the universe, but that the new race was so superior it'd been kicking our ass for generations.

When you got down to the survival level, people became completely unpredictable.

Even he had. He hadn't said a word about Portia's idea to create new nanomachines, machines that would attack the nanoharvesters. Because he didn't believe in the plan? Or

165

because he was protecting Portia? Or because he wanted to hide information from Maddox?

He liked to think it was none of the above. If he were rationalizing, he would say it was because he hadn't decided it was worth pursuing.

But somewhere, in that long and tense meeting, he had decided. He was going to tell Portia to go ahead with the new plan. If he could trust Maddox—and he wasn't sure he could—then the military was working on the same path as NanTech. If that was the case, then Portia was free to work on the new nanomachines.

He wished he could find out for certain, but he would lose too much time trying to crack the military's secrecy policies.

Survival took risks. Calculated risks, but risks to be sure. Portia wanted to deal with human technology. She felt more comfortable with it. And he knew that a scientist working in a realm she felt comfortable in made more progress than a scientist who worked in an unfamiliar place.

"You coming, Leo?" Britt asked from the door.

"Yeah," he said. He had a lot to do. And the first thing on his list was contacting Portia Groopman.

May 25, 2018
5:47 A.M. Central Daylight Time

142 Days Until Second Harvest

Vivian Hartlein leaned against a tree three blocks off Union Street in Memphis, watching. The morning air still had a damp chill, but she knew the summer heat would fall, thick and heavy, by noon. She hoped to be on her way north in that little truck she'd had Jake buy her. Forty-year-old Ford—rebuilt, of course—but not with none of them electronic

166

parts. No tracers, no nothing. Simple, old-fashioned combustion engine, just like God intended.

But she couldn't leave yet, not without knowing that her plan was started right.

From this morning on there'd be no turning back.

This morning the government would start paying for the deaths of her family. And for all the other millions of people it had killed. And this time they wouldn't be able to blame it on no aliens.

The street in front of her was tree lined and landscaped. A full two blocks away stood the Internal Revenue Service. It was in a four-story older building, made of granite, looking gray and solid and mean.

She studied the building one last time, taking in all the pictures of what it looked like. She wanted to remember every detail. The tall windows, the columns, the stairs leading in, the stone foyer beyond.

She'd never been in the building. She never paid no taxes, and Dale didn't neither. They got by. Government didn't even seem to notice they wasn't in the system. That was because they made sure they was as outside it as possible: no ID, no bank accounts, no active social security number. No way she'd give money to a corrupt and evil government. Especially now, now that they done killed her family.

Even as she was planning this, she never went inside. Two blocks away was as close as she had ever gotten. But she'd seen the plans, helped in guiding those who was going to help her do right. She had convinced them all.

Now she wanted to remember.

This morning was only the beginning.

She glanced at her watch as two cars, both sedans, moved down the street toward her. She pretended to be looking the other way as they passed.

There was less than two minutes left.

Another car pulled up in front of the IRS building and stopped. Even from two blocks away she could see a man in the passenger seat and a woman driving. Two kids was strapped in safety seats in the back. Vivian remembered when she'd driven her daughter around like that. And how she'd never gotten the chance to drive her grandbabies anywhere.

And she never would now. Thanks to the government and all their lies.

The man kissed the woman in the car lightly, said something to the children, then opened the door. That was as far as he got, half in, half out of the car, his head turned to look at his children.

The front of the IRS building blew outward directly at the car.

Every window in the building exploded as a massive black cloud covered everything.

Vivian stared, making sure she would remember.

Even two blocks away the concussion of the blast knocked Vivian to one knee.

The ground shook under her.

Windows smashed in the buildings near her, raining glass on the streets and sidewalks.

The rumbling, roaring sound smothered everything.

She never took her gaze off where the government building had been.

Slowly, she climbed to her feet. She'd expected a feeling of joy. Or maybe excitement.

But she felt nothing.

She stared down the street of destruction in front of her.

The IRS building was gone, covered in a cloud of rolling smoke. Car and building sirens was screaming from all directions.

The IRS employee's car had been smashed into the wall of the building across the street and was burning. She couldn't see the little family at all.

168

She thought about the children and felt nothing. She had cried all her tears for her babies. Now, everyone else would know what she'd been through.

War meant sacrifice. The Bible said an eye for an eye. A child for a child. Two grandchildren for her grandchildren. A daughter for her daughter. A father for Jake's father.

With one more look at the building, she turned away. Around her, people were running toward the destruction. But she walked quickly in the other direction.

She'd planned other shots in this war, and she was going to make sure they were done right.

7

June 5, 2018
10:22 Universal Time

131 Days Until Second Harvest

The command chamber inside the warship was large and round, a perfect circle. Cicoi stood at the entrance, his upper tentacles rising in astonishment as they had every time he had entered this chamber.

The command positions, circles built onto the walls and extended so that the officers seem to float by ranks, had all been repaired. The Commander's circle was in the middle on the only real floor. Before it were half a dozen round balls, all of which represented a different information feed about the third planet.

A cone-shaped command center encircled the Commander's position, with ten spots built into the board to rest upper tentacles during long battles. The entire design, using perfect shapes throughout, would relax a crew that had had a long space voyage or suffered a long tense battle.

Cicoi didn't want to think about the battles that had been waged from here. He knew enough of his people's history to know that those battles had been waged against either the North or the Center. Once upon a time, his people battled themselves.

Now they had a truce, built by circumstance and need. It was no longer as fragile as it had been when the Elders decided to save the planet, but there was still talk that if the survival situation ever eased, Malmur would separate itself into three distinct sections once more.

Cicoi wasn't here as Commander of the South. He was here as leader of the fleet. He had come to customize the command center for himself. This ship, the first warship to be fully repaired, would be the flagship for the new battle. His experience gained him the position of leader of the fleet. His youth had raised him above the other two contenders: the Commanders of the North and Center. The Elders believed that Cicoi had the reflexes, both mental and physical, to withstand a long battle. Since no one except the Elders had ever used this warship, true battle experience did not exist, and Cicoi had a hunch that the Elders were lying about the real reason they wanted him to lead.

They did think him more physically able: that was true. But they also thought him more malleable than the others, more willing to do their bidding.

And he was. Cicoi had always bowed to experience. He did not know the history of these ships well enough to know when the Elders had used them, but he knew from his Elder's sharp commands, barked to Cicoi from inside his own brain, that the Elder had once commanded the flagship himself.

Against whom or what Cicoi could not imagine—and was not even sure he wanted to.

The rungs leading to the command circle were built into the wall, and Cicoi had fallen in love with them immediately. He could wrap a tentacle around one and hold himself in place, while placing another tentacle above to pull himself up, or another tentacle below to ease himself down. After only a few weeks, he had already become so accustomed to this design that he moved along it rapidly, sometimes choosing to hang from the rungs while he gave orders to his repair crews.

They had looked at him with a mixture of fright and awe. The Elder had told him that the rungs had once been the latest design, the newest technology—the last new technology invented before the great move through the darkness of space—and there had been no time to implement it planetwide.

Cicoi wished their sun still existed. He wished he had seen the light and the plant life, and the waters Malmur once had. He wished all the buildings he frequented had had rungs instead of glide paths that broke down, or ramps that strained the tentacles, or even the awkward steps that had been cut into rock and tangled tentacles into awful messes.

The Elders had the wisdom of technology. Cicoi wished he had seen what other things their fertile brains could have created.

Even though the Elders had saved all of their lives—indeed, made it possible for Cicoi to be hatched.

And now, they made it possible for Cicoi to lead a fleet that would rescue his planet once again.

Cicoi grabbed a rung with his tenth upper tentacle and pulled himself upward, working his tentacles as the Elder had taught him: tenth, ninth, eighth, and so on, until it became time to repeat. His lower tentacles did not mirror, but floated free.

In space, the Elder warned him, gravity was sometimes lost on the warships—destroyed—or the energy from the gravity controls was moved to weapons or propulsion. The rungs made it possible for any command staff who were knocked loose or in the wrong place to return to their stations.

The stations were also models of innovation. In the harvester vessels, the circles were marks on the floors, as they were in the buildings planetwide. In the warship, there were tentacle hooks in the circles as well, so no matter what happened to the ship, the staff could remain in place.

Cicoi's upper tentacles twitched with anticipation. He longed to get this vessel spaceward. He longed already for the fight.

He glided across the floor and stood in the command circle. From this place, he could see all the other stations, above and below. Around him, if he needed it, the entire inside of the command chamber would become a viewer that would show him the vastness of space. He would see in three dimensions, pointing his eyestalks in all ten directions, including the lesser directions of above and below.

The Elder had told Cicoi to practice this maneuver so that he would not become dizzy at crucial parts in the battle. Cicoi had promised he would, and he had also ordered his team to do the same.

They would be ready. He would not underestimate the creatures of the third planet again.

Cicoi straightened all his tentacles and streamlined his body. He slowly raised his eyestalks, as he would before the formal order to launch the ship, and he turned them in the proper ten directions, feeling that half moment of dizziness as stalks two and seven went above and below simultaneously. Then he extended his upper tentacles, resting them on the console in the designated areas. His lower tentacles wrapped the rungs inside his command circle.

Never before had his body been fully utilized like this. He understood now why the Elder wanted him to practice.

Cicoi examined, from his post, all areas of his command chamber. This was the first time he had ever been inside it alone. First he had come with his Elder, and the command chamber had been a mess of collapsed circles, shattered rungs, and dust. The Elder had been distressed by this, his tentacles wrapped around his body, all but one of his eyestalks protruding as if he couldn't stand the sight of the destruction time had wrought.

173

All the other visits Cicoi had made had been to check on the progress of his repair team, and to learn how to run this command chamber. As the Elder taught him the tricks of the command circle, repair workers floated around them, tentacles clinging to rungs, or stations, or suspending them above work areas.

It had seemed like a pod-hive to him then, a child's pod-hive, safe and full of countless bodies learning how to move tentacles without tangling them.

Until now Cicoi had no idea this chamber was so vast. Or how much power it seemed to have in its glistening parts. It made him feel as if he could win anything, anything they faced, just by standing in this circle at this time.

And that, of course, was how he was supposed to feel. The comfort of circles, the confidence they gave.

But now the repair crews, trained as the Elder taught them through Cicoi—and in the process giving Cicoi more power than he'd ever had before—had moved on to the other ships. They had to work at full strength. Cicoi spared all the workers he could for this, but even that fell short.

The warships were so badly neglected, the damage time had caused so terrible, that the amount of work to fix them was tremendous. Even with this repair crew working at full ability, no more than ten warships would be ready by the time Malmur was in position to launch them.

Cicoi was taking a large risk moving this many workers to warship repair. Malmur needed a new harvester ship. It needed to absorb all the energy it could from this Pass around the sun. It needed to make provisions for the problems that had occurred last Pass.

And now the Elders were siphoning off more of the workers, making them work on the Sulas. The Elders wanted as many Sulas as possible. Instead of two harvests, the Elders wanted to do three, and that would take millions and millions of addi-

174

tional Sulas to replace the ones lost each harvest. The Elders had programmed the Sulas so that they would eat quicker, which would enable the extra harvest, but it also meant that they would use additional energy.

Cicoi's people were working all the time, with very short rest breaks. As the Elder said, sleep was something that happened in darkness, not light. Still Cicoi knew most of his people would rather have their stalks in their pockets once per decaunit. It kept them fresh. He worried about errors.

He worried about a thousand things.

He even considered asking the nonfertile females to leave the pods and come to work, but the training would be terrible. Still, there were easy jobs that even an untrained worker could do. Suggesting such a thing, though, was close to heresy, and he feared doing it.

If things got much worse, however, he would ask that the females become involved.

His tentacles were growing tired. His eyestalks were quivering slightly. Holding this position was much more difficult than he had thought.

He snapped his eyestalks into their pockets and relaxed his lower tentacles. Then he let his upper tentacles rest against his sides.

He had much to do before he met with the Elder again. Cicoi needed to check the newest batch of Sulas, the ones designed not for the third planet, but for the dead fourth planet. In this last Pass through this particular solar system, the harvester ships would make a stop at the fourth planet as well, and strip it of raw materials.

Cicoi hoped the materials on the fourth planet would be worth the effort. The loss of energy in this last effort had been tremendous. Workers reassigned. New parts for these warships. New Sulas.

Cicoi did not know what the plan was. He had tried to ask

175

several times. But the Elder had told him he would learn what he needed to when he needed to.

Only, Cicoi was beginning to believe he would never learn of the plan. And he feared he was trusting in the wrong place. The Elders had lived in a time of unlimited energy. They hadn't experienced an entire lifetime of deprivation.

Cicoi had. And he knew the cost of each bit of energy used. If it wasn't replaced, then the Malmuria would die off slowly, unable to support new pods, new life, new anything.

Malmur would be dead.

And it would be his fault.

June 5, 2018
3:10 P.M. Eastern Daylight Time

131 Days Until Second Harvest

"Lunch," Bradshaw said as he backed through the door of Portia's lab at NanTech. He held one large greasy white bag, and balanced a drink holder in his left hand. Portia's giant cup of Surge had spilled twice, and his fingers were sticky. He'd have to wash them before he got any work done at all.

Not that he was really working. Sometime in the last month, he had gone from being the adviser on fossils to the fetch-and-carry man for Portia Groopman. She didn't seem to notice and he really didn't mind. There wasn't much for a nearly retired professor of archaeology to do anymore, anyway.

After Leo Cross first got in touch with Bradshaw, a year earlier, the first six months had been heady. Suddenly archaeology had a relevance to modern society—more of a relevance than it usually did. So many archaeologists mouthed the old trope: You won't understand your present if you don't understand your past. But few believed it. Bradshaw found it ironic that the thing that discredited him—the alien nanomachines

176

he found fossilized decades ago—were the things on which all of society depended today.

Now, since his training had again become moot for the moment, he stuck close to Portia, helping in every fashion that he could. He had begun to feel responsible for her. Portia's parents were mostly absent. They felt that since Portia had found a profession she loved, and was making more than enough money, she could take care of herself. And she could. She had always done so, even when her parents' medical expenses had far surpassed their teachers' salaries, and caused them to get thrown onto the street. Portia had always found ways to survive.

But Bradshaw believed people needed to do more than survive. He believed they needed affection and caring and a useful purpose. Portia had affection from her coworkers and a useful purpose. But she didn't really have anyone to care for her.

Until him. He saw himself as the grandfather she had never known. Although if he really and truly were her grandfather, he would buy her a house, with a soft comfortable bed, and make her sleep in it once in a while. He was probably the only person who knew that Portia had lied about having an apartment. She slept at NanTech, showered at the health club across the street, and often bought her food from vending machines.

The least he could do was make certain that she was well fed. He'd actually set the chime on his watch to go off every three hours, and he supplied either a snack or a meal, whichever was necessary.

This time, he was bringing lunch. He'd found a superb deli two blocks away that made sandwiches of a kind he'd never seen. Stacked with meat, lettuce, tomatoes and whatever other vegetables he wanted, cheeses, and some kind of sauce that was to die for, all on a caraway rye that caught in the teeth and

177

lingered on the tongue. The smell of these sandwiches alone could pull Portia away from her research long enough to eat, and today, he was counting on that.

She'd been working nonstop all night long. He couldn't get her to quit and sleep. He'd finally gone home around eleven— he was of no use to anyone if he didn't sleep—and when he woke up, feeling guilty, at 4 A.M., he called. Portia answered, wide awake. No, she hadn't slept. No, she didn't know what time it was. And no, she didn't care.

She kept the shades in the lab drawn so that it was perpetual night. The lights made everything look washed out. Portia had her own lab at NanTech—she was that valuable to the company—and it had her usual collection of stuffed animals lining the walls. The computer systems were elaborate and the screens were huge. Much of the actual work was done by computers, with robotic arms that had different tools for the smallest bits of work.

She was sitting at the main desk, two large computer screens turned toward her. Her hair was mussed, its stylish do so long overgrown that it was ragged. She wasn't the composed girl he had met half a year before.

"I got roast beef for you," he said, coming around the table. "Lots of spicy mustard as usual. Extra cheddar, like usual, and they were saving a beefsteak tomato for you so that you'd get a really thick slice."

"Mmm," she said, not because the food sounded good, but because she had heard his voice and had to respond.

That response used to fool him, but it didn't any longer.

"Lunch," he said again, coming through the opening between the tables. He was about to set the white bag down on the empty tabletop when she said, "Don't!"

He frowned at her.

"I've got the nanoharvesters out, and I don't want anything near them. Especially anything that smells that good."

178

"The nanoharvesters." He went to the refrigerator and put the sandwiches inside. His stomach was jumping. She had said she wouldn't get the alien machines out until she had a prototype. "You had a workable idea, and you didn't tell me?"

"I made the breakthrough after you crashed," she said. "This morning, over—what the hell were those things?"

He thought of the incredibly gooey donuts they'd had this morning: thick whipped icing, cream in the middle, chocolate underneath. "I don't know what they're called," he said. "A Dunkin' Donuts specialty I've loved since I was in grad school."

"They had Dunkin' Donuts then?" she asked, teasing him about his age as she always did. But he could tell her heart wasn't really into it.

"You were making the excuses as to why you weren't going to tell me about the prototype."

"Oh, yeah," she said. "This morning over the Dunkin' Donuts specialty you love, you wanted to talk about that little incident in Coeur d'Alene, Idaho. So I let you."

His mood slipped a little. After talking to Portia, he'd been able to put his upset in the back of his mind. Now she reminded him of it.

Four bombs had gone off the day before in a home just outside Coeur d'Alene, killing a husband and wife. The neighbors were closed-lipped about what happened, but a few folks from the town said there had been a lot of suspicious activity lately, and a lot of outsiders coming into Northern Idaho. There was talk, the locals said, of an attempt to overthrow the government, and a specific group, which the husband and wife belonged to, was involved.

The bombing of the IRS building in Memphis was just a first step in that plan, many believed.

The antigovernment group's leader, Vivian Hartlein, was a

179

grandmotherly type who had lost her daughter and her grandchildren in the alien attack on California. She'd sounded reasonable enough, and had even laughed at the idea of overthrowing the government. But she had said, in the interview Bradshaw had watched, that she didn't understand why so many people had "swallowed the story of an alien attack."

This was the beginning of something, Bradshaw knew. And he only hoped it would fade away before the aliens returned.

"Earth to Edwin," Portia said.

He looked at her.

"Still thinking about the idiots?"

"I guess," he said. "I've seen too many of them in my lifetime."

"Yeah, well, they never really hurt anyone except themselves."

"Spoken like a true twenty-year-old," he said.

She looked at him, somewhat hurt. She always commented on his age, but he never commented on hers. And never in such a derogatory way.

"I'm sorry," he said. "I was in Oklahoma City on business during the bombing. I saw what idiots like that can do, and I've never forgotten it."

"What bombing?" she asked.

He felt a small stab to the heart. Of course she wouldn't know. She hadn't even been born yet, and her education was anything but formal.

"Never mind," he said. "What do you have?"

"A prototype," she said. "I was about to test it. Want to watch?"

He'd watched two other tests of her prototypes. They had consisted of a small Portia-made nanomachine on one side of the big computer screen—the machine was blown up to a hundred times life-size, of course—and an alien nanoharvester on the other. Theoretically, the Portia-made machine was supposed to demolish the alien machine, but in both cases nothing happened.

And Bradshaw had had to calm Portia down afterward and get her back to work. It wasn't that she was angry so much as extremely frustrated. This was the first time she'd ever had to make more than one attempt at solving a nanotechnology problem that she'd put this much time into.

The troubles of prodigies, he'd thought more than once. They never learned patience.

"All right," he said. "But after the test, you eat."

"Yes, Gramps." She kicked out a chair beside her, and he sat on it.

The alien nanoharvester was already on the screen. Its strange shape and eerie markings looked more alien every time he saw them.

Portia bent over the microscope part of her computer and, using an extremely tiny tool that looked like a miniature tweezers, placed something on the slide.

A round, gray nanomachine appeared on the edge of the computer screen. The Portia-made machine was a lot more aesthetically pleasing, with its precise and sensible design, and Bradshaw was starting to ruminate on the differences between species, when suddenly Portia's nanomachine began to move.

"Oh, shit," she said, but she sounded pleased.

It seemed to slide across the screen like a magnet heading for steel, and attached itself to the alien nanoharvester. Portia's machine quivered and Bradshaw suddenly realized that this looked like sex to him, sex between two incompatible insects—like a ladybug trying to mount an ant.

The thought gave him shudders.

"Oh, God," Portia said.

Finally her nanomachine stopped quivering. She looked at

some numerical specs that had been running on the other screen, and let out a whoop.

The sound made Bradshaw jump.

"Edwin!" she said. "We did it!"

He smiled at the "we." He hadn't had anything to do with it, as evidenced by the fact that he didn't know how she knew she'd succeeded.

"Well," he said a bit cautiously, "I know you got your nano-machine to attack, but how do we know that it killed the alien machine?"

"Edwin," she said, sounding disappointed in him. "I showed you how the power grids worked last time."

She had, too. He had understood the theory. One of the few breakthroughs she had been able to make on the alien nano-harvesters was to read their energy signature. She had shown him how, but he hadn't understood it then. He certainly didn't understand it now.

"My machine drained the energy from theirs. Look!" She pointed to the information running down the other screen. "That's all mine. And see the spike? That's where it absorbed the energy from the alien machine."

She clapped her hands together like a child in front of a surprise birthday cake. Bradshaw grinned.

"This is so wonderful. I conquered the molecular atomic attraction problem last night, but I just guessed on the energy signatures. And bingo, bango, bongo, we've got it!"

"Do we tell Leo?" Bradshaw asked.

"Not until we repeat this experiment half a dozen times," she said, leaning forward.

He put a hand on her shoulder. "You've made a break-through," he said. "You deserve lunch."

She waved a hand at him. "No time."

"No time for passing out from hunger either." He tugged at her arm. She didn't move. "Come with me, or I'll bring the sandwiches over here and contaminate your nanoharvesters."

182

She stood instantly. "You don't play fair, Edwin."

He grinned. "I want our resident girl genius to continue wowing the troops."

"There aren't any troops," she said.

"There's me."

"Do I wow you, Gramps?"

"All the time," he said, clapping her on the shoulder. "All the damn time."

June 5, 2018
8:45 P.M. Eastern Daylight Time

131 Days Until Second Harvest

Leo Cross's security bracelet bumped against his wrist. The plastic itched, and he wasn't used to wearing anything on his right side. His wrist'puter was on his left, and it had taken him years to get used to that. But the bracelet was a small price to pay to be here now.

He was in Britt's main lab, surrounded by nearly twenty scientists. A dozen more sat in a special viewing room, with a few special guests. Britt had used her guest pass to invite Mickelson. She had brought Cross into the main area as an adviser.

Hayes and Shane were on the floor, looking as uncomfortable as Cross was. It was all he could do to keep from standing beside them. He was dodging scurrying people, doing his best to stay out of the way.

This wasn't his kind of science. His kind of science involved digging and thinking and a few computerized tools. But Britt's involved computers everywhere, large screens that relayed information, and smaller equipment for telemetry. Speakers stood on one side of the room, wired into even more computer hardware, to amplify any ambient noise, although no one really expected there to be any.

They were going on-line with a probe, launched five days ago on an intercept course with the tenth planet. The probe was outfitted with equipment that would send all sorts of information back to Earth, from simple things that Cross would have thought of like visual and audio scans, to more complicated things such as devices that measured temperatures and surface composition. There would be infrared scans, and energy scans, and all sorts of other things that no one had bothered to tell him.

What he did know was that this was only the first of five probes. The second probe was launched three days ago, and would come on-line tomorrow. The next one would be launched in two days, with the remaining probes launched in rather quick succession.

The hope was that all of the probes would land on the tenth planet. The predicted best-case scenario was that one of them would get through.

Cross knew that Britt was worried that none of them would get through, that the aliens would have some sort of orbital defense of the planet. Cross doubted it, though. Never before had those creatures been attacked, at least not by humans.

Britt was moving from screen to screen, completely focused on getting everything ready. She lingered near the audio area, leaning toward the mathematical readouts. Cross took a step closer. He had seen the trials on this equipment and knew enough to recognize wave patterns and the Fourier Scale, but some of the other work looked completely unfamiliar to him. The physics of sound never interested him very much, not until now, when it suddenly became important.

Another scientist moved past him. Cross had long ago stopped looking at little name badges attached to the lapels. There were just too many people here he didn't know. Early

184

on, Britt had tried to introduce him, but he must have gotten that blank overloaded look, because she soon stopped.

"Coming on-line now," said the middle-aged redheaded guy up front with a starburst tattoo on his right cheek.

Cross looked at the screen directly before him, just like the others did. Numbers and figures ran across the screens.

"Put the telemetry on One," Britt said. "I want visuals on-screen only."

She had warned Cross she would do that. There were particular scientists trained to read the telemetry. Everyone else found it annoying and distracting.

"No sound except the probe itself," said one of the women.

"Readings near the probe are exactly what we expect in space," said someone else.

"Visuals coming on-line now," said the redhead.

Cross felt the muscles in his back tighten. The screens went blank for a moment, then filled with the blackness of space. Blackness and stars. He wondered how many other aliens were out there, how many other cultures existed on how many distant worlds, worlds he couldn't even see, not with the help of probes or oversized telescopes.

He had never expected, in all his years, to learn that aliens existed. And even if they had, he wouldn't have expected them to be so hostile.

So far the probe showed nothing new. But Cross didn't expect it. It was a miracle to get the information back. Ultimately, though, he wanted images of the tenth planet. He wanted to know what the surface looked like, what else the aliens had built besides spaceships and nanoharvesters. He wanted to know as much about them as he did about the ancient cultures he'd been studying his whole life.

The blackness of space was taunting him.

All over the world, in war rooms just like this, scientists were looking at these images, and wanting more.

Suddenly science had become the key to everything. And

185

humans had to work together to solve scientific puzzles that five years ago they hadn't even known existed.

More scientists were linked now than ever. More information was being shared than ever before. For the first time in its existence, the Earth was united in a common goal.

8

June 15, 2018
6:02 Universal Time

121 Days Until Second Harvest

The command center inside the International Space Station was a pile of ancient computers held together by buckets and bolts. Every time Gail Banks entered it, she half expected to see a pan beneath the so-called ceiling, collecting water drippings, like the house of her childhood. Badly constructed roof, walls that were falling apart, and parts that never should have been glued together. The station was like that, and as more and more modules were built on, no one thought to move the command center. Occasionally one of the countries that worked on the station sent up new computer equipment and it was cobbled onto the rest. The result was a hacker's paradise, which made a by-the-book woman like Banks want to pull her hair out.

Especially at a time like this.

She needed to launch three hundred missiles, and she only had enough equipment in the command center to handle a hundred at a time. She was relying on the shuttles to provide backup. Fortunately, though, her ISS team was a prepared group of hackers, and they had managed to jury-rig something. She wasn't happy with it, but it would do.

Her staff was scattered at the various posts. They were top-notch, well trained and ready. She'd already briefed the backup shuttle pilots and the mission control folks back home.

They were as ready as they were going to be.

She peered at the nearest monitor. The image she had chosen to watch was a real-time image of the missiles hanging in space. She was going to have three staggered launches, one hundred each launch. If she hadn't been so rushed, she would have moved the damn command center to a more sensible part of the ISS, and she would have waited until Earth sent her better equipment.

But she had known when she took this job the need for haste, and she had known she would have to jury-rig things. She did receive permission, when this was all over, to develop a new command center on the ISS, and she did put in requisitions for new equipment. Unfortunately, none of the changes would come when she needed them.

And she prayed that she wouldn't need them later.

This project had to work. She'd given her whole heart and soul to it.

As she watched, the countdown started behind her. How many times had she listened to countdowns like this, getting ready to launch missiles—fire rockets, so that shuttles could go into orbit. Never before had she experienced it while she was in orbit, or while the missiles were in orbit.

She had this horrible fear that some of the missiles wouldn't make it out of Earth's gravitational well. It was a fear she admitted to no one, although she did ground two Ukrainian missiles after examining them herself. They'd clearly been dug out of a silo that was built in the 1950s, and there was no way she would let them contaminate her project.

Her project. She let out a sigh and stood up.

"General?" one of the women said. "Everything all right?"

"I can't watch a launch on a monitor," she said. It always made her feel as if she were out of the loop somehow. Of course she usually felt that way when she wasn't hands-on. Command really wasn't her thing, but she knew how to organize people and she had been promoted to this place. Sometimes she still longed for the days when she was the one with her hand on the joystick, in control of the plane rather than the entire project.

She went to the nearest porthole. In this part of the ISS, the portholes were exactly that, large circles of thick, clear, scratched plastic that offered a distorted view into the blackness of space beyond.

Still, she could see the missiles hanging out there in space, a safe distance away from the station, their cylindrical shapes ghosts against the darkness.

"General, you can't see clearly from there."

"I can look at the replay on the monitors and I'm not going to read the telemetry," she said. "I trust you to let me know if anything is going wrong."

There was too much telemetry for one person to monitor anyway. Her staff had maxed itself out, with as much information as possible on all of the screens.

She clasped her hands behind her back.

The countdown continued.

Flares of light appeared at the base of some of the missiles— the older ones going through several launching stages.

Her breath caught in her throat. Her heart was pounding. They were actually going to do this. Goddammit. She had pulled it off. She had thought the task impossible when they assigned it to her.

"Three," the computerized voice droned behind her.

"Two."

"One."

"Launch!" Banks said in her firmest voice.

189

"Launch commencing," the computer voice responded, and her staff murmured its acknowledgment of that.

The blackness in front of her flared into brightness so blinding she had to resist looking away.

One hundred missiles, launching at the same time.

Fires burned beneath their bases and together they moved slowly, then quickly picked up speed away from the station, heading after a quick orbit around Earth into the vastness of space.

Red and green comm trails danced in front of her eyes, remaining even when she closed them. She felt her heart pounding. She opened her eyes again, and saw bits of color remaining against the backdrop of space, but she wasn't sure if that was another trick of her ocular nerves.

"Report," she said, turning around.

As they had been trained, her assistants called out the information she needed.

"Group One, green."

"Group Two, green."

The countdown continued through all twenty groups. Only four missiles had failed to fire, and she had expected that. They were the oldest missiles in this particular batch. There were more in the next wave of missiles, but she didn't have time to have the oldest ones double- and triple-checked. There was no time at all, actually.

Telemetry covered the screens before her. The warheads were alive, their codes already programmed in. Some of the missiles even carried old-fashioned warheads that detonated on impact, just in case the energy-draining shields of the alien ships affected all of the other missiles.

Warheads.

Nuclear missiles.

She had never in her life thought she would be the one to give the codes to launch them.

But then, she had always expected that, if they were launched, they'd be launched at other humans, at Earth.

She went back to her porthole. The other missiles hung in their orbits, awaiting their launch sequence.

She had two more waves of missiles to launch. Soon every warhead that human beings could get into orbit under short notice, every missile that even had a prayer of working, would be hurtling into space.

She turned to her crew. "Prepare second launch countdown." Then she turned back to stare out at the blackness of space.

Earth's greatest hope rested on her shoulders, and she had done all she could.

She prayed that would be enough.

June 15, 2018
2:31 A.M. Eastern Daylight Time

121 Days Until Second Harvest

Food is sleep, Britt Archer thought to herself as she studied the cold pizzas in their greasy boxes that someone had left in the back of the lab. She had a choice of cold pepperoni, cold sausage and mushroom, cold vegetarian, and cold pineapple with anchovies. Of course, there were only a few pieces of the first three, and almost the entire pineapple and anchovies. Archer grimaced. If there was anything worse than a pineapple and anchovy pizza, it was a cold pineapple and anchovy pizza.

But she had to eat, because she certainly wasn't going to sleep, not in the foreseeable future.

She grabbed the last slice of pepperoni, and then took a slice of vegetarian for good measure. The three pots of coffee

191

she'd made someone get from the nearest Starbucks were already gone. She'd used some French roast, finely ground, to make a pot in the lab's machine, but it wasn't the same. Besides, her nerves were jangled. She must have had enough caffeine to wire the entire Pentagon.

The Pentagon. She snorted slightly. Maddox could have warned her. Archer had thought the two of them had the beginnings of a friendship. To get a phone call this afternoon from Jesse Killius was bad enough. Someone could have told her sooner that her entire staff, plus everyone else she could muster in all the different labs all over the country, would be working well into the night. It was common courtesy.

But Archer was beginning to sense that courtesy and secrecy didn't go well together at all. She hadn't even felt comfortable enough to tell Leo what was going on when she had to cancel their dinner plans. She had to rely on the good all-purpose dodge, telling him that "something" had come up.

Yes, something had come up. Twenty probes that she had known nothing about were suddenly sending back telemetry, and her people had to monitor all of it. Twenty probes, in addition to the other probes her staff was in charge of.

Twenty *secret* probes. Where the hell had they come from? And who launched them?

And from where?

Dammit. She'd thought the entire world was working together. She didn't understand the point of secrecy. Did the government think that the aliens had planted spies among the general populace? And if so, how had they hidden those silly tentacles?

Archer shook her head slightly. She was getting punchy. She took a bite of pizza, thinking the pepperoni was fine cold, if a little greasy. Her stomach rumbled. She had no idea when she had last eaten.

Special probes One through Twenty. She cursed each and

every one of them for robbing her of her semidecent night's sleep. And her dinner with Leo. How come she finally discovered a man who understood her and at that moment the world decided it was on its last legs? Was someone trying to tell her something?

"Dr. Archer," Odette Roosevelt, one of her best researchers, said. "Those special probes are sending us signals."

Archer shoved a bit more pizza into her mouth, set the plate down, grabbed a napkin, and wiped her face and fingers. She crossed to the nearest monitor.

She'd had to give a speech tonight, too, the one she hated. Her staff all had high-level security clearance and it was because of days like this one. Her speech had been the usual song-and-dance about confidentiality, not speaking to the media on pain of death, and oh, yeah, no leaks. Nothing left this room without Archer's say-so. And she received permission for that from above.

Killius, who was the one to tell Archer that she and her staff had to spend the night together, did say that the information would be released to all the war rooms worldwide the following day.

She slipped into the chair in front of the monitor, staring at the images that came from Probe One. With the punch of a button, she could switch to telemetry, but she wasn't ready, not yet. She was frowning at the images, trying to make sense of them.

Some sort of movement, something in space. But what?

"Special Probe Number Two is now on-line," Roosevelt was saying, and the screen before Archer split so that she saw two slightly different views of the same images. Space, yes, but a lot more than that. The shapes were cylindrical, and they were moving.

What the hell was this?

"Probes Three, Four, and Five are coming onboard together," said Tom Cavendish, one of her other assistants.

The new images appeared on Archer's monitor. She gasped, as the picture before her finally made sense. She was staring at rockets heading out of Earth's orbit. Heading into space.

A lot more than twenty of them.

"My God," she whispered.

Then she felt a flare of anger. She had been part of the Tenth Planet Project from the beginning and no one had bothered to tell her of this? No one had bothered to tell Leo? This was what Maddox had been so secretive about. What the hell were they doing with rockets?

"Dr. Archer," Roosevelt said, her voice softer this time. "Do you see this?"

"Yes, I do," she said.

"Probe Six is coming on-line," Roosevelt said, in a more businesslike tone.

Probe Six didn't add much to the picture that Archer already had. She frowned. What was going on? Why launch so many probes and all at the same thing?

"We have Probe Seven," Cavendish said.

Probe Seven's view was of the top of one of the rockets. Archer felt a sudden chill. That couldn't be right. She punched a few keys, magnifying the new image.

"Jesus," Roosevelt said softly. "Is that a warhead?"

"What the hell is going on?" one of Archer's other assistants said.

"I guess we decided to take control of things," Cavendish said.

Archer's mouth was dry. Take control was an understatement. "How many missiles do you think we have here?"

"I'm guessing more than fifty," Cavendish said.

"Probe Eight is on-line," said someone from the far corner of the room. Archer didn't even try to identify the voice. She

194

was still looking at the U.S. Government stamp on the side of that missile.

"Those are nukes, aren't they?" said Melissa Carter, Archer's newest assistant.

"Yeah," Archer said. Nukes. Heading into space.

She raised her head as if she could see through the ceiling, into the sky above. Then she stood, feeling more unsettled than she ever had in her life.

Nukes.

No wonder this had been a secret.

Not from the aliens, but from humans.

She thought about the destruction she and Cross had watched less than a month ago, the black dust, the melting people, the screaming. She'd even dreamed about it—or more accurately, had nightmares about it. She had vowed that she would do everything within her power to prevent that from happening again.

Her power didn't include nukes, but human power did. Humans had the ability to defend themselves, and some of those ways were uncomfortable to say the least.

She was feeling ambivalent about this, and she at least understood it. Imagine if this had been announced. The peaceniks would have been protesting, and those nutcases who had blown up the IRS building in Memphis, along with their friends all over the country, would have been calling this a big government conspiracy and using it as a way of rallying their sick programs.

They were getting enough help as more and more people started figuring out that the tenth planet was going to have to pass Earth again.

No. The secrecy had been right. And it was her job, at least for the time being, to keep that secrecy until someone else told the world.

"Probe Nine on-line," Cavendish said.

"Probe Ten right behind it," Roosevelt said.

195

Archer swung her chair forward, divided her monitor among all the views, and also brought in the telemetry.

It was going to be a very long night.

June 15, 2018
12:00 A.M. Eastern Daylight Time

121 Days Until Second Harvest

The curtains were closed in the Oval Office, the thin sheers not enough to stop the light from the cameras from reflecting in the bay windows. Grace Lopez, the president's chief of staff, was standing behind the antique partner's desk, arguing with the White House correspondent for CNN. He wanted to close the blue curtains, and she wasn't going to allow it.

Grace Lopez was a short, round woman with curly gray hair, and a manner that reminded Mickelson of his second grade teacher—a woman who had terrified him throughout his grade school years. If Grace Lopez wanted something done, then someone had better do it.

But the lights were a problem, and President Franklin had been insistent: he wanted to make his speech from this room. The television reporters were suggesting the Map Room or even the Press Room, but Lopez was having none of it.

She would have to compromise, though. Even Mickelson knew that no vid reporter worth his salt would record in a room with that kind of reflection.

He turned his back on the argument and watched the White House press corps prepare for the big speech. The pundits had been guessing all evening about what the president would talk about. Fortunately Franklin hadn't announced that he was even giving a speech until dinnertime, or the punditry would have gone on for days.

Mickelson's palms were wet. He was wearing what he privately called his duck suit—the next step down from a tuxedo. It was an Armani suit, black, with a stylish long coat, and matching trousers. He wore a round-collar shirt to follow the modern style, and he felt as if he were choking. But at some point in the evening, he would go in front of cameras himself. The president had spent the entire day briefing his Cabinet. He planned to send them out, like troops, to mount a verbal assault defending his chosen plan of action.

General Maddox and the other Joint Chiefs were still in the president's study, going over last minute details with the president and his press secretary. Which was why Lopez was doing battle with CNN.

Other Cabinet members were scattered about the south end of the room. The secretary of agriculture was pretending to be interested in the musty books that lined the bookshelves, while the secretary of defense stood silently, her hands clasped before her as if she were waiting to be graded on her posture. Mickelson wondered if he looked as uncomfortable as she did.

"I don't like this." Tavi Bernstein, director of the FBI, stopped beside Mickelson. She was a slight woman who wore her dark hair in a conservative knot at the back of her neck. She, too, wore a long waistcoat, but instead of pants, she had on a knee-length skirt that showed off surprisingly good legs. Mickelson had once considered dating her, until he listened to her résumé during her confirmation hearings. The woman had been a special agent in undercover work for half of her career, and the other half she had run, with an iron fist, some of the most elite units in the agency. She was smart, and tough, and she intimidated him more than anyone else he had ever met.

"You don't like the speech?" Mickelson asked. They were keeping their voices low, so low that it was almost impossible to hear each other. But with this many members of the press around, it was always better to be cautious. In fact, Mickelson noted, they were both keeping an eye out for the errant boom mike or passing reporter.

"I haven't seen the final draft of the speech," Bernstein said. "But I spent all of yesterday arguing that he shouldn't make it at all."

"People have a right to know—" Mickelson started, but Bernstein waved an impatient jewel-covered hand.

"Spare me the liberal bullshit," she said. "We're at war. And it's time we acknowledge it. This country is a powder-keg, and no one outside my department seems to understand that. Everyone else is looking skyward."

"That's where the danger is coming from," Mickelson said.

"Not for a few more months. Right now, we're running triple the number of hate crimes and conspiracy arrests. We got a tip, fortunately, that led us to a huge supply of anthrax just outside Denver last week. And so far we've managed to stop five more bombings like Memphis."

Mickelson turned his head so that he could see her face. She raised her eyebrows.

"Don't look so serious," she said through her teeth, then smiled, obviously for the benefit of all the reporters in the room. "And don't look so surprised. We're not broadcasting any of this, except to a handful of folks."

"Not even Cabinet members?"

She shrugged. "You have enough on your plate, Doug. The anthrax thing is one of many my office has been dealing with since that damn planet appeared. My people are working harder than they've ever worked, and on more cases, from more areas, than ever before."

"What the hell do you think is going on?" he asked.

She looked at him for a long moment, then turned her gaze pointedly on the reporters. "How long do you think we have?"

He glanced at his watch. "We're only fifteen minutes late at this point. No one's left that office yet. They're fine tuning. I think we've got five minutes at least."

"Yeah, and ball-buster Lopez hasn't acquiesced yet," Bernstein said. "What the hell is she thinking? The drapes have to be closed if they're going to do a press conference in here at night. It doesn't matter if they haven't been closed since the Kennedy Administration."

Mickelson grinned. "I think I saw a photo of LBJ with them closed."

"Yeah, to keep the glare off all his television sets."

They both laughed, and Mickelson thought how rare it was to have someone else who knew the details of modern American history. He would wager they were the only two people in the room who knew that right where half the press corps was standing, President Lyndon Baines Johnson had had a console with three television sets built in, one for what was then every network.

That good ole boy from Texas would certainly be surprised now. Hundreds, maybe thousands of channels, not counting all the video on the Web, and the low-wattage stations. Now there was so much noise, Mickelson was amazed anyone heard anything. He knew that Franklin's press people spent most of the evening making certain that all the networks knew this was the most important speech in Franklin's career— maybe in the world. Even then, Mickelson doubted if more than half would carry it, and those would have pundits dissecting everything instantly afterward.

He was scheduled to appear on NBC and its subnetworks. He had no idea where Bernstein was supposed to lend her two cents.

She led him out the door and into the office of Franklin's private secretary. There was a crowd here, too, but none of them were reporters. More Cabinet members were here, waiting, and some of the deputy officials.

"Okay." Bernstein pulled him into a corner near a Remington statue of a cowboy on a horse, purchased during the Reagan administration. "You wanted to know what's going on? Here's what I think. I think people are terrified, and they don't know how to express it. They're also feeling helpless. We've had a huge rise in voluntary military recruitment. But that's not helping like it usually does in war. This threat is an unknown, it comes from the sky, and it seems all-powerful."

"So the speech should help," Mickelson said.

"Oh, for sensible people, maybe," Bernstein said. "But most people aren't sensible, not in the way we want them to be. And those crazed groups out there are spreading the word that the aliens aren't real. So when Franklin uses the 'n' word—"

Even in this more private room she didn't dare say nukes. Franklin had impressed on all of them the need for secrecy on this point. Mickelson had been avoiding discussing it all day.

"—who are those crazies going to believe is being attacked? If they don't believe aliens exist, there's only one other answer."

"Some international target."

"Fuck, Doug, sometimes your job colors your vision," Bernstein said. "No. We're not talking rational folk here."

"Used to be," he said softly, "the rational people were the ones who *didn't* believe in aliens."

She smiled grimly. "Well, times change. And our crazy friends aren't going to be worrying about an international target. They're going to be worrying about a local one. They know that we've been on their butts and so have the ATF, and the U.S. Marshals. They're going to think this is some kind of code."

Mickelson still didn't get it. "Yes, but you're talking about a fringe element."

Color rose in her cheeks. "That's what Franklin was say-

200

ing. He's so focused on the skies he's forgetting about the homefront. He does this and I guarantee that cities'll be burning in the morning."

Mickelson let out an exasperated sigh. "Why are you telling me this now? Why didn't you bring it up at the Cabinet meeting?"

"Because I've been talking to Franklin about it all week, and he didn't want the dissent at the damn meeting. He says, and I quote, 'What happens here doesn't matter a rat's ass if we don't get rid of those aliens.' "

Mickelson bit his lower lip. In his own way, Franklin was right. What happened in the next few months didn't matter if the aliens returned. A lump formed in Mickelson's stomach. His shoulders were so tight, it felt as if he'd snap every muscle in them simply by moving.

"You agree with him, don't you?" Bernstein said.

Trapped. Mickelson glanced at the door. Some of the reporters were in position, but Lopez was still arguing over the drapes. What a weird stalling tactic that was.

"Don't you?" Bernstein asked.

There was no way she was going to let him off the hook. "Yeah," he said. "I do."

"Damn," Bernstein said. "He listens to you. I was hoping you could get him to call this off at the eleventh hour."

"Sorry, Tavi," Mickelson said. "I think in this case, we're on the right path."

He left her side, feeling more uncomfortable than he had in days. There were no good options anywhere. And now the missiles had been launched.

He stepped back into the Oval Office just as Lopez closed the drapes. The reflection disappeared. She walked across the room, and let herself through one of the many doors. The CNN White House correspondent was shaking his head as if he hadn't seen anything like that for a long time.

Bernstein entered and pointedly went to a different part of the room from Mickelson. What had she expected? Yeah, he and Franklin went way back, almost as far back as he and Cross did. Franklin and Mickelson were both Rhodes scholars, and were in Oxford at the same time. They'd been part of a small enclave of Americans—it wasn't a popular time for Americans abroad—and they had stuck closer together than they would have if they had been going to graduate school in the States.

But Franklin hadn't chosen Mickelson just out of loyalty. He had chosen Mickelson to represent the U.S. abroad because he and Mickelson had similar views. Bernstein had been promoted from within the ranks. When the director's job came open, she had been the natural choice for it. But Mickelson had been chosen from the outside, and he had done his best to serve both his country and his president.

Which he was also doing now. Bernstein had presented her argument. Franklin had rejected it. End of story.

At that thought, the door to the president's study opened, and Franklin walked in, flanked by the members of the Joint Chiefs of Staff, and his press secretary. As Franklin approached the desk, lights went on all around him, illuminating that entire section of the Oval Office. Even the cracks in the ceiling were visible.

Franklin took his chair, and the others joined the throng behind the cameras. If viewed only from the cameras' undiscerning eye, it looked as if Franklin sat alone in front of windows hidden by lush blue drapes, an American flag and some lovely ferns in the background.

"Can we have a camera test, Mr. President?" one of the reporters shouted.

"We already did that," Lopez said. "Let the president start."

The lump in Mickelson's stomach grew heavier. All day, the discussions around the Oval Office had been about the speech. If human beings survived, this would be the signature speech of the Franklin presidency. Every adviser, every member of the president's staff was conscious of the fact that they were making history here.

And they were conscious of the fact that with each decision, they could be writing the end of history as well.

Mickelson made himself take a deep breath.

A TelePrompTer had been set up in front of the camera, a bow to the fact that this version of the speech had been cobbled together at the last minute.

Franklin stiffened his shoulders.

His press secretary was looking at her watch. She would give him the signal to start from off-camera.

Mickelson scanned for General Maddox. She was standing near the door that led into the president's office. She was in full dress uniform and, for the first time since Mickelson had met her, she looked nervous.

The press secretary's finger came down, the red lights on top of all dozen handheld cameras came on, and Franklin was beginning the speech that would define him.

"Good evening, my fellow Americans, and citizens of the world."

Franklin's voice quivered just a little, and his eyes widened just slightly in surprise. He was nervous.

Mickelson couldn't remember the last time he'd seen Franklin well and truly nervous.

"I speak to you today not only as the president of the United States, but as the representative of many of the leaders and governments of this world, with full support from the United Nations."

Good start. Mickelson's back stiffened. Now for the tough part.

Franklin held up a piece of paper. "I hold in my hand a declaration of war against the inhabitants of the tenth planet.

This declaration has been signed by all the major governments of the planet Earth. Last night, in a secret Security Council session at the United Nations, this declaration was presented as a resolution and passed unanimously. Later today, it will be formally approved by the general session."

Mickelson stole a glance at the U.S. ambassador to the United Nations. She had her hands folded in front of her. He'd helped her prep for last night's debate, only to get a call from her later with the report that there had been none.

The nations of the world were united on this. He should have mentioned that to Bernstein.

Although he doubted she would have appreciated it.

"At 6:05 Greenwich Mean Time today," President Franklin was saying, "the combined nations of this planet launched a counterattack against the tenth planet from orbit. Over a period of one hour, three hundred and six nuclear-tipped warheads were launched on an intercept course with the tenth planet. A few more will be launched over the next few weeks, until the launch window closes our opportunity for such action."

Mickelson's throat was dry. He wished he didn't have to be here. He wanted to be in some Georgetown bar, near the university, listening to the seniors react to the speech. He had no idea how this was playing in Peoria, let alone Beijing.

He hoped it was playing well, because there was no way to turn back from this course.

The president paused for a few moments, then went on. "It will take the fastest of this massive first wave of missiles sixty-three days to reach an intercept point with the tenth planet as it comes around the sun and heads back toward our planet."

Franklin was looking pale in the bright light. He was talking about the largest nuclear attack ever made. And, bless him, he looked as disturbed by it as a leader in time of crisis could.

Mickelson dry-swallowed. He resisted the urge to glance at Bernstein. Goddamn her. Why'd she have to come to him at the last minute? She had made him uncertain, and he couldn't be, not with his own television appearances awaiting him after this. He had to sound like a positive member of the team, something he was usually very good at.

Franklin lowered his voice to a confiding tone. "I know all of you watched what the inhabitants of the tenth planet did on their first attack against Earth. Many of you lost loved ones: parents, children, grandchildren. We all saw the damage these hideous weapons did. We were affected unevenly, but we were all affected. Earth is our home and it has been violated. We rise up now in self-defense."

Heartstrings. Mickelson nodded. Someone had had the good sense to use hot-button words like "home" and "violation." Franklin had even skirted around the concept of motherhood. If this had been a strictly American speech, Mickelson wondered, would there have been a mention of apple pie, too?

He shuddered and glanced at Bernstein. That cynical thought was courtesy of her.

Or was it? Maybe it was his own way of distancing himself from the emotional content of Franklin's speech. Mickelson had vacationed on the California coast. He'd been down the Amazon, and he'd even been to the places in Africa that had been destroyed. He hadn't lost friends or family, but he had lost *places* and in some ways that was just as bad. Maybe worse. Because humans believed places outlasted everything. In Europe, cities existed for a thousand years. In Asia and the Middle East, several thousand.

And the aliens had destroyed that feeling of security, the fact that some things lasted through time.

Mickelson took a deep breath. Calm. He had to remain calm.

"We cannot allow a second such attack to occur as the

205

tenth planet comes past us again," Franklin was saying. He had raised his voice again. He was speaking with force, no longer the friend and confidant, but the world leader. "All of the governments of the world have been working together, and will continue to do so, to fight the aliens on all fronts. The strike today was just the first. There will be more."

More. Jesus. A part of Mickelson had hoped that this one attack would be enough.

Franklin was looking directly at the camera. He looked more confident than he had when he began this speech. His tone was firm again.

Or maybe, just maybe, it came from the heart.

Mickelson braced himself.

"This is an historic day," Franklin said. "It is the first time the entire planet has gone to war against a common enemy. I had never imagined such a day, but it has arrived. We did not ask for this war. We do not want it. But be assured, we shall win."

Franklin continued to stare at the cameras. Then the red lights above them went out. Mickelson started with surprise. No traditional ending. No "thank you and good night." Just a declaration of power.

The reporters weren't even shouting questions. They looked stunned. Franklin stood, walked to the study, and closed the door behind him.

The Oval Office was incredibly quiet, considering how many people were in it.

Mickelson gathered himself. He had to go to the press room so that he could be the third wheel on some NBC panel talk show. He had to move.

But he didn't want to. Even though the president was gone, the air was still fraught with import.

We've finally done it, he thought. *We've finally declared war.*

Against an enemy they didn't know. An enemy they didn't understand. An enemy they'd never really seen.

Franklin had spoken with confidence about their chances. Mickelson wasn't sure if that confidence was real or not. But he knew that, for the first time since the tenth planet had started destroying sections of the Earth thousands of years ago, Earth finally had a realistic chance of fighting back.

And maybe, just maybe, they could win this.

Section Three

FINAL COUNTDOWN

9

August 1, 2018
10:01 A.M. Eastern Daylight Time

101 Days Until Second Harvest

As Leo Cross pushed open the double doors leading into Britt's main lab, he felt like an outsider about to enter a closed town. He took a deep breath, trying to overcome the feeling, but he couldn't really shake it.

Even though Britt had gotten him a permanent pass into the building a month ago—the day after the president had given his famous "We Are at War" speech—Cross still didn't know anyone but Britt by name. He wasn't consulted by the other scientists and he was constantly treated as "the boyfriend."

It was a new experience for him. All his life, he had been the center of attention, he had been the one that others had looked to, he had been the one with other people hanging on his arm.

Right now, he wasn't really hanging on Britt's—he was doing work—he just wasn't getting results. He spent a lot of time in his office, and in his workroom at home, studying information from all the different groups working on the various aspects of the Tenth Planet Project.

211

Movement seemed so damn slow. Slowness had never bothered him in the past, but now it did. Everyone was looking at the missiles as the things that would save the Earth, but Cross wasn't by nature an optimist. Nor was he a pessimist. He quantified things, hypothesized from information presented to him, and waited for results.

But with the missiles, he couldn't do that.

He threaded his way through the desks and computers and scientists hunched over them, studying telemetry or turning the streams of raw data into visuals. Britt had placed a large screen in the center of the room—a flat screen that had images on both sides. Right now it was running numbers, and no one was looking at it. At other times he had been in the lab, it had been showing images from various probes, sometimes the best or the prettiest. And a few times, late at night, it showed those images that could, when someone connected the dots with a white line, be made to look like something else—usually something juvenile and extremely funny.

A few of the scientists had looked up as Cross entered, but no one greeted him. Sometimes when he showed up, they looked at him as if he were the enemy. He took Britt away, when the rest of them had to remain, and he had a hunch they saw that as unfair somehow.

Britt was standing between two of her assistants, one hand on each desk, having an earnest conversation. He stayed well back, knowing better than to interrupt her work.

She had gotten thinner in the last few months, and the lack of sleep had hollowed out her face. The prettiness that had so appealed to him when they first met was lost to stress and burnout. She was still attractive, but she wasn't fresh faced, wasn't the energetic woman he had fallen in love with. He was beginning to worry how much more of this she could take, but he didn't know how much of his worry was coming from his love for her and how much of it was actually based on some intangible that he could see but not define.

Everyone who had reached the national—or international—level in science as Britt had done, had gone through weeks and months like this, just in their schooling, not to mention their jobs. But never did something like this happen when so much else was at stake.

He'd seen an article in the *Washington Post* about the extreme rise in stress-related diseases worldwide since the tenth planet unleashed its destruction on the Earth. The conclusion of the people who sent out the data was that everyone was under more stress now than ever before, and that there was little anyone could do about it except accept it, and move on.

Helpful advice for some people, for whom not being able to identify the actual problem made things worse, but rather ridiculous for the rest of the world—people like Cross.

Still, he wasn't really concerned with the rise in stress rates worldwide. Just the way that it manifested in Britt.

She wasn't getting much sleep, sometimes as little as two or three hours a night, and never more than five. She forgot to eat, unless someone ordered into the lab, and she was drinking way too much coffee to keep herself motivated.

"At least," Constance had said to him when he complained one morning over a solitary breakfast, "Dr. Archer gets some protein and calcium and solid calories from those coffee concoctions she drinks. They may not be healthy meals, but they're better than that swill we used to drink before someone invented Starbucks."

Maybe. But Cross didn't like it anymore than Britt had when he had been the one under such pressure.

She had vowed last night that she would get a full eight hours sleep. He had known then that she didn't have to be in the lab that morning, so he had conveniently shut off the alarm. He would let her sleep as long as her body dictated, and then he would feed her a big, healthy meal.

But they hadn't been asleep an hour when the phone call

213

came in. Dr. Archer was needed in the lab. The telemetry from the first probe was coming back.

Cross, who had been only partially awakened by the call, argued that she didn't have to go in, that the probes had been sending telemetry all along. Britt had snapped at him as she got out of bed and stumbled around searching for clothes that this particular probe was sent on a flyby of the tenth planet. She had instructed her staff not to disturb her unless the probe was sending in imagery from the planet itself.

That had gotten Cross out of bed, his head feeling like a melon that had just been split, and he had dressed with her, grabbed them both apples from the kitchen, and driven her to the lab.

Once there, he'd waited an hour before he asked to see the visuals, and he got a cold stare from all the scientists involved. This particular probe was sending the visuals back encoded along with all of the other information, and it would take a while to turn that code into actual pictures.

A while turned out to be hours.

Cross, who hated waiting around anyway, decided he was of no more use at the lab and went back to bed.

Alone.

He still had forgotten to set the alarm, and he had awakened a lot later than he had planned, grumpy, tired and out of sorts. At first he thought it was because of Britt's defection in the middle of the night, and then he wondered if it was because he had so little to do with the important events at the moment.

And then he realized that neither was correct. He was worried about what the probes would find. Sometimes he was afraid they would locate huge cityscapes like the ones he had seen in science fiction films. Sometimes he was afraid they'd find that the creatures in the ships were only the beginning; that there'd be a greater, more diverse race—all of it threatening— on the planet's surface.

214

And sometimes he was afraid they'd find nothing at all.

He wasn't sure which he could deal with, but he knew, the closer the probes got, the closer they all came to gaining more information, the more uncomfortable he got.

The biologists working on the alien corpses hadn't found much that was helpful. They knew so little about this creature that they didn't even know if the specimens before them were young or old, and they were having a hell of a time finding gender characteristics. There didn't seem to be any obvious kind.

The aliens were, at the moment, a dead end.

Britt finally looked up from her conversation, saw Cross, and smiled. He warmed. That smile made all his discomfort float away. Yeah, the others here might see him as an intruder, but they weren't Britt, and it was her lab.

"Leo," she said. "Come with me. I have something to show you."

He hadn't told her about his fears. He hadn't discussed them with anyone. He followed her toward a large console that had multiple monitors. They formed a circle, and she sat in the middle of them, and pulled a chair over for him.

"The planet is still on the far side of the sun, just outside of Venus's orbit," she said, "and it's too far away for our scopes to pick anything up. The information we're getting from the flyby has been relayed to the satellites, before it came here—the distances are amazing!—but we are getting information."

She glanced over her shoulder at him. Her eyes were bright with excitement, but he knew her well enough to know that the data streams were possibly what had excited her. He was past marveling at technology. He wanted to find a way to defeat those aliens, and he wanted a way to do it quickly.

He hoped that the nuclear weapons would do it. There was a chance, a pretty good chance, that they would. Three hundred of them pounding into this planet would end just about everything here with a nuclear winter.

A slight frown creased her forehead apparently at his lack of response.

"The sun," she said as she turned back toward the screen, her tone slightly cooler, "is still creating some interference, so what we're getting here is preliminary. But I thought I'd show you our first up-close-and-personal views of the tenth planet."

She punched a few keys, and an image formed on the monitors. It formed slowly, like images used to in the early days of computers, unfolding as pieces of data were transformed into images.

Cross's breath caught in his throat. This first image was a distant one, and it was familiar. It was a blackness, a round blackness, in space. It almost reminded him of the award-winning photos he saw of eclipses: a black hole in an active sky.

Nothing. His worst fears were coming true. He was going to see nothing.

He leaned over Britt's shoulder, afraid that if he said anything it would reveal his disappointment. So he tried to show interest in other ways, by focusing on the image before him, by moving closer to it.

Britt punched a few more keys, and that image disappeared. Another appeared just as the first one had, scrolling up. This one showed the same blackness, only larger. Then another appeared and another, each as the probe got closer to the planet.

The final image was quite close, and it was just of blackness, with the hint of something glinting against an edge.

"It seems odd to me," Britt said, "that this close to the sun, the planet looks black. It's really there. It's a solid mass. We're getting other readings that show it does have a surface, and

216

that there are some energy readings on the surface, but it's almost as if there's a shield in place that we can't get beyond."

Cross pulled his chair closer to the screen. He was staring at that glint. It looked like an angle, a large angle. He put his finger on it. "Can you blow that up?"

She did. The image was larger, but grainy, and it told him nothing.

"What kind of shield could that be?" he asked.

She shrugged. "I'm not even sure it is one. I have never seen anything like it. The other planets in this solar system don't look like this. Nothing in our databases prepared us for this."

Just like nothing had prepared them for the attack on the Earth, for the spaceships, and for the appearance of the aliens themselves.

Cross leaned back and templed his fingers. "The biologists are saying that these creatures emerged from an ocean, just like we did. Only they kept their tentacles and their eyestalks. They've found evidence that these creatures need water to survive, just like we do. I'm not an astronomer, but shouldn't we see evidence of water on this surface somewhere?"

"If that is the surface," Britt said. "We're not picking up any readings of shielding, but then, their technology is so different from ours."

"What if it's not technology?" Cross asked. "What else could it be?"

"Nothing that would form life as we know it," Britt said. "And these aliens have to be related to life as we know it. They build machines, they congregate in groups, they obviously communicate with one another. Life can't form without water and light, at least not life that we understand."

Cross sighed. He wasn't sure he could deal with the frustration. "Are we going to have another flyby before one of those probes goes down to the planet's surface?"

"One or two," Britt said, "depending on how things work."

"Are any of them going to go closer?"

"Yes," she said.

"Maybe that will give us more information." He looked at her. The excitement in her eyes had dimmed a little. "Unless I'm missing something."

"Just the fact that we're close, Leo." Her voice was low so that the other team members couldn't hear her. "We're actually looking at the planet itself, getting readings from it. That's a good thing."

"Intellectually I know that," he said. "I guess I'm just impatient."

"So am I." She patted his hand. "But the only way we're going to learn anything is to keep studying."

He grinned. "You sound like my old professors. They hated it when I leapt over weeks of experimentation with an accurate hunch. They always made me prove it."

"And that's why you went to archaeology instead of the hard sciences, isn't it?" she asked. "Because hunches are valued there."

His gaze met hers. She knew him too well already. He leaned in, and kissed her, then he rested his forehead against hers.

"Can I buy you lunch?" he asked. "You look like you're wasting away."

And then he caught his breath. He turned toward the screen, but the image on it was the first one.

"What?" Britt asked.

"Let me see that close-up again," he said.

She punched keys, and the final image appeared, its small glint taunting him from the corner.

"Shit," he whispered.

"This planet is on a long elliptical orbit," he said.

"Yeah?"

"And that means, for long periods of time, it's in the cold

darkness of space, no light, no nothing. And the temperatures on the surface would be incredibly cold, right?"

Britt frowned. "Yeah."

"But the biologists are saying that these creatures started out like we did. So their planet should have an ocean at least, and oceans don't happen on incredibly cold planets. They are ice, if they exist at all. Life doesn't emerge from the ice into the primordial goo."

"I guess," Britt said, sounding even more confused.

"Something changed for these creatures," he said. "Something major, and they were technologically advanced enough to deal with it."

"Maybe they have incredibly short life spans," Britt said. "Maybe they only exist during their time around the sun."

Cross shook his head. That didn't feel right. Or did it? Creatures with incredibly short life spans spent those lives gathering food, and reproducing. It wasn't conducive to making tools or industrialization, but he was basing this on an Earth model. What if, for the aliens, time went faster?

There was no way he could know that, no way he could prove it. But a shiver had run down his back.

"You have a hunch," she said.

He nodded. He didn't like it, but it made complete sense, no matter what was going on for those aliens.

"Britt," he said. "We're their food source."

"I know they harvest nutrients, but—"

"No, listen to me," he said. "What if they had some kind of technological disaster that destroyed their planet? What if something they made created that blackness? What if enough of them survived? Why would any creature go to such great lengths to create spaceships and nanoharvesters if this were something they didn't really need?"

"What are you saying?" Britt asked.

219

"I'm saying that I'll wager we are the key to their survival. Not humans. Earth."

She looked at him. There was something sad in her eyes. "I don't want to know that if it's true, Leo."

"Why not?" he asked. "It explains so much."

"Yes," she said. "It does. But it also means that in the end, it's us against them, and whoever wins the conflict is the only one who survives."

Cross nodded. He stood. "Yeah," he said. "It means that. It also means that they're not going to be deterred by half measures. If I'm right, they're going to keep coming until they have nothing left."

"Then I hope you're not right, Leo," Britt said.

But he didn't really pay much attention. He had to tell Maddox his theory, and he had to prepare her. She wouldn't like the lack of evidence, but he'd learned enough about her over the last few months to know that she would hear him on some level. She would continue to prepare for the worst.

Britt was exactly right. The Earth was in a fight to the death. And only the strongest, most creative species would survive.

August 1, 2018
19:31 Universal Time

101 Days Until Second Harvest

Cicoi wrapped his upper tentacles around his workstation inside the Command Building of the South. He hadn't been able to go back to Command Central, not since the Elders had shown themselves. He preferred to work here.

The warships were coming along, but his workers were getting tired. He had them on rapid rotations, with little pod

220

time, but that wouldn't work forever. The strain was beginning to show on his people; the extra work had become a burden. He wished he could awaken more of the sleepers, but he didn't dare. They hadn't gathered enough food on the last Pass to make awakening others possible.

The plans for the next Pass were shaping up well. He and his assistants had been going over the maps of the third planet, looking for the most fertile areas. That was old habit; the Elders wanted him to take as much as possible. But he didn't want to send the harvesters down to an area that was inferior to some other area. Even though the Elders wanted him to pluck the planet bare, he knew—and they knew—that they only had resources enough to harvest a large part, but not all, of the planet.

The Elder had been lurking all day. Something was bothering him, but he was saying nothing. Cicoi was actually grateful for that. He was getting tired of having the Elder constantly in his head.

"Commander." His Second was standing before him, all eyestalks extended, eyes facing forward in a circle, the position of respect.

"What?" Cicoi asked, not pointing a single eyestalk toward his Second. He had specifically asked not to be disturbed. How much time would pass before someone understood that when Cicoi asked not to be disturbed it meant to leave him alone?

"The creatures from the third planet have sent something hurtling our way."

"Another probe?" Cicoi asked, trying to keep the exasperation from his voice. The probes had led to a huge argument with the Elders. Cicoi and the other Commanders had agreed that sending a ship out to gather energy from the probes would waste more energy in fuel than they would receive. The Elders weren't so worried about the probes'

221

energy as they were about the information they would send back to the third planet.

Every time we think them primitive, Cicoi's Elder had thought to him, *we learn they have grown tremendously since the last Pass.*

Grown yes, but probes and information were not a threat. Cicoi didn't want to worry about the creatures until Malmur was much closer.

"No, Commander," the Second said. "This seems much bigger than the last few probes that we have monitored."

That caught his attention. He raised two eyestalks. His Second was also poised on top of his lower tentacles, and not balanced well. He was tottering slightly.

Cicoi waved an upper tentacle, signaling his Second to stand down. His Second did, with obvious relief. His eyestalks remained in a position of respect, however.

"Bigger?"

"Yes, Commander."

With his sixth upper tentacle, Cicoi activated a vision ball. It rose between him and the Second. "Where?" he asked.

"Coming from the third planet."

Cicoi had the ball show him the area of space and saw a shape, cylindrical, and quite large, heading in their general direction. Then he pulled out two other eyestalks and held them close to the vision ball. Not a single cylinder. But several.

They were too far away to count.

"These are too large to be probes," he said.

"Probably not," said his Third, who had come up beside the Second. The Third's eyestalks were also in a position of respect. "Probes can come in all sizes."

"But we have monitored their probes," Cicoi said. "None were this large."

"We cannot assume everything about the third planet is uniform."

Cicoi lifted three eyestalks straight up, eyes pointed at the ceiling. It was a sign of disgust. He had studied the third planet from his podling days. The creatures of the third planet preferred uniformity in function and design. It pleased their aesthetics. Just as it pleased the Malmuria.

Cicoi let his eyestalks drop as the thought dissipated. He had tried not to think of any similarities between the third planet's creatures and Malmuria since he had been accepted into the military.

"We must be suspicious of difference," he said. "Monitor these cylinders. When they get closer—"

We will die.

The Elder had returned. Cicoi withheld a curse, and finished his sentence. "When they get closer, we will see if we must take other action."

His Second and Third both raised their upper tentacles in a gesture of respect, and turned away. Then Cicoi left his workstation and went into the antechamber. He did not like having conversations with the Elder in public. It felt too revealing.

"If you think we will die, then tell me what those things are," he said.

I do not know, the Elder's strange voice was inside his head yet again. Cicoi hated this method of communication. *But we have underestimated these creatures too much. We cannot let the cylinders get close.*

"What do you propose we do?"

Send ships to intercept. Rob them of their energy as you have done with other space debris.

Cicoi remembered the vision ball. He saw the shapes, but the energy readings beneath were small, at least from a distance.

"We have the same problem," he said. "It would use up too many resources. We would not get enough in return."

Knowledge is something, the Elder said. *Without it, too many mistakes are made.*

223

"You mean, I make too many mistakes."

You and all of your young kind, the Elder said. *Somewhere along the way you have become dangerously cautious. If we had been so dangerously cautious, our race would be dead now.*

There was a lot of history in those words, some of which Cicoi understood and some he did not. He did know that it had taken courage for the leaders of the South, Center, and North to band together, to get the Malmuria to work together as a species, despite their differences. It had taken a great risk to throw Malmur out of its orbit as its sun went nova instead of building the ships that some had suggested, ships that would have scattered the people among distant stars.

"What do you think these are?" Cicoi asked.

You have said yourself they are too big for probes, at least of the kind we have seen, the Elder said. *Think strategically. Obviously the creatures of the third planet can. You have sent probes into space to find out all you can of your enemies. If you were to send something else, what would it be?*

"A weapon?" Cicoi felt all of his upper tentacles rise in horror.

We have thought of them as primitives for too long. And they were, when we first began coming to this planet. But they no longer are. They have space travel and cities and societies. They have reason, and they have obviously found a way to codify their history. They have looked at the record, my young friend, or perhaps they have an oral tradition that warned them. They know we never come for just one Harvest. They know we are going to make another. They are going to strike first. It is a way some creatures have of defending themselves.

"You sound like you have sympathy for them," Cicoi said.

The Elder floated before him. Cicoi hadn't seen the Elder until then. Where had he been? Behind Cicoi? Or did Elders have a way of being present without being visible?

I did not have sympathy for them when we first came to the third planet. In those dark days, they were not different from other life-forms on that planet. But they have proven themselves smart and strong, and they have shown that they are worthy opponents. In my day, before we lost our sun, a worthy opponent was all we sought.

"Going into space at this time would waste energy we cannot afford to lose," Cicoi said.

You sound like your compatriots in the North and Center. The Elder's eyestalks were rotating. Cicoi had learned that was the Elders' way of expressing disgust. *Cautious to the end.*

"Caution has its place," Cicoi said.

But not here. Not now. If I am right and you are wrong, we lose more than a bit of energy. We lose lives we cannot afford to give. Perhaps we lose everything.

"Do you believe the creatures of the third planet have that kind of power?"

I would not have believed that they had discovered space travel, the Elder said. *But they have, and now we must contend with that.*

Cicoi felt his upper tentacles droop. "What if I'm wrong? What if these things are probes?"

Then absorb their energy as you have done with so many other things. The trip will be worthwhile, just for that.

The Elder did not understand the kind of waste he was promoting. His time had been so different. He had not been born to limited resources, to long periods of darkness and cold. He did not understand.

"Every time we do something like this," Cicoi said, "we jeopardize lives."

The Elder wrapped his upper tentacles around his torso. *We jeopardize the entire planet whenever we pocket our eyestalks and refuse to see what is around us.*

225

Cicoi flapped four upper tentacles in distress, but the Elder didn't seem to notice.

You will send ships to intercept those cylinders. Warships.

"But we've only gotten a few ready and we need them when we approach the third planet."

You will send warships, the Elder said.

Cicoi pocketed his eyestalks in protest.

No matter how much you deny, you will listen to me. You may have experience with deprivation, but I have experience with war. We are in danger from those creatures. You must acknowledge this and head it off.

"I'm not wasting the energy of the South's warships on this mission," Cicoi said.

The other commanders will send ships. They will do as they are told. So will you, the Elder said.

"This is a mistake," Cicoi said.

Yes, your plan is a mistake, the Elder said. *I am amazed we did not catch these cylinders sooner. We should have destroyed the probes as I wished. Now we will pay the consequences.*

Cicoi kept his eyestalks pocketed for a long moment, but said nothing. There was nothing else to say. He had lost, and he knew it.

Finally, he raised a single stalk. The Elder was gone. Cicoi let his tentacles droop. Lost energy, lost resources, and all for a bit of curiosity. Curiosity that could have been satisfied if they only waited.

But he would do the Elder's bidding. He would take the five functioning warships into space, and he would examine those cylinders.

He only hoped he would get enough energy from them to make up for at least half of the waste.

August 1, 2018
6:45 P.M. Eastern Daylight Time

101 Days Until Second Harvest

Mickelson loosened the tie around his neck. The fifteenth formal dinner he'd had to attend in a row. It was beginning to get tiresome. In a day or so, he would call Cross and see if Constance could whip them up something wonderful and old-fashioned, something impossible to get at the fancy restaurants where he had to take other diplomats.

He longed for this whirlwind to end. But he knew it wouldn't. Not until the missiles hit the tenth planet.

He wished he could take the tie off, but he couldn't. He'd had this meeting scheduled for two days now. The president wanted to touch base with his key advisers, something he'd been doing off and on since the missiles were launched. The first meetings were held in the Oval Office, but Franklin had been inviting more and more of his advisers. So tonight's was being held in the Roosevelt Room.

The Roosevelt Room was across the hall from the Oval Office. Lopez had left the door open, and had placed beverages and snacks on the center of the large table. A few advisers were already inside. Mickelson peered in, wished he hadn't loosened his tie at all, and then crossed the threshold.

He had loved this room early in the Franklin administration. Then Franklin had gotten the bright idea to restore the room's original furnishings. When those couldn't be found, he settled for some mid–twentieth century couches and chairs along the side, a grandfather clock in the back corner, and a plastic-looking conference table that someone said was an antique from the 1960s.

To Mickelson, the table was an affront. It didn't go with the fireplace, which was original to the West Wing, or the lovely

227

arched door. Mickelson had complained loudly about the table and the mixed decor as well as the soft orange color of the wall, and the burnt orange color of the rug. He had complained so loudly and so often that Franklin had finally hauled out a photograph, which dated from the 1970s, of the room, and it looked just like it looked now. Ugly and mismatched and uncomfortable.

It wasn't until someone told Mickelson that Franklin's predecessor had redecorated that Mickelson understood Franklin's decision to make the room his own.

Still, Mickelson wished he would have improved it.

The advisers who were waiting were O'Grady and Bernstein. Lopez was down the hall, but she would join them as well. Mickelson looked at the makeup of the group and already knew tonight's topic: the state of the world since the declaration of war.

He suppressed a sigh. His job had actually gotten easier since war was declared. All the usual hot spots had cooled. No one wanted to be fighting among themselves when the aliens arrived. Issues weren't settled, of course, but that didn't matter. Right now, issues such as historical boundaries and trade agreements had been made moot. No one knew if they would even have a country three months from now, let alone borders to argue about.

Bernstein looked up from her conversation with O'Grady and her gaze met Mickelson's. They hadn't talked much since the night of the president's speech. Mostly Mickelson had avoided her. He didn't really want to talk to her. She intimidated him, attracted him, and made him feel foolish all at the same time.

It didn't help that her prediction of civil unrest had come true.

But not as bad as she had said it was going to be. There had been a march on Washington, peaceniks who didn't believe in the use of force, such a nonevent that no news station carried it. There had been five bombings, one in Denver, one in Chicago, one in New York, and two in Los Angeles, all government buildings. There were two assaults on military installations. And one attempt, in Washington state, to sink a fleet of ships in Puget Sound.

The image from those few days after the declaration of war that stuck with Mickelson was of a woman running from a bombed and burning IRS building in Los Angeles.

He could see it as if he were there. He remembered every detail of it shown on the news.

The woman's clothes were on fire, and she carried a child in her arms. He had heard she'd been there visiting friends she worked with, showing them her new baby.

A news crew was in the street and caught her running from the bombed building.

The faster she ran, the more the flames engulfed her.

The image of pain on her face was something Mickelson would never forget. He had thought of it over and over, trying to understand it.

Pain.

And intense fear as she tried to save her child.

Finally, as the flames engulfed her, she had gone down on her knees in the street. A passerby and the news broadcaster had tried to beat out the flames with coats, and as they had, the woman had offered them her child in a burning blanket.

The newscaster badly burned his hands taking it.

Neither the woman nor the child survived.

The unrest had lasted for days, then slowly faded.

But the memory of that woman and child would never fade for Mickelson.

Bernstein crossed the room and stopped in front of Mickelson. She touched the loosened knot of his tie. "You know, you should really commit. Either tighten it or take it off."

"If I take it off, I fail to show respect for my commander

229

and chief," Mickelson said only partly sarcastically, "and if I tighten it, I swear I'll choke to death."

"Oh, you have room," she said, and started to tighten the knot.

He stopped her by placing his hand over hers. Her skin was softer and warmer than he'd expected. "It's not the room," he said. "It's the idea."

She smiled a little. Then she moved her hand and dropped her gaze. "I suppose you think I'm an alarmist."

He could have lied, but he didn't see the point. "Yeah."

"I was wrong about the reaction to the speech. I thought people would take to the streets. I'm not wrong about the unrest."

"We're at war," he said to her. "We've been attacked as a world. We respond as a world."

She shrugged and turned away.

O'Grady had heard part of that. "If she knew her history, she'd know that people rally after their homes have been violated," he said.

"I know my history," she said, turning back to face O'Grady. "Who was this room named for?"

"Gosh," O'Grady said. "I have a fifty-fifty shot here, and the West Wing was finished in the 1920s, so I'm guessing the namesake of the teddy bear, Mr. Theodore Roosevelt, our twenty-sixth president."

"And what did his cousin, our thirty-second president, call this room?"

"Hell," Mickelson said, "if it was decorated like this."

O'Grady looked blank. "How the hell should I know that?" he asked.

"The Fish Room," she said. "He called it the Fish Room because he felt stupid calling it the Roosevelt Room."

"That's not history," O'Grady said, "that's interior decoration."

Her eyes narrowed. "I know my history," she said. "I

230

probably know it better than you. I know that the United States rallied when we were attacked at Pearl Harbor. I know that England, when it was bombed in the very same war, came together as a nation. I know that Afghanistan rebels, in their determination to drive the Soviets off their soil, helped destroy an empire. I know all of that. It's basic stuff."

She leaned in closer. "But I also know the history of extremism, and I know that when it's unchecked, especially in times of war, we're in trouble."

"So what are you suggesting?" O'Grady asked. "Taking all the UFO nuts who appeared over all the years and putting them in internment camps?"

There was a silence in the room at that moment, and O'Grady's last comment sounded louder than O'Grady had clearly intended. Over O'Grady's shoulder, Mickelson saw Franklin in the doorway, his face dark.

"Internment camps aren't anything to joke about, Shamus," he said.

O'Grady flushed a deep red and turned. "I didn't mean offense, sir."

"Yes, you did. You meant to offend Director Bernstein, and I won't have it. We're under too much pressure for your normal wry humor."

O'Grady nodded. Mickelson wished he could blend into the orange wall. Tempers were short, patience was frayed. These conversations never used to happen with Franklin's advisers.

"I take it you're talking about the lack of dissent," Franklin said as he approached the head of the table. The others did as well. Mickelson put his hand on the leather upholstered chair, with the brass buttons holding the fabric in place. By the time the meeting was half over, he knew, those buttons would be creating welts in his back.

"Actually, Mr. President," Bernstein said, "what prompted

Shamus's remark was my observation that extremism in times of war should not go unchecked."

Franklin shot her a withering glance. "Director, you've warned me of riots and dissent, which are simply not happening. Except for those small bombs which were, I grant you, distressing, we've seen nothing since I made my speech."

"That worries me," Bernstein said. "The hate mongering has grown, sir, and so has the discontent. I'm afraid that things are actually being planned."

"And I am not going to worry about a threat that may or may not be real," Franklin said, effectively closing the door on that conversation. "What are you seeing in Europe, Doug?"

Mickelson resisted the urge to bring his hand to his tie knot and tighten it. "It's about the same, sir," he said. "No great dissent, a lot of cooperation. There's been some moaning that the United States has taken the lead, but in Europe at least, no one seems to mind."

"In Europe, at least," O'Grady repeated. "Which means that people mind elsewhere."

"Asia mostly," Mickelson said. "China in particular. But right now they don't see any way around it. My sense is, from the heads of state I've spoken to, that most countries are relieved that we're taking the front position."

"So that if we fail, they can blame us," Franklin said.

"But we won't fail." Lopez was in the room. She had pulled the door closed. Mickelson fought a surge of irritation at her comment. Since the speech, she had become Franklin's greatest cheerleader. Mickelson had never really thought that that had been the position the chief of staff should take.

Franklin, too, apparently found the comment a tad too obsequious. "We might," he said. "Nothing is guaranteed until those nukes blow that planet out of the sky."

His metaphor was mixed, but that was the only problem

232

with his statement. Mickelson agreed heartily with it, and he'd never considered himself a hawk—that is, not before the tenth planet arrived.

"What about our borders, Shamus?" Franklin asked. "Are we having any problems?"

O'Grady shook his head. "Even the illegals have slowed. Right now, people are sticking close to home. It's my sense that no one is looking at their own problems. We're all looking at the heavens, waiting for those nukes to go off."

"Yeah," Lopez said. "I saw in one of the vid chats a kid say that he hoped you could see the explosions with the naked eye."

"I doubt we'll be able to see them with the large telescopes," Mickelson said. "From what I hear, the only information we're getting is from the probes."

"And it's good enough," Franklin said. "Right now, everything is a go. No problems so far. And that's all that matters."

"We're in the calm before the storm," Bernstein said. Her pessimism was beginning to grate on Mickelson's nerves.

"Maybe," O'Grady said. "Or maybe we're catching a break."

"I think those aliens have thought of us as easy targets for so long, we'll whup them with sheer surprise alone," Lopez said.

Mickelson let the conversation drift around him. That's how these meetings had been ending up. Endless discussions of the possibilities of success. It seemed like Franklin needed almost nightly reassurance that he had taken the right course of action. Mickelson thought it was interesting that in all of these meetings he'd attended, Maddox or other members of the Joint Chiefs hadn't been here, nor had the science advisers. The people who were still working on ways of defeating the tenth planet when it got closer to Earth hadn't stopped their work, nor did they debate the success of the missiles.

They went on as if they had a deadline, an important one. Mickelson wondered if they knew something he didn't.

"You're quiet, Doug," Franklin said.

"Yeah," Mickelson said. "One too many diplomatic dinners, I guess."

Franklin raised his eyebrows slightly. "Is it that, or something more profound?"

Bernstein was staring at him. O'Grady was studying his hands. Lopez was watching Franklin.

"We keep acting as if we expect the other shoe to drop," Mickelson said. "I guess I'm wondering when it will."

O'Grady shook his head. "I think we're not used to the time between action and result."

"Huh?" Lopez said.

Franklin also looked confused, but Mickelson got it.

"Yeah," he said. "I suppose we'd always assumed if we'd launched nuclear missiles, we'd know what got hit and when within the hour. We'd know if we'd wiped out our enemy, or if we had simply made things worse. But this time, we're waiting weeks."

"I hadn't thought of that," Lopez said softly.

"It's turning Bernstein into a Cassandra," O'Grady said. "And—"

"Watch it," Bernstein said. "Cassandra was right."

"Tavi," the president warned.

"I'll stop," she said. "Although I shouldn't."

Franklin sighed. "We are spinning our wheels. It doesn't feel right to work on domestic problems, and there seems to be little foreign work we can do. I guess you're right, Shamus. We're waiting, and none of us are very good at that."

"I'd like the wait to be over," Mickelson said.

"Me, too," Lopez said.

234

Franklin looked at both of them. "I only want the wait to end if we get the result we want," he said.

"You think there's a realistic chance we won't?" O'Grady asked, sounding a bit surprised.

"I'd be a fool if I counted on anything," Franklin said. "As bizarre as this is, we're fighting a war here."

Mickelson's heart was pounding. He hadn't heard Franklin this pessimistic since the initial attack.

"I trust you have backup plans," Bernstein said.

Mickelson knew of some of them. He was surprised she didn't. Then he realized that, with her dire and incorrect warnings, and the domestic focus of her job, she probably had no need to know.

"Oh, we have plans," Franklin said. "But if this is the first volley in a protracted struggle, we're in trouble."

Then, as if realizing that he was being too pessimistic, he stood, and put his hands on the table. "I'm glad you all came," he said. "We're ending now so that Doug can finish taking off his tie."

This time, Mickelson's hand flew to the knot. Franklin gave him a wicked grin and walked out of the room. The others stood too.

"You think he's scared?" Bernstein asked.

Mickelson thought for a moment. He assumed everyone was scared. They'd be fools not to be.

"I don't think that's an issue," he said. "He's doing his job, and that's all that matters."

"I guess." She looked at the open door, the one Franklin had disappeared through. "For the record, the reason I'm focusing on the domestic problem is I believe this nuke thing is going to work."

Mickelson gave her a sharp glance.

She shrugged. "I've been studying nuclear scenarios my entire career," she said. "No planet can comfortably survive three hundred nuclear explosions on its surface. No planet."

Her words buoyed his mood. It surprised him, that she wasn't as pessimistic as he had thought. He smiled, really smiled, for the first time in weeks.

"You know," he said, "I'd never thought of it that way. You're exactly right."

And he left, knowing that, for the first time since the destruction of the California coast, he was going to get a good night's sleep.

10

August 12, 2018
12:31 P.M. Eastern Daylight Time

94 Days Until Second Harvest

Vivian Hartlein fixed the strap on her vest where it bit into her side. The vest weighed almost thirty pounds and made it hard for her to breathe. And climbing the steps up into the Capitol Building had been slow. With the extra weight she felt like an old woman.

Over the vest she wore a long raincoat, even though there had been no rain forecast. She knew no one would pay her no mind. With the raincoat and the slow walk, she looked like a crazy old lady, not the leader of a group doing its best to bring down a godless government.

The warm afternoon sun beat on her, the vest heavy, as she climbed the long set of stairs toward the Capitol Building. The images of her daughter kept her going. Cheryl and them grandbabies, turned to black dust.

One foot at a time, one step at a time, she climbed until she was close to the security checkpoint. She didn't plan to try to get past them deluded guards. With so much explosive strapped to her, she knew she had no chance of getting through, no matter how she looked.

She stopped and rested, pretending to stare at the view behind her. The day was almost cool for August, and she was thankful the humidity was low. She wasn't sure she could have climbed those stairs on a really hot summer day. Not with this much weight on her.

Since the president had declared war on them made-up aliens, she'd lost more and more of her people. No matter how much proof she had, no matter how much talking she did, they slowly stopped listening to her. The government poisoned their minds. They saw all the media stuff as proof. Slowly they started to believe that the aliens was real, that they was coming back.

It don't matter what's goin' on with our government, Jake'd said to her that last day. He'd been her last soldier, the one she'd thought she could count on, her rock when her husband Dale didn't come back from California. *Right now, we got to ignore what's going on here because them aliens'll be back.*

They ain't no aliens, she'd said.

He'd looked at her sadlike. *They is, Vivian,* he'd said. *And right now, it's our planet that we gotta defend. When the aliens is gone, we'll go after the government. But not till then. Can't you see that?*

She tried to see what they all saw. But it was lies. All lies. So clear that she wondered why she was the only one that saw it. She'd removed the log from her own eye, but she couldn't seem to get the mote from her neighbor's, even though the Bible promised she could. She was righteous, and sometimes the righteous had to stand alone.

Above her the Capitol dome towered into the sky, a symbol of all the lies. All the murdering lies.

The death would just continue if truth didn't break through.

She had left messages, long letters and tapes, telling everyone the truth.

The truth would set them free. She just had to shock them into seeing it.

238

Her death, her strike against the very heart of the government, would rally those who'd strayed. They'd use her death to keep the fight going until the truth prevailed.

Her hands were shaking as she eased them into the pockets of the raincoat. In the left pocket was a picture of her daughter and her grandchildren. It was the only picture Vivian had of all of them.

She pulled it out and stared at it. With her right hand she grasped the trigger to the explosives. There was enough to blow a two-story hole in the side of the Capitol. And she would never feel a thing.

By the time the first siren wailed, she'd be in heaven, holding her grandbabies, and hugging her little girl.

With one more look at their picture, she turned and moved directly to the security checkpoint leading into the building.

The man in uniform smiled at her.

She smiled back—and pushed the trigger in her pocket.

August 12, 2018
1:01 P.M. Eastern Daylight Time

94 Days Until Second Harvest

Leo Cross sat in the hard lab chair, General Maddox beside him. It felt strange to see the general, in her uniform with her perfect posture, sitting in Portia Groopman's lab at NanTech. The stuffed animals, the scattered equipment, the expensive machinery, combined with General Maddox's presence, made this seem like they were three adults sitting in the bedroom of an incredibly rich, incredibly spoiled teenage girl.

Albeit one who had amazing talents.

Portia, her eyes bearing the same shadows as everyone else's, no longer looked so young. There were strain lines around her mouth, and an older look on her face.

239

Edwin Bradshaw—who had been trying to make certain that in addition to all the work she did, she got sleep and food—was standing toward the back of the room, arms crossed. Jeremy Lantine and Yukio Brown stood beside him, mimicking his posture. Both of them seemed somewhat nervous, even more so when they saw General Maddox.

The general was here on Cross's invitation. Portia had said she had found a way to stop the alien nanoharvesters, and Cross wanted to make sure the government knew about it. He didn't want to invite any of the science advisers. He felt that, if Portia was right, this would fall under the purview of the military. No one was better for the job than General Maddox.

After all, she was the one who had helped Cross get the harvesters to NanTech in the first place—through such a circuitous route.

The entire group was staring at the screen in front of them. On it, several alien nanoharvesters, blown up to one hundred times life-sized, were being attacked by the nanomachines Portia had designed. She had shown her five guests several different experiments. The first with one nanoharvester and one nanorescuer, as Portia was calling them. The nanorescuer had scuttled across the screen and landed on top of the nanoharvester. Then she had shown the same experiment with two, and so on, but these experiments were controlled. Each nanoharvester was lined up with a nanorescuer. Then she had run a series of experiments showing the harvesters already dissolving bits of grain. The nanorescuers still shut down the harvesters.

Those experiments were impressive, but this last one was the important one.

In it, she had placed a bunch of nanoharvesters on her slide and now had just finished putting an uncounted number of nanorescuers beside them in a large group.

Then she leaned back to watch.

The nanorescuers separated from their pack and each went

toward a different nanoharvester. When they reached the harvesters, the rescuers attacked one by getting on top of it and shutting it down.

When Bradshaw had first described this to Cross, he had said it had reminded him of insect sex, and now Cross agreed. But he wished that Bradshaw hadn't put that image in his head.

There were fewer rescuers than harvesters though, and once the individual rescuers had "killed" their harvester, they didn't move on. The other harvesters were untouched, and presumably remained alive.

Portia shut off the monitor. "And there you have it," she said. "The strengths and weaknesses of the nanorescuers."

Maddox leaned forward. "This is quite impressive," she said, and Portia smiled. "I never thought we'd be able to neutralize those things."

"And neutralize them once they're activated," Cross said. "You're amazing, Portia."

"Don't compliment her too much," Lantine said, "she might expect a raise."

"For this," Maddox said, "she should own the company. If our first method of attacking those aliens fails, then this one will certainly save us all. Congratulations, Ms. Groopman."

Portia was grinning like Cross had never seen her do. She seemed to enjoy the compliment from Maddox more than from anyone else.

"You did see the problem, though," Portia said.

Maddox nodded. "I am less concerned about it than I probably should be. I'm still stunned that you've found a way to stop these hideous things."

"Obviously," Cross said, "we're going to have one rescuer for each harvester. What kind of money are we talking about here?"

"Money isn't the issue so much as time is," Brown said.

"And resources," said Lantine.

241

"Resources?" Maddox asked. "We're talking about things a fraction the size of a flea. How much resources can it take?"

"It's not size that matters, General," Cross said. "It's our ability to make enough. Am I right, Portia?"

She nodded. "There's a few labs in this country that have the capability of building these things. A few more in Britain, some in France and Germany and Japan. I'm not sure about the other countries. Even though nanotechnology has come into its own in the last few years, we haven't been mass producing much of anything. It's not like we can take someone off the street and have him assemble pieces of a nanorescuer. It takes some specialized skills."

"Oh," Maddox said.

"However," Bradshaw said. "I have some ideas."

Maddox turned to him.

"Science schools like MIT and Cal Tech have entire nanotechnology divisions. They have postdoc students whom we can hire, and other students whom we can train."

"There are many universities with some excellent nanotechnology researchers," Brown said. "We just have to grab them and their best students now."

"And then do this worldwide," Portia said. "We need each country to have enough of these things so that they're prepared."

Maddox nodded. "That's the real problem, isn't it?" she said. "We have no idea what is enough."

"Well, actually," Bradshaw said, "we can get a fairly good estimate if we do some basic math."

"If they attack in the same numbers as before." Portia looked at Bradshaw and Cross had the sense this was the continuation of another discussion from long ago. "If they attack in larger numbers, we're in trouble."

Cross studied the now empty monitor. He was remembering the black dust, the videos of the blackness falling from the sky, the people screaming—

"We have one more problem," he said. "We have to be able to launch these rescuers before the harvesters do much damage."

"That does present a problem," Maddox said.

"No," Brown said. "Launching won't help us at all. These nanoharvesters destroy too much too fast."

Cross was afraid of that. He felt all the muscles in his shoulder tighten. They hadn't created something that was too little too late, had they?

"So what do we do?" Maddox asked.

"We dust." Portia spoke quietly.

Maddox looked at her with a perplexed expression. "Dust?"

"You know, like crop dusting. We spray the areas we think will be affected with the rescuers. We give people rescuers to carry on themselves, and then we hope we're right."

"My God, Ms. Groopman," Maddox said. "Do you know what kind of scale you're suggesting?"

Portia smiled. "I know it's a much grander scale than I usually work on," she said, "but, yes, General Maddox, I do."

Cross leaned back. One step forward and two steps back. If resources had been a problem before, they were a disaster now. There was no way he could see anyone manufacturing close to enough rescuers by the time the tenth planet returned.

If the aliens were still alive.

But there were still four days before the missiles were scheduled to hit the tenth planet.

"I hope those nukes work," Maddox said. "Because the amount of work this plan will take is something I'm having trouble imagining."

"We can do it," Bradshaw said.

Maddox turned toward him. "I appreciate optimism, Dr. Bradshaw, as long as it's well founded."

"I think it is," Bradshaw said. "We just have to take things one step at a time."

At that moment a young-looking man with blond hair came running into the room. He flicked on a television sitting on a table against the back wall, then turned to them, his face red, his eyes wide. "I think you're going to want to see this."

On the screen was a scene Cross had hoped he would never live to see. Smoke was pouring out of a huge hole in the side of the Capitol Building. Under the picture were the words *Capitol Bombed.*

As if fighting the aliens wasn't enough, they still had to fight each other.

August 12, 2018
14:32 Universal Time

90 Days Until Second Harvest

The warship worked better than Cicoi could have imagined. He stood at his command post, his upper tentacles resting on the controls, his lower tentacles wrapped around the circle, and his eyestalks extended. He had practiced enough that he did not get dizzy despite the long amounts of time he had to stand in this position.

His staff was scattered along its various positions, some of them clinging uncomfortably to their posts. Those members he had to make a note of because they had not trained as he had requested. He would not be able to use them in the upcoming missions to the third planet.

"Commander," his Second said. "We are approaching the first cylinder."

Cicoi waved a single tentacle, initiating visuals. He saw tentacles rise and fall in surprise all around the command center. The images of space surrounded them, except for an ugly projectile heading in their direction.

"Can we tell what it is?" he asked.

"It is not a probe," his Second said. "It has many functions, but there is a concentration of materials in the tip that seem—"

"Forgive me, Commander," said his Third, "but the materials when combined could explode."

"Explode?" Cicoi felt himself float slightly. He tightened his grip on the circle. So the Elder had been right. This was a weapon. "Harvest the energy from this cylinder, and instruct the other ships to do the same. Then send a message to the fleets led by the Center and North informing them of this."

"We will expend more energy in the message," his Tenth warned, "than we will receive from the cylinder."

"I know," Cicoi said.

He watched as his staff performed their functions. His Second stopped suddenly, his upper tentacles tangling.

Cicoi felt his own upper tentacles rise slightly. He forced them back down. "What is it, Second?"

"I am getting readings that indicate many more cylinders," his Second said.

"How many more?"

"At least eighty in this first group. Some had simply arrived in advance of the others," his Second said.

"First group?" Cicoi did not like the sound of that.

"I am getting shadows, readings from at least two more groups," his Second said. "They are larger than this first group. And very close behind."

"Larger?" Cicoi knew he shouldn't repeat, knew it made him sound powerless, but he had not expected this.

The Elder had, though.

"And you believe them all to be weapons?" Cicoi asked.

"I am confirming this now," his Ninth said. "I have run the materials and the speculations about them. The weapon inside is crude, but extremely powerful. If all of those weapons hit Malmur, we will lose everything."

Cicoi nearly lost his grip on the circle. How could these

creatures have gone from such a primitive place to having the ability to destroy Malmur in the time it took to do one Pass?

"Send this information to the fleets of the North and Center. Have the Command on Malmur launch our harvester ships. We must absorb energy from these cylinders," Cicoi said.

"Some of the energy in these cylinders is dormant," said the Eighth. "Many of the cylinders have been propelled here, and are approaching us with momentum only."

"Surely the weapons have energy signatures," Cicoi said.

"Not enough for us to use," said the Eighth.

"We can absorb some of the energy, Commander," his Second said, "but not all of it. We do not have enough ships."

"Then we must divert," Cicoi said. He pressed the controls with the tips of his tentacles and saw what was causing his staff to pocket their eyestalks. Even with all the harvester ships deployed, even with the fleets of new warships, they did not have enough power to attack all of the cylinders.

Some would get through.

He felt his own eyestalks wilt, but it took all of his composure to make certain that he did not pocket them. He had to think.

He straightened his eyestalks, and pointed one at his Second. "I want you, and the Third through Fifth, to see which of these cylinders have the smallest weapons. Those we will not pursue. The others we will handle as best we can."

They raised a single eyestalk in response.

"Remember," he said, "make your measurements accurate. The ones we ignore are the ones that will hit our homes."

His voice shook at that last. He wished the Elder had come with him, but the Elder had not. The Elder had said it was up to Cicoi to greet this threat.

But, as had been the case with the third planet, the threat was greater than expected.

246

And, Cicoi worried that no matter what he did, the threat would destroy them.

August 16, 2018
7:32 A.M. Eastern Daylight Time

86 Days Until Second Harvest

The lab was full. Scientists, guests, dignitaries, and of course, the actual researchers who belonged there. For the first time, Cross felt like one of the gang. He at least got nods of recognition from the researchers who seemed to view everyone else with suspicion.

Britt was at one of the control stations. She was working on several things at once, and Cross knew better than to ask what they were. He was staring at the large monitors scattered around the room, the flat screens holding the key to the future.

Today was the day. The papers and newscasts for the last few days had alternated between images of the bombing at the Capitol Building and the attack coming on the tenth planet. The attack on the Capitol had been put down to one lone extremist who thought the aliens were fake and the government had killed her kids in California.

At the moment Cross wished the aliens were fake. Or that he would just wake up from this nightmare. But neither seemed to be the case.

He kept staring at the screens.

The images coming back from the tenth planet were somewhat strange. Cross thought he caught glimpses of black alien ships in space, and so did several of the researchers, but it was tough to confirm. They were almost impossible to see, and the readouts that the lab was getting from the missiles gave conflicting information.

Two of the six monitoring missiles had gone dead in the last hour, which Cross saw as confirmation that the aliens were out there in space trying to stop Earth's attack.

He didn't like that.

But it was expected. It was the reason so many missiles had been sent, why some were to explode on impact, with no energy source onboard for the aliens to drain. The aliens trying to stop the attack had been expected. Cross just had to remember that.

His stomach was jumping, and it wasn't from the four cups of coffee he'd had since he arrived.

This time, when Britt had gotten the expected middle-of-the-night call, he had come with her.

Cross had answered. He'd been lying there, unable to sleep, as he had for the past two nights.

Everything rested on those missiles.

Everything.

For the first time, when he said the fate of the world was in balance, he meant it. If the missiles didn't strike, didn't wipe the aliens out, Earth's chances of survival were poor, even with Portia's rescuers.

Now a number of the monitoring missiles had gone dead, and there were alien ships out there.

It was expected, he knew. He kept reminding himself, yet he was getting a horrible feeling that all this waiting, all this planning, had been for nothing.

Then, on the screen before him, a blinding flash.

The screen seemed to go white.

The entire lab lit up with the intense light from the screens.

The tenth planet showed up for a moment in relief, like a shiny black surface catching the reflection of a flashbulb.

That image was frozen in his mind.

Black screens covering the entire planet, and one explosion ripping a massive hole in those screens.

"Oh, my God," someone said.

248

"Was that—?" someone else asked.

Then there was another flash.

This time the second flash lit up the glowing mushroom cloud of the first before the planet disappeared into blackness again.

And then another flash as a third atomic blast hit the tenth planet.

And then another.

So much light was coming from such a far distance away that Cross had to shade his eyes from the screens.

"We're doing it," Britt said. Then she shouted it. "We're doing it!"

Two more bombs exploded.

Cross watched.

Stunned.

He'd never seen nuclear bombs go off in real time.

His reaction was mixed. Stunned shock, and a weird elation. He hadn't thought it possible.

He had thought they would fail.

No, he had believed they would fail.

Three more flashes, and then, abruptly, the pictures got cut off.

There was a moment of silence.

People continued to stare at the dead screens.

Researchers pushed buttons on their monitors. Britt checked to see if the satellite relays were working. They apparently were, for when she turned around, a grin was on her face.

"We did it," she said again.

And a cheer went up, the loudest cheer Cross had ever heard.

It took him a moment to realize his own voice was in the mix, raspy and joyful and full of relief.

They had done it.

They.

Had.

Done.

It.

They had attacked the tenth planet.

They had fought the aliens in a second battle.

And this time, Earth won.

11

86 Days Until Second Harvest

Cicoi was the last to leave his warship. He took the glide path to the staging area, his tentacles drooping, his eyestalks hanging near his torso in complete disgrace. He should have listened to the Elder. He should have listened sooner. He should have planned for this.

Fifteen of the cylinders had gotten through the ships and had hit Malmur.

Fifteen.

The destruction was more than he could think of.

The images of those explosions sending odd-shaped clouds into the atmosphere were burned into his memory.

Two pods were gone.

An entire sleeping chamber, with thousands of unawakened Malmuria, had been vaporized.

Eight harvest ships were destroyed and, in some ways, worst of all, vast areas of energy collectors had been ruined.

And none of that counted what the radiation released by the cylinders might do. It was unfamiliar to Malmur and possibly toxic.

His planet was in flames.

251

The black surface of his home was lit by fire for the first time in any memory.

He had seen some of the fires from orbit as he returned home.

In disgrace.

He would offer himself to the recycler, and try to serve his people as best he could by converting himself to energy.

No.

He wilted farther.

His Elder was here.

Waiting.

We cannot lose more of our kind, particularly to a misplaced sense of shame. You did listen to me. You diverted or destroyed all but fifteen of their cylinders. There were at least three hundred. Imagine if they had gotten through.

The Elder appeared in front of him, tentacles floating. Cicoi thought such a cavalier attitude at this time was almost as bad. Thousands had died. Thousands more probably would die once it became clear that the energy reserves were gone.

As if the Elder had heard the thoughts, it said, *We cannot mourn. We are not done fighting yet. Yes, we have lost thousands. But millions still live. And for their sakes, we must go to the third planet and take what we need. Only then will Malmur survive.*

Cicoi knew that. There was logic in it. "But we have no way to defeat the creatures of the third planet," he said.

You think they are great because they've attacked us? You know nothing of war. They were primitives when we first came here. They are nothing compared to us. The Elder moved closer to him, waving eyestalks in front of him. *They have probably used all of their weapons to attack us. And they are no match for the Sulas. We must get to the planet. We must take everything we can. And then we must never return.*

"But how can we do this now?" Cicoi asked. "We have lost Malmuria. We have lost ships. We have lost recyclers, and

252

energy collectors, and storages. We do not have time for repairs."

We make the time, the Elder said. *We cannot rest until we have what we need. We will defeat them, and we will do it my way.*

Cicoi let his eyestalks droop even farther. He knew that he did not deserve to live. His curse was that he could not have an honorable death after this great defeat.

He had to live on.

He had to live on with the memory of those explosions ripping his world apart.

He had to live on with the memory of the fires burning.

And in living on, he would do everything he could to save his people—and his home.

August 16, 2018
8:18 P.M. Eastern Daylight Time

86 Days Until Second Harvest

"All that pessimism, Bernstein, and we won," Shamus O'Grady said.

Doug Mickelson eased himself away from the conversation, but not so far away that he couldn't hear. They were in the Oval Office at Franklin's invitation, along with the other Cabinet members, the Joint Chiefs of Staff, a few of Franklin's closest advisers, and the First Lady. Despite the champagne, this gathering was not billed as a celebration. It was, instead, something else. What, exactly, Franklin hadn't made clear yet.

"I wasn't pessimistic about the bombs," Bernstein said. "I *told* Mickelson that. That's why I've been talking about the domestic situation."

Mickelson moved even farther away from the conversation. The Capitol Building had been attacked. In many ways, Bernstein had been exactly right, yet they had all done what they had needed to do.

He glanced around. There weren't any real conversation groups he wanted to join. He heard a lot of discussion of policy, for the first time in months—and a lot of laughter, also for the first time in months. From various groups, he heard "Ka-boom!" as someone's hands rose.

The papers were running picture after picture of the atomic bombs exploding on the black, panel-covered surface of the alien world. Pictures with headlines saying WE WON!

It had become clear to him that the moment when the missiles hit the tenth planet would become one of the defining moments of this generation.

Maybe of all human history.

Franklin's approval ratings in the nation and worldwide couldn't be higher. The United States suddenly was the most popular country on the globe for organizing and carrying out this mission. Even though other governments were involved, everyone knew where the credit belonged.

"You're not drinking your champagne," Maddox said softly.

He turned. She looked both tired and relaxed. This had been an incredible strain on her. "Neither are you."

She shrugged. "I have made it a policy to never toast a successful bombing raid."

He started. He hadn't thought of it that way. "It does seem like bad form, doesn't it?"

"When you think of it in those terms," she said. "But that's really not why everyone's celebrating."

"We struck back," he said.

She turned her head slightly. "You know, you're the first person I've spoken to who actually understands the difference."

"Between what and what?"

"Winning a battle and winning the war."

254

He set his glass down. She did the same as the door from Franklin's private secretary's office opened. An aide came in, and handed Franklin a downloaded hard copy. Franklin squinted at it, then had the aide close the door.

The room grew silent. This, then, was what they had been waiting for.

Franklin took an extra moment, and then looked up. He waved the paper. "It's a damage assessment report," he said.

Mickelson felt his shoulders stiffen. A hard look came over Maddox's face.

"It seems," Franklin said, "that it's better than we thought. We thought that if the aliens fought back—and it's now clear they had spaceships in the area, attempting to destroy our bombs—we'd be lucky if one or two hit the surface. Fifteen— or five percent—of the missiles we sent up there hit and exploded on their planet."

Mickelson found himself breathing shallowly.

"We've hurt them," Franklin said. "We've hurt them badly. Let's hope they'll think twice before coming to us again."

Everyone in the room cheered.

Franklin raised his glass and proposed a toast.

Mickelson grabbed his and feigned a sip, but he felt unsettled.

He made his way through the crowd, to Franklin's side. "Mr. President," Mickelson said, as usual finding it uncomfortable to greet an old friend that way, "you know as well as I do that they will still come back."

Franklin nodded.

"Then why did you say that?"

He turned to Mickelson. "Because we need hope, too, Doug."

"Hope won't prevent the tenth planet from coming close to the Earth again in eighty-six days."

"No, it won't," Franklin said. "But it just might give us enough energy to fight the next battle—and win it, too."

255

August 16, 2018
9:51 p.m. Eastern Daylight Time

86 Days Until Second Harvest

The sounds of celebration echoing over the city were dying down. Leo Cross sat on a lawn chair in the enclosed yard of his D.C. house. Britt sat beside him. They'd finished one of Constance's wonderful dinners and a bottle of wine, and this time, when they went to bed, Cross was unplugging the phone.

The world could do without Britt Archer for one night.

"Sounds like people are getting tired of partying," she said.

"Sounds like," he said.

When the images of the bombs exploding on the tenth planet were broadcast all over the world, people took to the streets in joyous celebration. Confetti fell, fireworks went off, there was screaming and shouting and general mayhem. It reminded Cross of the pictures he'd seen of New York City the day that someone declared World War II had ended, only this time, the celebrations happened worldwide.

In Washington, a cheering crowd had gathered outside the White House, ignoring the damaged Capitol Building. But Cross knew that the damage was part of this battle. And that there was going to be more before the war was over.

"I would have thought the celebration would continue for days," Britt said.

"People know," Cross said. "The tenth planet still has to orbit close to us. There's still a threat."

He looked up at the clear sky. Stars winked against the blackness. Who'd've thought that something that happened so far away would affect them like this at home.

"At least now those damn aliens know how it feels," Britt said.

Cross looked at her. She seemed fiercer than she ever had. "They're just trying to survive like we're trying to survive."

"I don't give a damn about their reasons," Britt said. "They hurt us. We hurt them. Maybe they'll go away now."

"They can't, Britt," he said. "They need Earth's resources. Those aliens are going to come back even stronger. We didn't destroy them, we only hurt them, just like they hurt us. Just like they have been hurting us every two thousand years."

She sighed. "I know you're right. I just wish you weren't."

"I wish I wasn't either."

They both stared at the stars for a long moment.

"So we fight," Britt said finally.

"We fight," Cross said. "And it'll be the most important battle we'll ever fight. We have no other choice. The planet can't support both races."

"One of us must win," Britt said, softly.

Cross didn't reply. There was nothing to say.

Epilogue

August 17, 2018
6:21 A.M. Pacific Daylight Time

85 Days Until Second Harvest

Danny Elliot slipped out of the house and onto the quiet street. All of the adults were still asleep. His mother had been up forever last night, drinking and laughing and celebrating for the first time since the black dust came. In the last few months, they had managed to put their lives back together, but his mother hadn't laughed.

She said the aliens got what they deserved.

Finally.

Danny watched the bombs hit the tenth planet over and over again. The images made him a little sick inside, but he wasn't going to say that. Instead he sat, quiet, wondering if that's what the aliens saw when they dropped all that stuff on San Luis Obispo.

He adjusted his backpack and crossed the street, past the still-full houses and into the Zone. The patrols didn't happen as often anymore, and the dust had long ago turned to a thick black mud, solid from the rains. It had packed down into something like concrete, except in areas closest to buildings or under trees where the wind had blown it.

He knew of a couple of places like that.

Maybe he should have called Nikara, but he didn't. Their friendship didn't feel the same anymore, not without Cort. The three of them balanced, but when Cort died the day the dust fell, the balance died, too. Nikara and Danny fought a lot, and there was no longer anyone to referee.

Danny'd said something about that to his mom, and she had looked at him sadly.

"It's not the fighting," she said. "Cort's presence will always be a ghost between the two of you."

Maybe.

But yesterday, Cort had been avenged.

Atomic bombs had been dropped on the aliens.

In all the stories Danny heard, in all the vids he saw, ghosts went to their final rest after they'd been avenged. And even though he didn't want to lose Cort—the living, wonderful Cort—Danny didn't mind losing the dead one.

He wanted to get the image of Cort, lying on the couch sick with the flu, melting under the black dust like those people on TV had, out of his mind. He needed to think about the friend he'd known, not the way Cort had died.

And this morning, he'd woken up with a way to do it.

It didn't take long to reach the house that he and Nikara had climbed up to, that day in April. It was easier to get to now that the military wasn't patrolling that much. They weren't as afraid of the dust. They knew what it was, knew that it wouldn't hurt anyone, or so they said. So they didn't really guard it anymore.

The rhododendron bushes no longer had flowers. Instead, thick green leaves covered them, making one side of the white house look like a forest. The trellis they'd climbed a few months ago was hidden by climbing roses and out-of-control growth.

He slipped past all of it, catching a bit of ocean breeze, inhaling the salty scent.

Cort had loved living in this part of town. Cort would stop

them sometimes and make them smell the ocean, or look at the way the roses had grown over the summer. Cort said it didn't matter what kind of house you lived in, or what neighborhood you lived in, as long as you noticed what nature provided nearby.

What nature had provided here was a shelter.

Danny went around the house and into the backyard, right up to the beginning of the black dust. A giant rhododendron grew right on the edge. It would provide what he wanted.

The blackness looked less threatening now. Maybe because he was used to it, or maybe because he knew it would never come again. But he still wasn't going to walk on it. Walking on it would be like walking on Cort.

Danny took off his backpack and reached inside. He had taken a jar that Cort had given him last year. It was obsidian and smooth, a magic jar, Cort had said. They both didn't believe in magic anymore, but it was nice to pretend.

Danny'd had the jar beside his bed ever since Cort died.

Danny pulled the stopper and carefully set it on the top of his backpack. Then he grabbed a ladle he'd stolen from the kitchen, and slowly lifted a branch on the rhododendron. A branch on the side toward the destruction.

There was real black dust underneath, blown there by the winds off the ocean. Black dust and bits of other things, things that Danny'd always imagined were bones.

Ashes and bone.

Bits of Cort.

Carefully, using the ladle, Danny scooped up as much of the dust as he could and poured it into the jar. It was painstaking, disgusting work, but it was important.

Too many people had died in April. Too many went unaccounted for, and too many had just disappeared. Cort's entire family—his dad, and his mom, and his dog—had died that day, too. And when entire families went, no one bothered with a funeral. Danny had heard that Cort's grandparents, who lived in Minnesota, had had a memorial, but that had been too far away. No one in Minnesota even knew Cort.

But Danny had. Danny and Nikara and a lot of other kids. And it wasn't right that they didn't really get to say good-bye.

Danny stoppered the jar, and then took out one other container. He felt weird using his mom's Tupperware, but the guys would understand. He filled it, too.

That container he would take to the ocean. They'd have a service, and he'd throw Cort's ashes into the sea where Cort would want them.

But Danny was going to keep some in the jar, for remembrance.

For Cort.

Danny finished and climbed out from under the rhododendron. Then he leaned up and stared at the cloudless blue sky. He held the jar aloft and, imagining that black alien planet, the one where the bombs hit, he said, "Yesterday was for Cort, you bastards."

He wondered if, somewhere deep down, they had known that. He imagined that they did.

He put the jar and the container in his backpack, then he stood. For a moment, he stared at the blackness.

Then he turned his back on it.

Forever.

85 Days Until Second Harvest

Watch for *The Tenth Planet: Final Assault*

DEAN WESLEY SMITH was a founder of the well-respected small press Pulphouse. He has written a number of novels—both his own and as tie-in projects—including *Laying the Music to Rest* and *X-Men: The Jewels of Cyttorak*.

KRISTINE KATHRYN RUSCH is the Hugo and World Fantasy Award–winning former editor of *The Magazine of Fantasy and Science Fiction*. She turned to writing full-time two years ago. She, too, has written a number of original and tie-in novels, including the *Fey* series and *Star Wars: The New Rebellion*.

Printed in the United States
by Baker & Taylor Publisher Services